What Readers Are Saying about the Men of the Saddle Series

"I have never read a book by this author that I didn't
enjoy all the way through."

• K.N. •

"*The Peacemaker* is an entertaining mix of memorable characters,
detailed setting, and gentle humor, served up with a Christian message
that makes its point without being preachy. Who wouldn't share
Wynne's frustration at being jilted? What woman wouldn't fall
in love with Cole Claxton? Settle back with *The Peacemaker* for
a visit to the Old West and the lovable Claxton family. You can
always depend on Lori Copeland for a great story."

• B.W. •

"Lori Copeland has outdone herself with *The Peacemaker*.
The book is pure fun. . . . I enjoyed every step of their journey
along the road to true love."

/ • M.C. •

"*The Drifter* is yet another wonderfully written novel
by Lori Copeland and a great addition to the Men of the Saddle series.
I love how she combined this book into a western romantic comedy
that is sure to brighten your day."

• R.M. •

LORI COPELAND

MEN *of the* SADDLE

the Maverick

Tyndale House Publishers, Inc.
WHEATON, ILLINOIS

Library of Congress Cataloging-in-Publication Data

Copeland, Lori.
    The maverick / Lori Copeland.
        p. cm. — (Men of the saddle ; #3)
    ISBN-13: 978-0-8423-8690-6 (sc)
    ISBN-10: 0-8423-8690-4 (sc)
    I. Title.
    PS3553.O6336M38 2005
    813'.54—dc22   2005008031

Printed in the United States of America

11 10 09 08 07 06 05
9   8   7   6   5   4   3   2   1

HOPE DEFERRED MAKES THE HEART SICK,

BUT A DREAM FULFILLED IS A TREE OF LIFE.

PROVERBS 13:12,

New Living Translation

Kansas frontier, 1868

The early morning wind had a sharp bite to it, but overhead the sun shone brightly on the eastern rim. Cass Claxton guessed a man couldn't ask for much more in the first week of February. The sled zipped along the icy road, and a smile formed at the corners of his mouth. He set the brim of his hat lower on his forehead, and his cobalt blue eyes surveyed the endless expanse of Kansas sky.

The visit with his brother Beau and Beau's wife, Charity, had been good, but he was eager to get home before another storm hit. Winters in Missouri were contrary, but he didn't think they could hold a candle to Kansas blizzards. Beau had nearly lost his wife and baby daughter last week when a whiteout had taken them by surprise and almost cost them their lives. The good Lord had smiled on Beau that day. He'd lost one wife to a rattlesnake bite; Cass didn't think his brother could stand another tragedy.

No doubt about it—the newly formed Claxton family was blessed. Cass remembered the solemn way Reverend Olson had reminded the family that it had been nothing short of a miracle that Charity and Mary Kathleen had survived after being buried in snow for five hours by that sudden storm.

His smile returned when he thought about how happy his brother was now. And it was high time. It had taken a long time for Beau to get over the death of his first wife, Betsy, but thanks to the good Lord and a sweet little Kansas widow by the name of Charity, it now looked like he'd make it just fine.

The way Beau had loved his first wife and now Charity sometimes puzzled Cass. As far as women were concerned, Cass could take them or leave them. And he'd done just that, more times than he cared to admit.

There was no way a woman was going to hog-tie and brand him. He'd never met a woman he'd want to be around much longer than a week—with maybe the exception of Wynne Elliot. Now there was a woman.

The image of her crimson hair and dancing sea green eyes came back to haunt him. He probably should have married her when he'd had the chance, but there was no use crying over spilled milk. Cole, his eldest brother, had married Wynne, and Cass had to admit he'd never seen a happier couple.

Of course, Beau's wife, Charity, wasn't all that bad either. She'd make Beau a fine woman—no arguing that point—but marrying was the last thing on Cass's mind. He wasn't anywhere close to settling down and raising a family. He had a peck of wild oats to sow before any woman dragged him to the altar—if one ever did.

He gave a sharp whistle and set the horse into a fast trot. The runners ate up the frozen ground. He began whistling under his breath. Directly ahead he spotted four riders approaching. The horses were coming fast, their hooves thundering over the packed snow. Cass wondered where they were headed in such a hurry.

The riders drew closer and Cass frowned, noting that one of the arrivals was that infuriating *Susanne McCord.*

The woman had been nothing but a thorn in his side since the day he'd watched her throw a temper tantrum in Miller's Mercantile. He'd hoped last week's blizzard had gotten her, then checked his uncharitable thoughts. He'd like to make it out of Kansas without running into her again, but it looked like his luck had soured.

He decided to politely tip his hat and ride on by and was about to do just that when the foursome reined up in his path. Caught by surprise, Cass hauled back on the reins, bringing the sled to a sudden stop.

Leviticus McCord; his daughter, Susanne; Reverend Olson; and a large man wearing a tin star sat stiffly in their saddles, staring back at Cass.

Cass touched the brim of his hat. "Reverend."

"Mr. Claxton."

The horses danced about, breathing frosty plumes into the brisk morning air.

"What brings you out this way so early in the day?" Cass asked. Silently seething, he ignored the young woman on the dapple-gray mare. His blood still boiled whenever he thought of how Susanne McCord had hauled off and hit him between the eyes. Then the silly twit had had the gall to look him up a few days later, at his brother's house, and offer him the exorbitant fee of five—even six—hundred dollars to take her back to her aunt in Saint Louis.

He'd flatly refused and none too nicely. He wouldn't take Susanne McCord to a catfight, let alone back to Missouri, and he'd wasted no time in telling her so.

It had been dark by the time she had accepted his no. She had started to cry. She'd pleaded that she felt too faint and frightened to find her way back to town. Cass had had no recourse but to let her stay the night under Beau's roof, but he'd sent her packing at first light.

Now here she was again, looking down at him with that superior smirk that made him so mad he couldn't see straight.

"We're looking for you!" Leviticus interrupted before the pastor could speak.

"Me?" Cass's grin slowly faded. Why would Leviticus McCord be looking for him?

The sheriff motioned for Cass to comply. "Mr. Claxton, would you mind climbin' down off that sled?"

"It depends. . . ." Cass glanced back to Revered Olson expectantly. "What's going on?"

The reverend apologetically met Cass's gaze. "I believe you've met . . . uh . . . hummruph . . . uh . . . Miss McCord?"

Cass spared a glance in Susanne's direction. "I've met her."

Susanne nodded from beneath the veil of an ostrich-plumed hat, her violet eyes mocking him.

"Met her? *Met* her!" Turning scarlet, Leviticus shouted louder, "I should hope he's *met* her!"

Cass's eyes snapped to the irate father. "I've *met* her."

"Cass . . . uh . . . this is most difficult, son," Reverend Olson began in an uneasy tone. "Would you mind to step down for a moment?"

Susanne appeared to be sniffing loudly into a lace handkerchief. Her sobs shook her mass of waist-length blonde ringlets, and the silken strands of hair shone like spun gold in the morning light.

Cass wrapped the reins around the brake and in a lithe motion landed on the ground. Something was wrong. He could feel it. "What's the problem?"

The men dismounted and stared at Cass for a moment. Then Leviticus exploded, "*What's the problem?*"

Cass realized where Susanne had inherited her volatile nature. The five-foot-two retired circuit judge was now hopping around in the road with his fists balled into tight knots.

"*What's the problem?*" Leviticus repeated, pausing long enough to draw an indignant breath before shaking his finger under Cass's nose. "I'll tell you what the *problem* is, you . . . you young whippersnapper! You sullied my daughter, and you're going to be held accountable!" He stomped his left foot, nearly dislodging his felt bowler.

Cass shifted his stance to eye the judge sourly. "I've what?"

"*Sullied my daughter!*" Leviticus shrieked. "Disgraced, soiled, tarnished!"

Cass's gaze narrowed. "I know what the word means, sir."

"I should hope so!"

"Now, now, gentlemen, let's all calm down," Reverend Olson advised. "I'm sure we can settle this matter without hollering to raise the dead."

Cass met the pastor's eyes. "What is he talking about?"

The reverend looked to Susanne, then to Cass. "Well, it seems that you and . . . you and Miss McCord spent a night together recently. Am I correct?" Cass could see that the reverend sincerely hoped that he wasn't. The preacher was a friend of

Beau and Charity's, and Cass didn't like to see him so uncomfortable.

"Spent the night with her?" Cass shot a reproachful eye toward the woman in question. "No, sir, I did *not* spend the night with her—not like she's insinuating."

"Oh yes, you did!" Susanne accused. She sniffed loudly.

Cass shifted his weight a second time, and his eyes sternly pinpointed her. "I did not." He knew as well as anyone that her accusation meant war. A man didn't trifle with a woman in these parts unless he married her.

Susanne heaved a tolerant sigh and dabbed at her streaming eyes. "I told you he would take this attitude, gentlemen."

"Now hold on a minute." Cass turned back to Reverend Olson. "I don't know what she's told you, but nothing happened that night—"

"So, you *did* spend the night with my daughter!" Leviticus accused.

"I didn't spend the night *with* her. My brother and his wife were present—"

"She was gone all night!" Leviticus bellowed. "How do you explain that?"

"She was there because she felt too 'faint' to make the trip back to town. I was there . . . but so were my brother, Beau, and his wife. If you won't take my word for it, you can ask them. . . ." Cass's voice trailed off when he began to realize that the more he tried to explain, the more he appeared to incriminate himself.

Leviticus glanced pointedly at the sheriff, and Cass could see the wheels in his mind turning. The entire town of Cherry Grove knew that Beau Claxton had stayed with the widow Burk for months before he'd married her. Cass broke a sweat though it was a cold day.

"Papa—" Susanne turned watery eyes on Leviticus—"it would be a waste of time to ride all the way to the Claxton place; I'm feeling delicate this morning. The wind's so cold." She shivered. "You know perfectly well that Beau Claxton would say anything needed to protect his no-good brother." Her voice trailed to a whine. "Can't we settle this matter quickly?" She lifted one hand to her brow as if faint.

Cass shot her a scathing look. "Susanne, this is not funny." The seriousness of the situation was beginning to sink in, and he was getting uneasy. And mad. Just plain mad at the woman. "Nothing happened the night you stayed at Beau and Charity's, and you know it. I should have sent you packing, and I would have if you hadn't lied to me when you said you were feeling faint."

He shifted his attention to Leviticus. "Sir, your daughter approached me that night and offered me five hundred dollars to take her to Saint Louis—even upped the offer to six hundred."

Leviticus's face turned varying shades of scarlet.

"I said no." Cass didn't mind telling on the silly twit. Now Leviticus would see how thoroughly rotten a daughter he had.

The distraught father leveled his gaze on his daughter. "Did you do that, Susanne? Did you offer this man six hundred dollars to take you to Saint Louis?"

Susanne gasped, batting long black eyelashes. "Gracious no, Papa! Where would I get that kind of money?"

Leviticus turned to Cass. "Where would she get that kind of money?" Cass figured that Leviticus knew his daughter's penchant for lying, but he felt obliged to ask.

"I don't know!" Cass snapped. "She offered me money; she didn't say where she was going to get it."

"Mr. Claxton." Leviticus stretched to his full height. His diminutive stature wasn't all that intimidating, but it struck the proper respect in Cass. "Susanne doesn't have six hundred dollars. Great day, man! *I* barely have six hundred dollars! That's a fortune!"

"I understand, sir." He did understand. Six hundred dollars was a lot of money, and the little schemer had been lying about that, too! "But that's what she offered me—six hundred. . . ." Cass felt a sinking sensation when he began to realize that he was in deep trouble this time.

Leviticus straightened, tugging his velvet waistcoat into place. "If my daughter says she didn't offer you the money, then I must assume she's telling the truth."

"But she's lying!"

Leviticus shot his daughter an exasperated look but continued. "Whether she offered the money or not, she says you took advantage of her that evening, and I can't take the risk. You have to make an honest woman of her. Restore her integrity."

"Now hold on—"

"No, *you* wait a minute," Leviticus said, his eyes narrowing. "You're about to take a wife, son."

The conversation had slipped beyond the point of reason. Cass whirled and was about to climb back into the sled when he felt the barrel of a shotgun tapping his right shoulder. He slowly turned to meet the sheriff's cold, assessing eyes.

"You want to take a few minutes to reconsider your hasty decision, son?"

Cass froze. The clear implication in the man's tone made him rethink a quick escape.

"Son—" Reverend Olson reassuringly laid a hand on Cass's shoulder—"you best think this thing through."

"But, Reverend." Cass stared back helplessly. "I haven't been near Susanne McCord. . . . She hit me . . . and it left a knot the size of a goose egg." The reverend had to know the extent of what he was dealing with!

Reverend Olson nodded. "In Cherry Grove, we tend to take the woman's word in matters of this delicate nature. I'd suggest you marry the girl and then try to resolve the matter in a more satisfactory manner." His eyes indicated the overwrought father.

Marry Susanne McCord? Cass would rather throw a rope over the nearest tree and hang her!

Leviticus helped his daughter off the mare. She rested her slender hand on his arm. "You do believe me, don't you, Papa? I wouldn't story about an awful thing like this. I warned Mr. Claxton he'd surely be facin' my papa's wrath. That's what I said . . . but I do declare he wouldn't listen. . . ." She broke off tearfully and buried her face in a lace handkerchief.

Leviticus wrapped a protective arm around her trembling shoulders. "I believe you, Daughter." His chin firmed. "Sheriff," he prompted in a righteous tone.

The sheriff stepped up, and Cass looked at Reverend Olson pleadingly. "Are you actually going to let them do this to me?"

The clergyman sighed and opened his Bible. "Do you, Cass Claxton, take Susanne McCord to be your lawfully wedded wife?"

"No, I do not!"

Reverend Olson turned patiently to the bride. "Do you,

Susanne McCord, take Cass Claxton to be your lawfully wedded husband?"

She sniffed, daintily blew her nose. "I suppose I'll just have to, under these dreadful circumstances." Her lovely amethyst eyes peered at Leviticus woefully. "Don't you agree, Papa?"

Her father patted her hand. "You just relax, darlin'. Papa will see to it that your virtue is protected."

"*Virtue*—that's rich!" Cass exploded. "She doesn't know the meaning of the word!"

"Oh, Papa. He's just so dreadful. Do I really have to marry him?" Susanne peeked at Cass from behind her handkerchief.

"Lady, all you have to do is tell the *truth*—if you have it in you," Cass said through gritted teeth. He'd never raised a hand against a woman, but given half a chance, he'd gladly strangle Susanne McCord at that instant and worry about forgiveness later.

Reverend Olson droned on, apparently hoping to dispense with the unpleasant matter as quickly as possible. "Do you promise to love, cherish, and obey, till death do you part?"

"Welllll . . . I . . . I suppose I can . . . if I must. . . ." Susanne glanced at Cass. "I *do*."

Reverend Olson turned back to Cass. "Do you promise to comfort, honor, and keep her, in sickness and in health—"

"I wouldn't pull a mad dog off her!"

"—forsaking all others, till death do you part?"

Cass took a deep breath and closed his mouth. Nothing short of a miracle was going to stop this atrocity. Didn't the woman have one ounce of respect for marriage—for God's word? A man and a woman didn't marry lightly.

The sheriff lifted the barrel of the gun a notch higher. "Say you're gonna forsake all others till death do you part, boy, or I'll blow a hole through your chest."

"I will not."

The sheriff pressed the shotgun firmly against Cass's rib cage. Cass sent a frantic look at Reverend Olson.

Reverend Olson sighed. "You better say you'll take her for your wife, son. The marriage won't be legal otherwise."

The gun nudged him again. "Wanna live to see thirty, boy?"

Cass thought about it: death—or life with Susanne McCord. Still he didn't answer. He felt the gun press tighter in his side.

"All right! I do!"

Reverend Olson snapped the Bible shut. "I now pronounce you man and wife." He lifted his brows hopefully. "I don't suppose you'd like to kiss the bride?"

Cass stared stoically ahead. "I don't want to kiss the bride."

The reverend sighed. "I didn't think so."

Five minutes later, Leviticus stored the last of Susanne's baggage in the back of the sled.

"Take care of my daughter." Leviticus reached up to shake his new son-in-law's hand. Cass sullenly ignored the offer.

Leviticus laid a small pouch filled with several gold pieces on the seat beside Cass. "She's a good girl," Leviticus told him in a hushed whisper. "Just a mite determined at times."

Cass thought that had to be the understatement of the year.

Reverend Olson, the sheriff, and Leviticus remounted. With a nod, they prepared to leave.

"You be sure and write your papa the moment you reach Saint Louis," Leviticus reminded.

"I promise. You take care now! I love you!" Susanne McCord Claxton blew kisses.

The small party turned their horses and trotted off in the direction of Cherry Grove.

Cass whistled sharply, and the sled lurched ahead. "You are not going to get away with this," he warned.

Smiling, she slipped her arm through his. "I believe I just did, dear husband."

"Don't call me that."

"Why? I'll grant you permission to call me your wife . . . but only until we reach Saint Louis." She laughed merrily.

"I'll be calling you a lot of things before we reach Saint Louis," he promised.

"Tsk, tsk, such a sore loser! You should have accepted my gracious offer when I first offered it," Susanne pointed out, primly adjusting her skirts. "You'd have been much better off— six hundred dollars richer and still single."

"You don't have six hundred dollars!"

"But you don't know that for certain," she pointed out.

"Your own pa said you didn't."

"My own *pa* doesn't necessarily know everything," she reasoned. "You'll discover, Mr. Claxton, it's so much simpler to let me have my way."

"And you'll discover your conniving ways are going to be dumped on your aunt's porch so fast it'll make your head spin," Cass snapped. "I'll take you to Saint Louis, but once we're there this absurdity is over. This so-called marriage will be annulled. Immediately."

Susanne twisted in the seat and waved her handkerchief at Leviticus, who by now was a speck in the distance. "Bye-bye, Papa. I'll write real soon!" She turned back to the conversation. "And you'll find that all I wanted in the first place was to go to

Saint Louis." She heaved a sigh of contentment. "I'll be only too happy to have the marriage annulled, darling, the moment I reach my Aunt Estelle's. However," she said, pausing to smile at him, "it was truly a touching ceremony—wouldn't you agree?"

Rotten. Cass had no doubt about it. The girl was just plain core rotten.

CHAPTER 1

Six years later, Saint Louis, Missouri

Thunder cracked then rolled along the quiet residential street. A young woman hurried on her way, her hand placed strategically on top of her head to prevent the gusty wind from carrying off her plucky straw hat.

Susanne McCord didn't mind the inclement weather, but she did wish the rain could have held off for another thirty minutes. Fat drops peppered down on the cobblestoned streets, scenting the air with the smell of summer rain.

She smiled, thinking of the changes the past six years had brought. She'd arrived at her Aunt Estelle Merriweather's a spoiled, flighty, temperamental young woman yearning for fun and parties. Instead she had found a dedicated woman struggling to maintain a small orphanage in her home. Now her aunt was gone, and Susanne was in charge of the children.

Her shoes skipped gingerly over the gathering puddles, her eyes scanning the numbers printed on the towering houses. The three-story frame dwellings nearly took her breath with their lovely stained-glass windows and hand-carved doorways.

When lightning flashed as bright as a noonday sun, she peered at the address scrawled on a scrap of paper that was fast becoming soggy in her hand.

Her feet flew purposefully up the walk as the heavens opened to deliver a torrential downpour. Pausing to catch her breath, Susanne stood for a moment under the shelter of the porch eaves, watching the rain pelt down. She noticed the old lamplighter, already soaked to the skin, hastily making his way down the street.

She called out, inviting him to take cover with her. He turned and scurried up the walk, his head bent low against the driving rain.

"Terrible, isn't it?" Susanne commented as the white-haired gentleman removed his top hat and shook the rain off.

"'Tis for certain, little lass." He grinned and his wizened face broke into a wreath of wrinkles. He set his lantern down and extended a friendly hand. "Thaddeus McDougal here."

Susanne returned his greeting. "Susanne McCord. It looks like we're in for a good one." Susanne had never acknowledged her married name, nor did she ever plan to. Since their journey from Kansas to Saint Louis, she had not seen Cass Claxton again. They had parted on bad terms, with Susanne declaring she would see him again when hades froze over.

Thaddeus sighed. "Aye, it does at that, lass."

"Well, we can always use the rain."

"'Tis true, 'tis true." Thaddeus glanced about the massive porch, mild curiosity on his face. "Wasn't aware the old house had finally been sold."

"Oh, I don't think it has." Susanne noticed that the house was not in the best of repair. The porch sagged, the paint was peeling, and several shutters flapped haphazardly in the blowing rain. It didn't matter though—it looked beautiful to her. "I'm here to see about acquiring its use."

"Eh? Well . . ." Thaddeus's pale gaze roamed over the peeling porch ceiling. "Old Josiah would be upset if he could see his house now. Used to brim with love and laughter, it did." His eyes grew misty with remembrance. "Josiah never had children of his own, you know, but he took in every stray he could find. Fine man, he was. The world lost a bit of sunshine when Josiah Thorton was laid to rest."

"I never knew him," Susanne admitted.

"Fine man." Thaddeus sighed again. "Well now, little lass, why be you tryin' to acquire such a big old barn of a house?"

"I'm looking for a place big enough to be a home for nine children."

"Nine children!" Thaddeus took a step back, eyes wide. "Beg pardon, miss, but you don't look old enough to have nine wee bairns."

Susanne smiled at his obvious bewilderment. "I'm overseer of a small orphanage. The bank has been forced to sell the home we're presently living in, and someone mentioned that this house was empty. I've looked unsuccessfully for weeks for somewhere to move the children, so when I heard about the house I hurried right over." Her forehead creased with a frown. "I'm sorry to hear the owner's passed on."

Losing Aunt Estelle's house had been a blow, but running an orphanage was not a profitable business venture, and Estelle had been forced to mortgage her home for operating expenses.

Now Susanne was desperate to find somewhere to shelter the children.

"Aye, Josiah died about a year ago."

"Then his family will be disposing of the property?"

Thaddeus frowned. "Josiah didn't have any family—leastways, not that I know about. Rumor has it that he had a business associate, though. Could be he can tell you what's to be done with the house."

"And how might I contact this business associate?" Susanne hoped that wouldn't prove to be another time-consuming delay. The orphanage had to be out of its present location by the end of the month.

"Well . . ." Thaddeus stepped over to the legal notice nailed to the porch railing and peered through his wire-rimmed spectacles. "It says here that anyone wanting information about his property should contact a Mr. Daniel Odolp, Attorney-at-Law."

Susanne took a small pad from her purse and prepared to scribble down the address. "Does Mr. Odolp reside here in Saint Louis?"

"Aye, his office is close by." Thaddeus read the address aloud for her.

"Oh, that's not far."

"Only a wee jaunt."

"I wonder if Mr. Odolp would still be in his office."

Thaddeus reached into his waistcoat and took out a large pocket watch. He flipped open the case and held the face of the watch toward the receding light. "Depends on how late he works. It's nigh on six o'clock."

Six o'clock. Susanne doubted Mr. Odolp would be working this late, but since she'd be passing by his office anyway, it wouldn't hurt to check. "Thank you, Thaddeus." Susanne replaced the pencil and pad in her purse and reassessed the inclement weather. It wasn't raining hard—just a nice, steady drizzle. "I'll go by and see if Mr. Odolp is still in his office," she decided.

"But it's still raining."

Susanne shrugged and gave Thaddeus a bright smile. "I won't melt."

"Well now, you just might. You're an unusually pretty piece of fluff with that flaxen hair and those violet-colored eyes. If you had wings you'd look like an angel," he finished wistfully.

"A half-drowned angel, surely, but I appreciate the lovely compliment. It's been nice talking with you, Thaddeus." Susanne reached down and quickly removed her shoes and stockings, then her hat. It was senseless to ruin them. Her toes peeked out from under the hem of her skirt.

Thaddeus grinned. "A barefoot angel. Nice visiting with you, lass." He picked up his lantern. "I must be about my work. It'll be full dark soon."

Susanne watched the old lamplighter step off the porch. A chance meeting and now they would go their separate ways. One set out to light folks' pathways; the other to find a home for nine waifs and strays.

Aunt Estelle had been a devoted, God-fearing woman who had taken seriously the commandment to give a cup of cold water in Jesus' name. No child had been turned away from her door. When Susanne had worried about unpaid bills, her aunt had quoted her favorite Scripture: " 'Be kindly affectionate to one another with brotherly love, in honor giving preference to one another; not lagging in diligence, fervent in spirit, serving the Lord; rejoicing in hope, patient in tribulation, continuing steadfastly in prayer; distributing to the needs of the saints, given to hospitality.' Romans 12:10-13."

Estelle Merriweather had lived those words. She had been patient when times were hard, diligent in prayer, rejoicing in hope and believing that God would provide.

Susanne dodged another puddle. Well, she had been as patient as possible, which she acknowledged wasn't saying all that much, and the good Lord knew she spent a prodigious amount of time on her knees. But she felt the hope in her own heart was a feeble candle flame compared to the blazing torch of steadfast confidence that had filled her aunt's every waking moment.

Still, she had learned to trust in God's tender care. She sighed. Hope. It was all she had to cling to.

"Lord, I'm *hoping* you will help me get that house."

Saint Louis, Missouri, had been the gateway to the West for adventurers, explorers, traders, missionaries, soldiers, and settlers of the trans-Mississippi. Founded in 1764 by Pierre Laclede Liguest, a French trader, it began as a settlement for the development of the fur trade. One hundred and ten years later the area had turned into a thriving waterfront town where cotton, lead, pelts, gold from California, and silver from New Mexico poured through shipping lanes along the busy Mississippi levee. It was said that Saint Louis was admired for her hospitality, good manners, high society, virtue, and the sagacity of her women.

One such woman hurried through the night, intent upon her mission. Susanne could hardly believe her good fortune when she rounded the corner leading to the landing and saw the faint lantern glow spilling from a window of a second-story office.

Prominently displayed in bold black print across the window was DANIEL R. ODOLP, ATTORNEY-AT-LAW.

She covered the short distance to the building and climbed the steep stairs leading to the second floor. A few minutes later she tapped softly on Mr. Odolp's door.

"Yes?" boomed a deep voice that brought nervous flutters to Susanne's stomach. The man sounded like a giant.

"Mr. Odolp?"

"Yes!"

"I . . . I wonder if I might speak with you?"

Susanne heard a shuffling, then the sound of chair legs being scraped across a wooden floor. Heavy footsteps approached the doorway.

She swallowed, her throat gone dry. With only a small tallow candle splitting the shadows of the dark, narrow, forbidding hallway, she suddenly wished she'd decided to wait until morning to make her visit. Just as she was turning to leave, the door was abruptly flung open.

"Yes?"

The man standing in the doorway was indeed a giant, at least six feet five. Bushy dark brows nested over his beady black eyes. His face was pockmarked, and his jowls hung heavily on his neck. Sweat beaded profusely on his ruddy forehead.

Susanne thought he was the most unattractive and intimidating man she'd ever encountered.

"Mr. Odolp?" she asked meekly.

"I am Mr. Odolp!" he barked. "Good grief, woman, are you deaf?"

Susanne drew herself up stiffly, perturbed by his appalling lack of gentility. "No, sir, but I shall be if you continue to speak to me in that tone."

"You called my name," he boomed, "and I answered. You implied you wanted to speak to me, and when I opened the door, you asked *again* if I was Mr. Odolp. Naturally, one would assume you have a hearing problem."

Susanne jumped as he bellowed again.

"*Yes*, I am Mr. Odolp!"

"Well, you needn't keep shouting." She lifted her skirts and brushed past him.

He closed the door and stalked back to his desk, his eyes grimly surveying her bare feet. "Where are your shoes and stockings, young lady?"

Susanne glanced down and blushed. Her shoes were still in her hand, along with her hat and stockings. She must look as strange to him as he did to her. "I'm sorry . . . it was raining."

"What brings you to my door at this hour?" the attorney demanded, curtly dismissing her stammering explanations. He sat down and reached for a wooden box filled with cigars, selected one, bit off the end, and spat the fragment into the wastebasket. His chair creaked and moaned with the burden of his weight.

Susanne flinched at his lack of manners, but her demeanor remained calm. "I understand that you're handling Josiah Thorton's estate?"

"I am." The lawyer held a burning match to the cigar and puffed, blowing billowing wisps of smoke into the air.

The humidity in the room was stifling. Susanne fanned smoke away from her face. "I was wondering if Josiah's house is going to be sold."

"Which one?"

"Does he have more than one?"

Mr. Odolp turned his face upward and hooted uproariously. "'Does he have more than one?' You're not serious!"

"I'm afraid I didn't know Mr. Thorton personally."

"I'm afraid you didn't either." Mr. Odolp fanned out the match, propped his feet on top of his desk, and took a long draw on his cigar. "Exactly which house did you have in mind, honey?"

Susanne felt her hackles rise at his growing insolence. "The one on Elm Street. And my name is Miss McCord, sir."

"Well, what do you want to know, Miss McCord?"

"Some details about the house. For instance, who will be disposing of the property?"

"The house was jointly owned."

"By whom?"

"Josiah and his business partner." Mr. Odolp brought his feet back to the floor and stood up. He lumbered to the files and rummaged for a few minutes before extracting a thick folder. "Since Josiah had no immediate family, we're waiting to see if anyone steps up to claim his estate." Mr. Odolp grinned as though he knew his next remark would certainly shock her. "Josiah's partner wants to be sure there aren't any illegitimate Thortons waiting in the wings."

Susanne was taken aback by his speculation and annoyed at

his continuing impudence in a lady's presence. "And if there aren't?"

"Then the Thorton estate reverts to Josiah's partner." Mr. Odolp sighed, and Susanne detected a note of envy. "A sizable fortune, I might add. The partner will then decide what he wants to do with the property."

"Exactly how long will it be before a decision is made?"

"Six months or longer."

Susanne walked to the window and looked down on the rain-slicked streets. She pursed her lips thoughtfully. The house was exactly what she was looking for. Undoubtedly there were others available in town, but none so well suited to her purpose.

She'd hoped to stay in the house longer, but six months would be sufficient. If she could persuade Josiah's partner to lease the house to her for six months, it would alleviate her immediate problem. At least she and the children would have a roof over their heads until she could make other arrangements. "Would it be possible for me to speak with Mr. Thorton's business associate?"

"I see no need to bother him. What is it you want?"

Susanne turned from the window, meeting his beady eyes. "I would prefer to speak to the partner in private, Mr. Odolp."

"And he would prefer you to speak to me."

"Then let me phrase it differently." Susanne let a hint of coolness creep into her manner. "I *insist* on speaking to Josiah Thorton's business partner."

"You can't."

Susanne arched one brow. "Does the name Silas Woodson ring a bell with you, Mr. Odolp?"

"The governor?"

"Yes, the governor of Missouri." Susanne tapped her finger on her cheek thoughtfully. "You see, Uncle Silas would be quite distressed to learn of this conversation—"

Daniel Odolp's eyes widened. "Now, now, let's not jump to conclusions. I'll help you if I can." She could almost see him thinking that if the governor was the chit's uncle, he'd better be a bit more cordial. His manner changed abruptly. "I don't like to have my clients bothered . . . but in this particular case I'm sure I can bend my rules a bit."

He reached hastily for a pen and paper. "Now, I'll just jot down the name and address of Josiah's partner. There's no need to tell him where you got this information, of course—"

"None at all."

Daniel slapped the piece of paper into her hand. "How is your uncle these days?"

"Oh, very busy."

"I can imagine."

Susanne nodded. "He and my dear mama are brother and sister, you know."

"No, I didn't know."

"Well, I must be off, Mr. Odolp." She folded the paper carefully and slipped it into her bag. "Thank you for your cooperation."

Daniel rose and extended his hand, his manner noticeably more pleasant. "Always happy to oblige, Miss McCord. Must you be leaving so soon?"

Susanne smiled. "I do wish I had time to stay and chat."

"Stop by anytime. Always happy to visit."

"I will."

Susanne clutched her shoes, stockings, and hat as she

walked to the door. She'd pulled it off! Aunt Estelle would have disapproved of her tactics, but under the circumstances even she would tolerate this one tiny deception.

"Good evening, Mr. Odolp."

"Good evenin', ma'am. You say hello to the governor for me."

"I will. He'll be ever so pleased to hear from you."

Once safely outside, Susanne hurried down the steep stairway and out onto the street, still grinning from her victory. She did have one qualm—mainly that God might not approve of her methods. "Lord, I'm sorry if I sort of edged outside of the bonds of truth, but You know I just have to have that house. There is no other answer."

Pausing to catch her breath under the streetlight, she reached into her purse and carefully unfolded the paper the attorney had given her. Her eyes widened, and she felt a hot flush creep up her neck when she read the name printed in bold black letters.

Cass Claxton

Cass Claxton! She had to force back a rush of hysteria.

Great day in the morning! Cass was Josiah Thorton's business partner?

Late-afternoon sun spilled across the Aubusson carpets in the elegant room. Golden rays bathed the fine furniture and the tasteful art hanging on pewter-colored walls. Dark mahogany bookcases contained the finest array of world literature. Cass

Claxton was a wealthy man in earthly ways, but when it came to keeping a woman happy he was poor as a widow's mite.

"It is getting late," the young woman observed.

"So it is." He shuffled through a stack of papers, finding that his heart wasn't in the upcoming social event. Shadows had lengthened and turned to a rosy hue when Laure Revuneau eased from the window and approached the desk.

"*Mon cheri*, you will make us late for the party," she reproached. "Can this work not wait until morning?"

Cass lazily grinned at her, stemming her hopes of serious reprimand. "Laure, my love, I can think of a hundred things I'd rather do with you than attend another one of your Saturday soirees."

She sighed. "*Cheri*, I do not understand you at times. They are not merely *soirees*. My father is the French consul. I have many responsibilities, not the least being to uphold Papa's image."

He reached out and caressed the curve of her cheek. Drawing her into his arms, he kissed her. Kissing always silenced a woman's complaints.

"*Mon pauvre cheri*," she whispered when their lips finally parted. She sympathetically traced the tip of her finger around the outline of his lips. "Do you truly hate my parties so?"

"With a passion. So why do you insist that I attend?"

"Because, it . . . it is something a man of your importance should do."

Cass threw back his head and laughed heartily at her simplistic reasoning.

Laure affected a pout. "Do not laugh at me, *mon cheri*. Someday we will be called upon to host many parties in our own home," she reminded.

He tensed at her thinly veiled reference to marriage—her hints were coming up with unnerving regularity these days. "I'm sure your social responsibilities must be burdensome, but may I say you handle it with elegance and charm that other women can only envy."

"Oh, *merci, cheri.* I have wondered if you'd noticed." She moved gracefully across the room to adjust a vase of fresh flowers.

Cass sat down behind the desk, his eyes going back to the documents in hand. "Would it honestly upset you if I failed to attend the party tonight?"

Laure looked distressed but not surprised by his inquiry. He'd never enjoyed social functions so it couldn't have been a surprise to her. He watched as she carefully rearranged a large white magnolia. "You have pressing business?"

The sun's sinking rays formed a halo around her hair, making it appear as rich as black velvet. Watching her domestic efforts, Cass smiled. She was lovely, rich, and God-fearing. And he wasn't in love with her.

There had been many women in his life, and none could match Laure Revuneau's beauty. But marriage—his marriage— was the last thing on his mind.

"Business could wait," he admitted, returning to the subject. "I'm just not in the mood to socialize."

She tilted her head coquettishly. "You are not in the mood for my company?"

"My dear, you are lovely to look at, but I'm not in the mood for a party."

Laure finished the busywork, then turned and faced him. "I wish you would change your mind. Many of your business associates will be there."

"I thought it was some sort of charity function," Cass murmured absently.

"*Vraiment,* truly, but the guest list is quite impressive. I've invited everyone having the tiniest bit of social prominence—"

"And money," he speculated.

She laughed softly. "*Oui,* most assuredly those who have *richesse.*"

Cass knew her angle. He was arguably considered to be the most eligible yet the most unobtainable bachelor in town—and the young Frenchwoman was not unaware that he was a highly successful entrepreneur with valuable connections to the wealthiest people.

Cass had contacts that Laure drew upon regularly. Because of his various holdings in shipping, cotton, lead, and even silver from Mexico, he could be a real asset for a man in her father's position.

Laure's candid admission of where her values lay annoyed Cass. The last thing he wanted was to mingle in a smoke-filled room with the idle rich. "Why don't I make a donation to whatever it is you're supporting and let it go at that?"

Laure arched a supercilious brow, her smile tantalizing. "I don't want to press you for more than you can afford. I realize you have your own charities."

He frowned at her. "I don't know what you are talking about."

She smiled. "I met Reverend Dawson yesterday. He told me how grateful their church is for the new steeple you provided them."

Cass shrugged. "They needed a steeple. I had the money. Nothing to make a fuss over."

"And the new organ for the Methodist church? the wagonload of meat and vegetables for the Sheltered Souls Mission? Ah. I know your secrets."

"Not all of them, surely." He smiled at her. "That doesn't mean I have to attend every charity benefit in town."

Laure turned, and Cass noticed that her lower lip curled with displeasure. "Please, *mon cheri* . . . you must come . . . for me?"

Cass hated it when she—or any woman, for that matter—tried to pressure him. "Laure, I don't want to argue about this."

"But Papa will wonder where you are . . . and so will my friends!" She crossed the room and knelt beside the desk, grasping his hand. "Please! It will be the last party I will ask you to attend this week." She stared up at him, eyes wide with expectation.

"This week?" Cass shook his head with amusement. It was Friday.

"Say you will come, *cheri*." Laure lightly kissed the palm of his hand.

"Laure . . ."

"*S'il te plaît?*"

He sighed, realizing she was going to be stubborn about it. "All right, but I won't promise to stay the evening."

"*Merci beaucoup, mon cheri!*" Joyfully she wrapped her arms around his neck and kissed him breathlessly. "You will not regret it, *cheri*. . . . I promise."

He wasn't optimistic, but it was difficult to refuse her when she looked at him with those wide turquoise eyes.

"I will instruct Sar to prepare your bath." Laure rose and leaned over to kiss him fiercely. "Try to arrive before dinner. It will please Papa."

Blowing one final kiss, she hurried from the room, leaving a faint trace of her expensive French perfume in the air. When the study door closed behind her, Cass rested his head against the chair back. He didn't plan to hurry. He even toyed with the idea of going back on his promise to attend the party, but after mulling over the consequences such a reversal would bring, he concluded it wouldn't be worth all the tears and fury.

Afterward he would stop by the club for a visit. An hour or two of complete solitude. It had been a lucky day when his old friend, Josiah Thornton, had asked young, callow Cass Claxton to come to Saint Louis and be his business partner. Cass had worked hard and been instrumental in expanding their investments, and he'd prospered beyond anything he'd ever dreamed.

He leaned back in his chair, thinking that sometimes he longed for the old days on the farm with his brothers, Beau and Cole, and his mother, Lilly. In his drive for wealth, he'd neglected important things like family and nieces and nephews—and friends. It had been months since he'd corresponded with Trey McAllister, a man who had become like a brother in the days following the war. There were times when he felt the price for worldly pursuits had been too high. Cole and Beau were happily married, but love had escaped him. While he lived in an imposing house, its emptiness often mocked him.

Cass thought with dread of the evening ahead, but having convinced himself that his concession was the only way to keep peace, he got up from the desk and went in search of the waiting bath.

Shadows lengthened as the carriage carrying Susanne drew to a halt in front of an impressive rose red brick home. The railing of the house's charming cupola matched the one that ran the length of its wide veranda. To the left, a beautiful rose garden captured her attention. She had debated whether to postpone her business until morning, but then decided that since she was in the vicinity, she would approach Cass on her way to the charity function she was about to attend. She swallowed. Meet the lion in his den, so to speak.

Lion? Stubborn mule was more like it.

Susanne sat for a moment staring at the lovely old two-story home, wondering when her estranged husband had become so prosperous. But then again maybe he'd always had money. She realized she knew nothing about Cass Claxton other than the bits of information she'd been able to extract when he'd escorted her to Saint Louis six years ago.

Six years. Was it possible that the days and months had passed so swiftly? She felt the familiar guilt, remembering the way she'd tricked Cass so mercilessly. She was deeply ashamed of what she'd done when she remembered the selfish lengths she'd gone to to get her way, but at the time she'd been desperate. She had been certain that she couldn't have stood another moment in Cherry Grove, Kansas, and since Papa wouldn't hear of letting her travel to Saint Louis alone, she'd thought her only alternative was to use Mr. Claxton as a pawn.

She winced when she recalled the pall of black silence that had hung between them during the endless journey. Justifiably, he'd been furious and had spoken only when absolutely necessary—to bark a warning or issue her a brusque ultimatum. Then, on her Aunt Estelle's front lawn, he had dumped her—and that was the most charitable way Susanne could describe it—and tossed her the small pouch of money Leviticus McCord had given him following their shotgun ceremony.

He had issued one final, tight-lipped decree: *"Have this outrage annulled!"* A nagging twinge reminded Susanne that she had never gotten around to it. Not that she had taken her vows seriously—far from it—but she had never filed for the annulment. She'd assumed there was no hurry. Cass had returned to his home in River Run, and she'd felt certain that she'd never see him again.

A real marriage, a binding one, to Susanne's way of thinking, began with a snow-white wedding gown, a church, flowers, and a host of well-wishers, not with an embarrassed minister, a sheriff carrying a loaded shotgun, and a bewildered groom—a stranger—pleading for mercy in the middle of a dusty road. But she supposed she should have kept her promise and followed through on the annulment. Well, she was certain of one thing: Cass Claxton had not pined away for her. Most likely, he'd filed for the annulment the moment he'd gotten home.

Stepping lightly from the carriage, she instructed the driver to wait, then turned and proceeded up the flagstone walk.

A lovely dark-haired beauty about her age was coming out the front door. As Susanne approached, the woman greeted her softly, *"Bon soir, madame."*

Susanne returned her smile. "Good evening. Is Mr. Claxton in?"

"Oui." The dark-haired woman's eyes ran lightly over Susanne.

"Thank you . . . *merci.*"

The young woman distractedly responded, *"Pas de quoi. . . ."*

Susanne stood before the brass door knocker, fashioned

in the shape of a lion's head, trying to bolster her courage. She peered closer at the fierce image, thinking the symbol apropos for Claxton. She knew that what she was about to do would not be pleasant. Cass would not be pleased to see her again, and she couldn't blame him. But the needs of nine homeless children were far more important to her than a bruised ego.

She turned slightly to watch the striking young French-woman step into the waiting hansom cab sitting at the side entrance. Who was she? Susanne mused. A maid? She seriously doubted it, considering the woman's appearance and the cut of her stylish gown and cloak. One of Cass's lady friends? Apparently her dear "husband" was managing to amuse himself in his wife's absence.

The philistine brute!

She drew a resigned breath and reached for the brass knocker. Cass Claxton didn't scare her. Whether he was pleased to see her or not, they had business to discuss.

And please, dear Lord, let him be civil. I know what I've done to him is awful, but I'm willing to make amends if You will open the door for me. Thank You, Father.

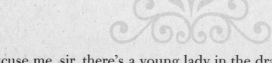

"Excuse me, sir, there's a young lady in the drawing room who wishes to see you." Sar's towering frame dominated the doorway to Cass's bedroom.

The black butler's height of six feet seven inches could be

disconcerting for all who were not acquainted with the man's genteel ways and impeccable manners. His hands were as large as ham hocks, his heavy features far from attractive. But anyone who knew Claxton's manservant could and would attest to his kindness and gentle heart.

For the past three years Sar had run Cass's household with a tenacious spirit and a firm hand. Cass commonly referred to Sar as his right arm, and no other man had so rightfully earned Cass's trust and respect.

"What young lady?" Cass kept his attention centered on the stubborn cravat he was trying to tie.

"She says her name is McCord, sir."

"McCord?" Cass sighed and irritably jerked the cravat loose. The name failed to register with him. "Can you do something with this thing?"

Sar stepped forward, and within a moment the task was effortlessly completed.

"I don't know how you do that," Cass reflected absently. "Would you hand me my jacket?"

"About the young lady, sir?" The servant retrieved the double-breasted topcoat and held it as Cass slipped it on.

Reaching for a hairbrush, Cass tried again to control the springy mass of dark hair still damp from his bath. "Tell the lady I'm indisposed. She'll have to make an appointment to see me on Monday."

"Are you feeling ill, sir?"

"I feel fine."

"The lady was quite insistent about speaking to you this evening."

Cass laid the brush down on the dressing table. "It's late; my business for the day has been concluded. If the lady wants to see me, she'll have to come back Monday."

"I'll convey your message, sir."

"Oh, and have the carriage brought around." Cass reached for the black top hat lying at the foot of the bed. "I'm ready to leave."

"Yes, sir." Sar bowed politely. "Will you and your lady want a bite to eat when you return, sir?"

"No. Miss Revuneau won't be returning with me. I plan to stop by the club later." Cass glanced up and flashed Sar an insightful wink. "You and Sarah Rose can take that evening walk early, can't you?"

A smile brushed across the man's face. "Yes, sir, I'm sure we can."

Susanne looked up as the butler approached. "I'm sorry, madam. Mr. Claxton is not receiving guests at this time."

"Oh?" Susanne's brow lifted with surprise. "Did you tell Mr. Claxton that *Susanne McCord* wishes to speak to him?"

"Yes, madam, I informed Mr. Claxton of your wishes."

"And he refused to see me?"

"Mr. Claxton requests that you make an appointment to see him Monday morning."

"Oh, he does, does he." Susanne shot a reproachful glance up the stairway. Did she dare try to sidestep this giant and force her way into Cass's bedroom? He had every reason not to see her, granted, but she'd come this far. If she left now she'd never find the nerve to come back.

She measured the manservant with a critical eye. He was twice—three times—her size. There was no way she'd be able to make it up the stairs without his stopping her.

"Then I suppose I have no other choice but to comply to Mr. Claxton's request." She nodded coolly. "Good evening."

Sar opened the door. "Good evening, Miss McCord."

Susanne was leaving by way of the front entrance when Cass left from the side entrance of the house. He paused momentarily to enjoy the early evening air. The temperature was beginning to cool; a bank of dark clouds hung in the west, hinting of rain before sunrise. Suddenly his attention was drawn to a young woman just entering a carriage at the front entrance. A flash of homespun cotton and the door to the carriage closed. Moments later the carriage disappeared in the gathering twilight.

McCord. Cass frowned as the name Sar had mentioned earlier popped unexpectedly into his mind.

McCord? Susanne McCord?

He quickly shook away the alarming thought. It couldn't be the same woman. God wouldn't do that to him.

Seconds later he stepped into his carriage, and the conveyance pulled away.

CHAPTER 2

The French consul's elegant mansion blazed with light when Susanne emerged from her carriage a short time later. She glanced down at her homespun dress, her best, but perfectly improper for the event. Money was scarce as hen's teeth at the orphanage, and food was needed more than fine dresses. The French consul had invited her tonight with the charitable intention of introducing her to men and women who would be only too happy to contribute to the small orphanage once they learned of the pressing need. Susanne was prepared to make the plea.

Yet she was in a foul mood. Her "husband's" lack of cordiality hadn't surprised her, nor had his insolence. See him Monday, indeed! She didn't have the time or tolerance to play silly games with him. She needed to face him, face his wrath, clear the air, and move on. He would never take pity on her, but he had seemed the type who loved children. Once on the road to Saint Louis they'd run across an entire family without shoes. He had promptly taken them to the mercantile and purchased each member a pair of the finest leather money could buy. Then he bought the children a large bundle of peppermint sticks. At the time Susanne had thought he was addled *and* rude, but later she realized he must be a man who believed and followed the Lord's command: "Love your neighbor as yourself."

Gathering her skirt in her hand, she started up a walk lined with towering hickory and walnut trees. Blooming roses heavily perfumed the air, and the occasional streaks of lightning in the west suggested more rain.

Susanne dolefully recalled how Slade Morgan had asked to escort her to the gala this evening. When she'd explained to him that she wanted to make a brief stop before the party, Slade had consented to meet her later. As it turned out, her stop had been so brief that he could have accompanied her easily. She nodded to a young couple who strolled past arm in arm and hurried up the walk.

She found herself wishing again that tonight's festivities were being held solely to benefit Maison des Petites Fleurs, or House of Little Flowers. But the small group of homeless waifs had been Aunt Estelle Merriweather's personal crusade, so the hodgepodge flock rarely received outsiders' attention. The nine children were regarded as less than ideal youngsters—street urchins who had stolen for survival, eaten their meals from garbage cans, and fought tooth and nail for the right to exist in a sometimes cold and callous world.

The memory of dear, colorful Aunt Estelle brought the first smile of the evening to Susanne's lips.

Estelle had had a heart as wide as the ocean. Susanne fondly recalled how her aunt, without a word of recrimination, had welcomed the frightfully overindulged daughter of her baby brother into her home six years ago.

Over the years Aunt Estelle managed to channel Susanne's zest and eagerness for life in more sweet-natured directions. She taught her niece the rewards of asking politely instead of rudely demanding. She had shown Susanne the wisdom and power of a twinkling eye and a gracious smile. And she had encouraged her to live her faith, not pretend it.

When Susanne put it all into play she had reformed practically overnight. Now God meant something to her other than words in the Bible. Their daily walks together were more precious than gold to her; she had given her life completely to serving and pleasing Him. She stopped stamping her foot and petulantly tossing her head of golden curls. No longer headstrong, she had become a lady. Estelle had watched a lovely young woman rise from the shell of the original Susanne McCord, like a beautiful butterfly emerging from its ugly cocoon.

Estelle had shown the same zeal and enthusiasm with the nine orphans. She saw them not as thieves and misfits but as needy children crying out for love. Society's lack of compassion toward these children had haunted Susanne's aunt. So one cold, snowy morning she had gone out into the streets, gathering the town's homeless young ones to her ample bosom, telling them something miraculous, something they had never, ever heard before. They were loved.

Aunt Estelle had confided that the dark eyes that had stared back at her with open skepticism had seemed forbidding. However, one by one, their small, dirty hands had clutched the material of her skirt, and like the Pied Piper, she'd led them down the streets of Saint Louis, past the shops and doorways of the town's most respectable and prominent citizens and into the first real home they had ever known.

She had found an elderly couple to attend to the children while she personally handled their religious training and the financial burden. She had taken in washing and sewing and extra baking in order to stretch the budget. It had been a rigorous undertaking, born of love, but she declared it had been worth her every sacrifice to ensure the boys and girls a decent childhood.

When Estelle had passed away a year ago, the awesome responsibility of keeping the small group intact had fallen to Susanne. At times, keeping the wolves from the orphanage door had seemed nearly impossible. Estelle had not been a rich woman, and she had left too little money to keep the orphanage operating.

Leviticus McCord had sent what money he could spare, but it was not enough. Estelle's house was heavily mortgaged in order to pay the orphanage bills. Finally the bank had been forced to sell it in order to settle her estate.

Susanne had been able to keep food on the table by first depleting the small inheritance her mother had left her, then by working as a seamstress. But now that they'd lost the very roof over their heads, she wasn't sure how much longer she could manage to hold on. *Hope.* The word Aunt Estelle had charted her life by seemed like a dim star, barely seen and vanishing when looked at directly. If Susanne couldn't talk Cass into letting her have the Josiah Thorton house she had no idea how they could carry on. She couldn't turn the children back onto the streets. Not after they had experienced a real home and been part of a family. She couldn't bear to think of that happening. No, she had to have that house. It was the only answer.

Harlon and Corliss McQuire, the elderly couple who helped look after the children, refused wages, insisting that they needed very little except room and board. Susanne knew the two of them had grown to love the children as their own, but she felt guilty about their working for nothing.

One fund-raiser like tonight's, and the children would be secure for a whole year, she thought wistfully, wishing again they didn't have to share the largess. However, she would settle for the lease to Cass Claxton's rose-bricked house. She stepped onto the large veranda.

Slade Morgan waited in the shadows of the portico. Susanne approached, and he stepped forward and bowed graciously to kiss her hand. "How lovely you look this evening, my dear." Slade was an encourager to her cause; they'd met one day in the park, and he was the force behind the French consul's efforts to obtain financial support for the kids.

Susanne broke into a smile. The charming, debonair riverboat gambler's easygoing manner and silver tongue managed to capture the attention—as well as the hearts—of most women. She prayed for his soul daily.

His effect on Susanne was no less energizing.

She curtsied demurely. "Sir, you're ever so kind."

Slade gazed back at her, fondness registering in his eyes. "Kindness has nothing to do with it. You are, without exception, the most beautiful woman here tonight."

"May I take that to mean you have already examined the other ladies in attendance?" she bantered, knowing full well that he had. A romantic relationship between them would never come to pass, but she thoroughly liked the man. He had been a solid friend these last few months. Many times he'd left baskets of meat and cheese and fresh fruit on the orphanage doorstep, fiercely denying that he'd been the benevolent soul responsible for the blessing. But Susanne knew where the bounty came from.

He feigned astonishment. "Are there *other* women present?"

Grinning, she looped her arm through Slade's, and he led her through open French doors into a large ballroom, where elegantly dressed men and women whirled around the floor to the strains of violins and harps.

The ballroom looked splendidly opulent. French-cut glass chandeliers flickered brightly overhead, their gaslight fixtures illuminating the rich red tapestries draped artfully at the great long windows. There were massive bouquets of summer flowers atop carved stone pedestals and priceless paintings on every wall. The marble floor was magnificent, having been polished until it reflected the pastel images of the ladies' gowns like a shimmering rainbow.

Susanne found herself thinking that she could care for her nine homeless children for the rest of their lives with a mere fraction of the money represented in this room.

"It's marvelous," she whispered under her breath.

"Stuffed shirts," Slade confided. "But rich ones."

Didier Revuneau spotted Slade and Susanne when they entered the ballroom. Taking his daughter's arm, he gently moved her through the crowd to greet the late arrivals.

"*Bienvenu,* my good friend, *bienvenu!*" The French consul reached out to grasp Slade's hand in greeting.

"Good evening, Consul."

"You have met my lovely daughter, Laure?"

"We've met." Susanne noticed that Slade's eye grazed the

lady with lazy proficiency. He bowed. "Good evening, Miss Revuneau."

Laure graciously acknowledged the greeting, her wide turquoise eyes openly admiring the handsome gambler. "Monsieur Morgan."

"Ah, such a lovely young flower you bring with you tonight." Didier's eyes were warm as he bowed and lifted Susanne's hand to his mouth, lightly kissing the tips of her fingers.

Susanne curtsied. "It is an honor to meet you, sir."

"Ah, but the honor is all mine, *ma chèrie.*"

"And who is this, Monsieur Morgan?" Laure's voice was soft but crisp as she demurely slipped her arm through Slade's with such a familiar ease that it made Susanne wonder exactly how well they knew each other.

It was rare for a man of Slade's reputation to be invited to such a prestigious gathering, but then Susanne knew that her friend was widely accepted in the community despite his questionable occupation.

Slade glanced affectionately down at Susanne. "Miss Revuneau and Consul, may I present Miss Susanne McCord."

"Ah." The host nodded. "From the orphanage, yes?"

"Yes. Thank you most kindly for your invitation."

Laure inclined her head demurely. "I believe Mademoiselle McCord and I share a mutual acquaintance."

"Yes, I believe we do." Susanne had the distinct impression that the consul's daughter might be better acquainted with Cass than she.

"Monsieur Claxton," said Laure.

"Monsieur Claxton," Susanne confirmed. So here was the

reason—and a decidedly lovely one—her husband had been indisposed earlier.

"Did you see Cass?" Laure asked.

"No," Susanne admitted, waiting to observe Laure's reaction.

"Oh." Laure's full lower lip formed into a pretty pout. "I am sorry."

"So was I."

"You are good friends with Monsieur Claxton?"

"I was there on a business matter."

Laure's expression was noticeably more guarded, but the tone of her voice remained pleasant. "Perhaps you will be granted another chance. Cass promised to come to the party. He should arrive very soon."

Susanne felt her pulse take an expectant leap. "Oh?"

"Yes . . ." Laure's attention was momentarily diverted by Susanne's rather plain attire. The dress was simple, but Susanne knew it was also becoming to her. "I was admiring your lovely dress earlier. Is it not the one shown in the recent issue of *La Modiste Parisienne*?"

"Oh, my, no. I could never afford to purchase such a gown. I'm afraid I only copied it," Susanne admitted.

"You *made* this dress?" Laure's brows lifted.

"Yes. I'm delighted you like it."

"It is exquisite," Laure complimented and then returned her attention to Slade. "You must promise me a dance later."

Slade inclined his head politely. "Of course; I would be honored."

"Enjoy the evening," Didier said. Susanne detected a merry twinkle in his dark eyes. "And your lovely lady."

"Thank you." Slade glanced at Susanne. "I'm sure I'll enjoy both."

The consul and his daughter merged into the crowd, leaving Susanne and Slade free to mingle.

"She is lovely, isn't she?" Susanne's gaze still lingered on the consul's daughter.

"Laure?" Slade chuckled. "Indeed, she is quite a woman." He eased her toward the refreshment table, where he poured two cups of cold punch.

"Slade . . ." Susanne was annoyed to discover that she was actually curious about Cass's relationship with the French beauty, though she hadn't the vaguest idea why. She had never considered Cass appealing—and they mixed like oil and water.

"Yes?"

"I was wondering about Miss Revuneau's friendship with Mr. Claxton."

Slade's eyes met hers with a look of amusement. "Friendship?"

"I was on my way to speak to Mr. Claxton earlier, and when I was coming up his walk I saw Miss Revuneau leaving."

Ordinarily, Susanne would have felt ill at ease prying like this, but she knew Slade wouldn't think her boorish—friendship had freed them to discuss their thoughts.

Slade's left brow lifted inquisitively. "Why would you be going to see Cass Claxton?"

Color flooded her cheeks. "I told you; I needed to discuss a business matter with him."

"And Laure was leaving?"

"Yes."

Slade's smile, brimming with male perception, confirmed the obvious. "I would guess they'd spent the afternoon together."

"Oh . . . they are seeing each other?" Susanne deliberately kept her inquiry casual. It really was none of her business. The moment Cass discovered that she was here sparks would fly. *Oh, Father, I don't want to be at sword's point with the man—grant me the temperament to handle our situation with gentleness and grace.* How many times had she prayed the simple prayer? God was not hard of hearing, and His memory was perfect, so why did she continually ask the same thing?

Thank You for answering my prayer, Father.

Now. That was that. She wasn't going to think about it anymore, but simply proceed as though she and Cass were able to talk sensibly and reason like adults. All she needed was the use of a house he owned— and only for a mere six months. Surely the good Lord would not have to work a miracle in this instance.

"I believe you could say that." Slade smiled.

It was Susanne's brow that lifted this time. "Seriously?"

"If Laure has her way. Cass has been a difficult man to get to the altar, but Laure is a determined young lady." Slade leaned closer and lowered his voice. "I've heard she's planning a Christmas wedding."

Susanne glanced at the dark-haired belle, whirling around the floor with one of her many admirers. "Oh, really? How interesting." *How* very *interesting,* she added under her breath. *So he had the marriage annulled and failed to notify me. The cad.*

Around ten, Slade suggested he go in search of more punch. Heat suffused the crowed room. Susanne agreed and drifted toward the veranda for a breath of fresh air while she waited.

She strolled along the railing, listening to the peaceful voices of nature blending in muted harmony. A full moon shone overhead; the earlier rain had vanished.

She allowed her thoughts to drift, feeling relaxed and more optimistic about the children. Somehow things always had a way of working out. If worse came to worst, she could always take the children to her father in Cherry Grove. Leviticus had mentioned in his last letter that he would be willing to provide a home for the orphans in Kansas, but Susanne feared Harlon and Corliss were too old to make the long trip, and she didn't have the heart to leave the couple behind. The children were family to her, and so was the elderly couple. It would be best for all concerned if she was able to keep her flock in Saint Louis, where Harlon and Corliss could remain a part of their lives.

She knew what Aunt Estelle would say. "Ask the Lord. He will direct your paths." She purely hoped He wasn't directing her path toward Cherry Grove, Kansas. Surely God could see it would be better for them to remain here in Saint Louis.

Straight ahead, Susanne saw a man step onto the veranda and pause to admire the evening. Light spilled from the ballroom, and she recognized Cass Claxton's familiar stance.

Proud.

Confident.

Her heart thumped in her chest. *Coward*, she silently chastened. *He's just a mortal man. And a bullheaded one at that.*

She paused, staring at her husband, taking in the head of curly dark hair and powerfully broad shoulders. The years had added an attractive, virile maturity to him. In fact, he now possessed devilishly good looks. He had been heavier when she'd last seen him, almost stocky from what she remembered, and now he looked leaner, older, and wiser.

More inflexible.

Unapproachable.

Dressed in black, with a gray-and-white-striped silk waist-coat, his polished boots showing not a speck of dust, Cass looked every bit the successful young entrepreneur he was reported to be. He carried his top hat in one hand while the other curled around a malacca cane—a rich brown walking stick made from the stem of a palm tree. How had the rough ex-soldier she had known been transformed into this picture-perfect dandy?

She stood quietly in the shadows, not ten feet from him, afraid to breathe. How would he react when he saw her? She was afraid she knew. He would be none too happy.

As though sensing that he was being watched, he straightened and turned.

And their eyes met.

Even the cicadas and tree frogs seemed to be holding their breath with strained anticipation as Cass and Susanne stood, staring at each other.

His eyes, even more of a vibrant cobalt blue than she remembered, narrowed as they coolly assessed her. Her cheeks warmed beneath his masculine appraisal.

Susanne stood immobilized, holding her breath, preparing for the explosion. Would he detonate with pent-up anger? Or would he turn and walk away without a word? She prayed that he wouldn't walk away. She didn't want to cause a scene, but for the children's sake she would if necessary.

His gaze centered on her, Cass calmly fingered his cravat. In

a voice as relaxed as if they had last seen each other only yesterday, he murmured, "As I live and breathe, if it isn't Miss
McCord. Hades must have frozen over."

Susanne McCord! Somehow her presence wasn't a total surprise.
Trouble was likely to show up anywhere, even at a private party.

"I heard you were here," she said, her tone calm.

Cass felt surprisingly in control of this sudden turn of
events. He was proud that he had sounded so casual. He
intended to be every inch the suave, sophisticated gentleman,
but wasn't sure he could pull it off.

Their gazes remained fixed—reminding him of wild animals
caught in a snare.

She was prettier than he'd remembered. Her once too-slim
body had rounded gently to form appealing curves. Only her
eyes were familiar, a defiant deep violet lined with long, sooty
lashes. She wore her hair differently—more refined and sophisticated than six years earlier—but he'd wager she was still the
devious little schemer.

"Looks like the rain has passed us by," he remarked, hoping
to keep the unexpected encounter as impersonal and brief as
possible. He hadn't seen Susanne McCord or thought about her
in years, but her appearance suddenly brought back the black
day six years ago when, at the wrong end of a shotgun barrel,
he'd been forced to marry the devious twit. Cass did not hold
the memory dear. He couldn't imagine what Susanne McCord

was doing here at Laure's party, but he didn't intend to stick around long enough to find out.

"It does appear that way." She edged toward him.

He debated whether she intended to block his way to the ballroom, and he hoped she would think otherwise.

Taking a second step closer, she said, "I'm glad you're here. I'd like to talk—"

He interrupted. "Make an appointment." Turning, he started back to the ballroom.

Boldly, she stepped forward, throwing her slight weight in his path. Once again their eyes locked.

Cass casually sidestepped, and she dogged his movement. He hadn't forgotten the misery she had dealt him when he'd angered her by deliberately blocking her path in Miller's Mercantile six years ago. Out of the blue, she'd ruthlessly brought him to his knees with one swift, retaliatory blow of her purse to his head.

Facing her, he said calmly, "You are blocking my way."

"I know—excuse me, but I do need to talk to you, and there's no sense in me making an appointment when I can say what I have to say and be done with it." A pleasant smile remained intact on her rosy lips, but he thought it seemed a trifle more forced.

"We have nothing to talk about—and don't try hitting me again."

Her cheeks flamed, and she had the decency to look repentant. "I wasn't going to strike you!"

The sharp exchange between the couple started to draw attention.

Cass glanced uneasily at the growing cluster of curious onlookers. "What do you want?"

"I want to talk to you."

"I'm busy."

"You are *not*."

Seizing her by the wrist, he pulled her back onto the veranda.

"Let go! You're hurting me!" She wrestled to free his hold as he sent a weak smile in the direction of the bewildered guests watching beyond the glass door.

Moments later he backed her against a baluster in a secluded corner of the porch. Their eyes locked in a glacial stare.

"What *are* you doing here, Susanne?" His face was inches from hers now, his voice ominously low.

"Let go of my arm," she demanded.

"Not until you tell me why you are here."

Dipping her head, she sank her teeth into the back of his hand, then twisted loose of his grip so swiftly he could do nothing but let go.

Sucking in his breath, he stared at the row of small, even teeth marks on the back of his hand. "You little spitfire," he hissed.

Her eyes met his. "You weasel! Is this any way to treat a woman you married?" She used both hands to straighten her gown.

Cass glanced over his shoulder, alarmed that her remark might be overheard and misunderstood. "What do you want, Susanne?"

She lifted her chin regally, snapped her fan open, and moved deeper into the shadows. "Why, dear, dear Cass, whatever makes you think I want something?" she inquired.

"Why, dear, dear Susanne," he mocked in a tone far from sweet, "because you always do."

"Perhaps if you had consented to see me when I came by your house earlier, you'd know what I want," she reminded him.

"I had no idea it was you."

"And if you had known?"

His eyes narrowed. "I would have set the dogs loose."

He noticed that his response didn't surprise her, but that only confirmed that she hadn't changed over the years. She was going to be as easy to reason with as a grizzly bear with a thorn in its paw.

"You should have made an effort to see who it was before you sent me away," she accused.

By now the curious guests had starting filing back into the ballroom. Cass made a mental note to extend apologies for the unseemly display. "I was busy."

"Yes. I met her on the way in."

He flashed what he knew to be a lazy, arrogant grin guaranteed to ruffle her feathers. "Then you understand why I didn't want to be disturbed."

She refused to take his bait. "Tsk, tsk. The woman must be desperate for male companionship." She dropped her voice, and he knew what she was about to add would cook her goose, but poor Susanne was powerless to let her opportunity pass. She didn't prove him wrong. "Once a weasel always a weasel."

She had to know that once she'd bitten the whey out of him she'd ruined any chance of civility now. Whatever she wanted, she'd just sealed her chances of ever getting it from him.

Cass fought the urge to strangle her. He knew it was useless to try and outwit her in a war of insults—he'd tried that six years earlier and had lost hands down. All he could do was stand his ground.

She watched warily as he ran a hand through his hair. "What are you still doing in Saint Louis, Susanne?"

"I live here, remember?"

"I remember." But he'd tried to forget. He assumed she had married and by now was in the process of tormenting her husband to death. "I thought you'd moved on by now."

"Ah, then you've thought of me over the years," she said.

A wicked smile curved the corners of his mouth. "Not even once." That wasn't true; he'd thought she would be civil enough to send him a copy of the annulment, but she hadn't. Other than that, he hadn't thought of her.

She sighed. "A pity. And here I thought you were pining away for me all this time."

Cass chuckled mirthlessly. "What a dreamer."

"I would think the more proper question is, what are *you* doing here in Saint Louis? I thought you'd be in River Run."

Cass casually set a booted foot onto the rail next to her and stared into the darkness for a long time.

"It's none of your business," he finally said, "but if you must know, I returned to River Run for a few months before an old friend wrote and asked me to join him in a business partnership here in Saint Louis. So I came back."

"Josiah Thorton," she murmured absently.

His eyes snapped back to meet hers. "How did you know Josiah Thorton?"

"I didn't. I just know that he was your business partner . . . and that he died, leaving you heir to his estate."

Cass didn't fancy her knowing anything about his business. "Where did you hear that?"

"Never mind how, I just did. Actually, it's Josiah's house that I came to see you about earlier."

"Josiah's house?" Cass studied her guardedly. "What about it?"

"I want you to rent the house to me."

"Rent the house to you?" Cass found the request odd, even for Susanne McCord. "I wouldn't rent my horse's leavings to you."

"Nor would I accept them," she snapped.

"Then what makes you think I would rent Josiah Thorton's house to you?"

"I know you won't rent *me* the house, but I'm hoping—and praying—that when you hear that I have nine children who desperately need that house, you'll be willing to at least listen to what I have to say."

For a moment silence filled the air as Cass slowly digested her words. Nine kids? Suddenly he threw his head back and laughed uproariously. His jollity continued to grow, and by the puzzled look on her face he could see that she was frantically reviewing her remark to see what was so amusing that it could send him into fits of mirth.

"What's so funny?" she challenged.

Cass pointed at her, his eyes filling with tears. "You . . . and nine children!" He slapped his hand on his thigh and broke into another boisterous round of laughter.

She watched with a jaundiced eye. "What's so funny about the children and me?"

As quickly as his gaiety had erupted, it came to a sudden halt. His studied her dispassionately. "I can't imagine any man living with you long enough to father nine children. Did you marry a simpleton?"

She smiled. "Yes. But that's beside the point. The children don't have fathers."

His jaw dropped.

"Not *that*," she accused. "They aren't *my* children. Technically."

"I didn't think so!" He burst into laughter again.

"If you can pull yourself together, I'll tell you why I have them," she said curtly.

"Oh yes." He wiped tears from his eyes. "I'm all ears."

"The children are orphans. My Aunt Estelle took them into her home to raise, and after she died I assumed responsibility for their care."

He'd believe that when it was announced that, through an unforeseen technicality, the South had won the war! "Of course you did! Grasping, conniving, spoiled Susanne McCord giving unselfishly of herself to nine homeless children. Sounds exactly like you, my lovely."

"You don't believe me."

"I couldn't hope to live long enough to believe you, Susanne."

"Then I suppose it would do no good to plead with you to lease Josiah Thorton's house to me?"

"None whatsoever." Cass was not a heartless man, and he regretted that innocent children would suffer from his refusal—if she was telling the truth—but the truth was foreign to this woman. He wouldn't help Susanne McCord cross the street, let alone rent Josiah Thorton's house to her. She was out of his life, and he intended to keep it that way.

"Mr. Claxton—" Susanne's eyes locked stubbornly with his—"I know you and I haven't exactly been friends." She stoically ignored the choking sound he made in his throat and continued. "But I fail to see how you could let our personal differences stand in the way of providing a home for nine helpless children. I *beg* you to reconsider. I understand you have accumulated wealth beyond what most people can imagine, and you surely have no need for such a large house. Please reconsider; I'm desperate."

"Come now, Miss McCord, if what you claim is true, and you've turned into an unselfish saint, which I don't believe for a minute, then why are you making it sound as if I'm the one responsible for the children's misfortune?"

"You have the house," she said simply.

He lifted his brows wryly. "There are no other houses in Saint Louis with twenty-four rooms?"

"I'm sure there are, but none so ideal and none that I can afford. I'm afraid I can only offer a pittance to repay you for your kindness and generosity." She nearly choked on the praise. "But the children and I will paint and clean and weed the gardens for a portion of our keep."

"What makes you think you could afford what I would ask?"

"I'm not sure that I can, for we have very little money. But when I saw the house, I knew it was exactly what the children needed, even though it's old and run-down and needs a mountain of repair. Why, no one would think about purchasing it in the condition it's in now. Of course, I had no idea you owned it—"

"I don't. It belongs to Josiah Thorton."

"But he's dead, and you're the heir to his estate and the one most likely to inherit it, along with the rest of Mr. Thorton's vast holdings."

Cass's eyes narrowed. "And who told you that?"

"I can't say who told me, but wouldn't it be to your advantage to have people living in Josiah's house, people who would maintain the dwelling until the estate is settled?"

"And what happens once the estate is settled? Suppose I have a potential buyer interested in purchasing Josiah's house. Would the kindhearted, generous 'weasel' then throw you and your nine little orphans out of the maintained dwelling?"

"Well . . . I'm not sure what would happen in that case." Susanne had learned long ago to take life one day at a time. "It's possible—if I can't find another house at that time—I might be forced to take the children to my father in Cherry Grove, but I don't want to do that right now. With winter approaching, the long journey would be extremely difficult for the elderly couple who helps me run the home," she confessed.

"I hate to hear that, Miss McCord, because I'm not going to help you." Cass straightened to face her. "It looks like you're going to have to trick someone else into helping you out of your mess this time."

She felt her temper rising. "You *can't* help me—or you *won't* help me?"

He grinned. "Both. I can't because Josiah's house is not mine to do with as I please—his estate won't be settled for months yet. And I won't because . . ." His eyes skimmed her insolently. "Well, I think we both know why I won't, don't we? Oh, by the way, I never received those annulment papers. Where are they?"

"You are heartless," she spat out. "Cold, uncaring. Selfish!"

"Weasel," he mocked. He touched his index finger to her chin in silent warning. "Watch it, sweetheart—your halo is wobbling."

She was going to explode. He'd really done it this time. Squaring her shoulders, she called out to his retreating form, "We don't *have* to have twenty-four rooms, you know. We can make do with far less!"

"Forget it."

"Don't you have *any* house you could rent to me and the children?"

"Not even one. Good evening, Miss McCord." He threw his head back and laughed merrily.

Susanne stamped her foot. Good evening, indeed!

The man was an intolerable muttonhead who was going to pay for his high-handedness.

And pay dearly.

CHAPTER 3

Susanne had reached the end of the line. Her options, slim at best, had run out. "I'm sorry," she told the children that night, "but we have no other choice. We must start for Kansas at first light Monday morning."

Susanne McCord did not quit, not when a matter touched her heart, and the children's plight tore at her compassion. She'd broached the lion's den and confronted the insufferable Cass Claxton twice, begging him to reconsider. On both occasions he had turned a deaf ear and told her in his most holier-than-thou tone that it would take an act of divine intervention for him to rent her a glass of water, to say nothing of Josiah Thorton's house.

She'd left enraged each time to scour the town for other prospects, praying for that divine intervention he was so smugly sure she'd never find.

And she hadn't found it.

Lord, are You listening? I really believed You'd help me get that house.

She'd been so sure keeping the children in Saint Louis was the best thing for everyone concerned. It wasn't as if her determination to coerce Cass Claxton into letting her have that house was a selfish desire or even a spur-of-the-moment decision. She'd prayed about it long and often. For some reason God hadn't seen fit to answer her prayers. How could she hold on to hope when her way seemed blocked every direction she turned?

She sat at the orphanage's round dinner table, hands folded, trying to gauge the reactions on the bright young faces. The children—Aaron, sixteen; Payne, fourteen; Jesse, nine; Doog, eight; Margaret Ann, six; the twins, Lucy and Bryon, five; Joseph, four; and Phebia, three—digested the news with solemn gazes.

The children knew of her diligent search to find a home large and inexpensive enough to house them. She also knew the worry lines on her forehead tonight told them that the miracle they had hoped for had failed to materialize. In three short days they had to vacate Aunt Estelle's house. The bank would take possession of their home and pass it on to the new owner. The children would be on the street again. That must not happen. They had learned to trust and to enjoy a fairly stable life. She could not and would not let them return to the sort of desperate existence they had once endured. There was nothing left now but to notify her father and arrange transportation to Cherry Grove. The challenge was overwhelming, even for a woman of her fortitude.

"Are we gonna ride in a wagon?" Jesse picked up an ear of corn and gnawed on a row of tender kernels. The late garden was producing nicely. Susanne would pick the last of the produce and take it with them.

"We have enough money to buy a wagon and a team."

Funds from her personal savings were meager but sufficient. "We cannot hope to find a wagon that will be large enough for all of us to sleep in, but we'll ask the Lord to keep the weather mild so that we can sleep on pallets beneath the wagon at night. Corliss and Harlon will sleep inside."

Susanne tried to read Corliss's reaction to the news as the matronly woman went about quietly dishing potatoes onto the youngest child's plate.

Phebia was the baby of the household, a gurgling, brown-eyed, chubby-faced tot who had been left on the Merriweather doorstep two years ago by a mother who could no longer care for her. Estelle had been eager to welcome a ninth stray into the fold, and the other children had joined in to help with Phebia's upbringing.

"I know it's not the ideal time to embark on a journey," Susanne admitted quietly, "but if all goes well, we should reach Cherry Grove in six to seven weeks."

She knew the journey would be long and arduous, but it was only the end of August, and she figured that with God's help, they would reach their destination before the first heavy snow. She was relieved to see both Corliss and her husband nodding as she spoke, supportive as usual of any request she made of them.

"How are we going?" Harlon asked.

"Well, the most sensible way to go would be to take a boat up the Missouri River to Westport, then buy a wagon and supplies to transport us on to Cherry Grove, but because of our lack of funds, we won't be able to do it that way. We'll travel by wagon, keeping to the main route crossing the state."

The old man nodded. "I'll see to getting the wagon and a team first thing in the morning."

"Thank you, Harlon. Wes Epperson, at the livery barn, said he might have one he'd sell cheaply." Susanne absently reached to cover Doog's fork in a mute reprimand when he prepared to launch a pea at an unsuspecting Bryon. "I think you'll like Cherry Grove," she told the children—although she herself had never been happy there.

When her mother died, Susanne had longed to return to the parties and gaiety of Saint Louis; she'd begged Leviticus to let her go back to Aunt Estelle's, where she'd spent much of her younger years. Leviticus had ignored his daughter's pleading and instead insisted she move with him to Cherry Grove to begin a new life. The decision had forced Susanne to take her own action.

Cass Claxton was elected to take her back to Saint Louis.

The marriage ploy had worked like a charm, though Susanne realized now that using such underhanded tactics had been reprehensible. She thought about her last encounter with Cass and knew deep down that he was absolutely right to resent her. She was no longer the irresponsible, willful girl she had once been, but she had to admit her earlier selfishness still disturbed her deeply. God had forgiven her, but she was slower about forgiving herself. Cass would never forgive her.

Now, when she most desperately needed Cass's help—or more accurately, when she needed the house he controlled—she knew she could never convince him that she had changed.

She sighed, and her father's words came back to haunt her: *"You've made your bed; now you must lie in it."*

"Will them Indians git us?" blond, gray-eyed Jesse asked. He wrapped a string bean around his forefinger.

Susanne smiled. "You've been listening to the big kids in the neighborhood again. They are just trying to scare you. There are no hostile Indians left between here and Cherry Grove, and I'm sure the good Lord will see us through."

Aaron, the oldest of the boys, said quietly, "Ma'am, what about the border ruffians?"

A shudder rippled down Susanne's spine. The threat from marauding gangs of ex-soldiers, both Union and Confederate, was still very real along the Missouri-Kansas border. "Like I said, the Lord is our shield. We'll be very careful to stay out of danger."

"It will be all right," Margaret Ann chimed in.

Susanne had always contended—out of Margaret's hearing range—that Margaret was a thirty-year-old trapped in a six-year-old's body.

"What may I do to help, Miss McCord?" Margaret inquired sweetly.

"I'll make a list tonight of duties that will be assigned to each of us. I'll have it completed by breakfast tomorrow morning." Susanne sipped her coffee, trying to read the children's faces again. She was relieved to see that they seemed to take the turn of events in stride. Over the years, under Aunt Estelle's tutelage, they had become exemplary kids.

Margaret and Payne stood up and began to clear away the dishes, while Corliss wiped Phebia's hands and face and lifted her out of the wooden high chair. She handed the child her favorite doll, Marybelle, and then swatted her lovingly on the bottom.

"Jesse, it's gettin' late. Time for Phebia and Marybelle to be off to bed."

"Yes, ma'am." Jesse pushed back from the table and led Phebia, who immediately popped her thumb into her mouth, out of the room.

"The wood box is gettin' low." Aaron reached into his pocket and slipped his cap onto his head. "I'll be filling it, Miss McCord, before I turn in."

"Thank you, Aaron," Susanne replied absently. She reached for the small slate and piece of chalk.

The remainder of the children dispersed from the table in an orderly manner. Harlon disappeared into the kitchen and returned with the coffeepot, lifting his bushy white brows expectantly at Susanne.

"I've had plenty, thank you."

Corliss bustled off to the kitchen to supervise the cleaning. Harlon sat back down at the table. The clock on the mantel chimed six times while he methodically scraped the bowl of his pipe. Susanne scribbled on the slate, deeply absorbed in making a list of supplies she would need to purchase for the long journey. Money was tight, but she had been known to stretch a dollar until it cried for mercy. Thanks to Cass, she would now have to stretch it until it dropped dead of overuse.

She knew very little about wagons and teams and the proper food to carry on such a long trip, but she had spent hours that morning at the general store, talking to an outfitter. Clifford Magers had explained to her that when she went to select a wagon, she must make sure that it was strong, light, and constructed out of well-seasoned timber—especially the wheels, since they would be traveling through a region that was exceedingly dry this time of year. He warned Susanne that unless the woodwork was thoroughly seasoned, constant repairs would be inevitable.

She'd have to travel light, he insisted, no matter how strong the urge to take along furniture, potted plants, iron stoves, and grandfather clocks. He emphasized that should she succumb to temptation, the heavy items would only have to be discarded by the wayside later in order to conserve the animals' strength for their long journey.

In selecting her team, Clifford advised mules rather than oxen because they traveled faster and seemed to endure the summer heat better. But when she'd gone to the livery later that day, she discovered that mules were priced higher than oxen.

Wes Epperson told her he thought she'd be smarter to buy oxen over mules, assuring her that oxen stayed in better condition and were able to make the journey in the same amount of time. He contended that oxen would be less likely to stampede.

Susanne would have preferred mules, but with her limited funds, she supposed oxen would have to be her choice.

She glanced up, aware that Harlon had been watching her for the past few minutes. She smiled encouragingly. "Is there something you'd like to suggest, Harlon?"

"Yes, ma'am."

Susanne laid the chalk aside and folded her hands over the slate. "I'm listening."

"Have you given any thought to the dangers a young woman and nine children will be facing once we're out on the trail?" he began quietly.

She sighed, sensing that all along Harlon had harbored misgivings about her decision. "I know there will be dangers, and I'm not happy about having to go, but taking the children to my father is our only hope of keeping them together."

"With all due respect, Miss McCord, I think we need a man— a good, strong man who knows the wilderness—to lead us on such a long journey."

Susanne sighed. "I've thought about that, Harlon, but I have no such man, and it isn't as if we're traveling to some faraway place like California or Oregon," she argued. "I'll have you to help me. You're a man."

"I'm an *old* man," Harlon reminded gently. "I can't do anything but hunt for game and haul freshwater to the camp each night. You need a young man, a man strong enough to protect you, wield a bullwhip, and drive a team of oxen."

Susanne realized he was right, but what choice did she have? She didn't know such a man, and her scarcity of funds prevented her from hiring anyone.

"Maybe we can hire a bullwhacker to drive the team," Harlon mused.

"I don't know a bullwhacker, and even if I did, I wouldn't allow such a bully to travel with us."

Everyone knew a bullwhacker was the biggest show-off on a wagon train. His casual brutality to animals was deplorable, and he usually kept the women and children in constant fear. "Besides, I can use a bullwhip myself," she said. A former suitor had taught her how to handle a bullwhip almost as well as a man. She'd become accurate enough to swat a fly off the rump of an ox before the ox even knew a fly was there.

"Well, 'course, it's your decision," Harlon conceded. "I just wanted to make sure you'd thought about what we're gonna be up against."

"I have, Harlon, and I agree with everything you're saying, but I'm afraid we have no other choice. We will have to make the trip alone." She reached over and squeezed his hand encouragingly. "Aaron and Payne are developing into strong young men, and they will be able to drive the oxen. And though they haven't had much experience with a rifle, I'm sure they will learn quickly. The girls will pitch in to do all they can. You'll see; we'll be fine." *Easy to say,* she reflected. She knew only too well the dangers involved, but she would have to take the risk.

Harlon drew thoughtfully on his pipe as she tried to convince him it would be a memorable journey. She knew what he was thinking—that it would be memorable, all right! Susanne knew Harlon had traveled with a wagon train back in the fifties, and he could still tell about the torrential rains, blazing sun, freezing winds, and the dust—miles and miles of swirling dust— that got into the eyes and clothes and food, tormenting the weary travelers until they thought they would lose their minds. She'd heard him talk about the flies and the sickness. . . . Well, it would be different this time. It had to be.

Since God hadn't helped her get the Thorton house, dare she hope He would guard them on this trip? *I'm sorry,* she mentally apologized. *It's not that I don't believe, because I do. I'm just not sure what You want me to do.* It hardly seemed possible that God would want her to set off this time of the year with nine children and an elderly couple traveling all the way to Kansas by themselves. Even she could see the enormous potential for disaster.

"You'll see; we'll make it just fine," she said again before turning her attention back to her list.

"Well, I hope so," Harlon muttered.

A few minutes later he pushed away from the table and slowly got to his feet. "It sure would make it easier if you had a husband to take us all to Cherry Grove," he said almost wistfully.

Susanne glanced up from the slate. "Yes, it certainly would make it easier."

"Well, don't be frettin' none over what I've said." Harlon

sighed as he stretched lazily. He shuffled over to wind the clock. "Me and Corliss will do everything we can to help get those young'uns to their new home. The good Lord will see us through. He always has."

"He always has." She nodded. "I've been praying about it, Harlon, and I don't think we have a thing to be concerned about." She was doing her best to keep up a good front, although truth be told, she was scared half to death thinking about everything that could go wrong.

Harlon nodded and announced he was going to turn in.

Susanne distractedly bid him good night.

The lamp had burned low when she finally blew out the flame. She closed her eyes and clasped her hands around her waist, trying to ease the stiffness in the small of her back. Harlon's earlier comment drifted back to her: *"It sure would make it easier if you had a husband."*

Reaching for the candle, she rose to make her way to the darkened stairway, thinking about his observation.

Suddenly her hand paused on the railing.

"It sure would make it easier if you had a husband." Harlon's words echoed through her mind again, taunting, offering an almost prophetic challenge. *"Someone who could take us to Cherry Grove . . ."*

Her feet absently claimed a second stair, then hesitated again. It *would* make it considerably easier if she had a strong young husband to help out. He could safely escort them, and they could all stop worrying. She stood in the darkness, scowling thoughtfully.

Well, maybe she *had* a husband—a good, strong, reasonably young husband who was more than capable of escorting them on such a journey. And why shouldn't he? Wasn't he partly to blame for her having to make the journey since he'd refused to rent her Josiah's house?

Susanne, there's no way on this earth that you could ever talk Cass Claxton into escorting you to your own lynching . . . well, maybe he would agree to take me to that, she amended grudgingly. But he would most assuredly refuse to take her, two seventy-year-olds in failing health, and nine homeless children to Cherry Grove, Kansas.

She took another step and then paused. No, he would *never* do it . . . unless . . .

Unless . . .

She smiled and then moved with purpose as she hurried up the steep stairway, confident that if she put her mind to it, she could find a way he would.

Maybe it was time to show that smart-alecky Cass Claxton that Susanne McCord *still* had the upper hand when she wanted it.

Monday morning dawned with a slow, steady rain dripping from the eaves of the Claxton estate. In the distance occasional thunder rumbled, but all in all, the gray, cool morning was ideal for working. However Cass found he had to struggle to keep his mind on the papers spread out before him.

He sat at his desk trying to concentrate while Laure sat watching him.

"Oh, *mon cheri*, why must you always work? Could we not go for a ride in the countryside?"

"It's raining, Laure. Don't you have mission work you should attend to?"

"Oh—I am not in the mood for mission work. Can we not have a picnic in the gazebo? It would be so lovely even though it is raining. Come—don't be such an old workhorse."

Moments later he found himself gazing into her turquoise blue eyes and admonishing her in what he hoped was his sternest voice. "What am I going to do with you?"

"Ah, but I am shameless when it comes to you, *mon cheri*." She smiled and lightly traced the outline of his lips with her forefinger. "Please? A simple picnic."

A sudden rap on the study door interrupted them.

Laure groaned when Cass shoved back and went to answer the summons. "Tell Sar we do not want to be bothered," she said.

Cass grinned and opened the door. "Don't be so eager, love. There is time for both business and pleasure." She frowned when a more persistent knock sounded.

He found Sar waiting with an envelope in his hand.

"Yes?"

"I'm sorry to bother you, sir, but a telegraph message just arrived. I thought you would want to see it immediately."

"Oh?" Cass took the envelope. "Thank you, Sar." He closed the door and crossed the room, opening the missive to peruse it.

"What is it, *mon cheri*?"

A frown creased his forehead. His eyes quickly scanned the puzzling message.

NEED HELP STOP COME AS QUICKLY AS POSSIBLE STOP BEAU

"Is it bad news?" Laure moved to stand by his side, her eyes searching the message over his shoulder.

"I'm not sure. It's from Beau."

"Your brother?"

"My brother in Cherry Grove. He must be in some sort of trouble." Cass absently pitched the piece of paper onto the desk and strode briskly toward the doorway.

"Where are you going?" Laure demanded.

"To Kansas." He flung the door open and shouted for Sar.

"*Kansas!*" Laure wailed. "But you cannot! You will be gone for weeks! And there is a party Friday night."

"You'll have to attend without me."

"But this is most terrible!" Laure ran out of the study, trying to keep up with his rapidly retreating form. "When will you be back? How long will you be gone?"

"Don't know, and I'm not sure," he murmured distractedly. "I'll let you know." Bounding up the stairs two at a time, he shouted, "Sar! Pack a bag! I'm leaving in five minutes."

"But, *mon cheri!*" Laure paused and slapped her hand against the railing angrily when Cass continued his ascent. "*Cherry Grove, Kansas?*"

Rain fell in heavy sheets. When Susanne received the wire answering her inquiry, she smiled grimly and destroyed the paper.

Father, forgive me. But I know no other way. I realize I have already broken another promise—to make amends to Cass and then to leave him alone—but there's no other way to get the children to Kansas. If You will see us safely to Cherry Grove I will step out of Cass's life forever. And this is one promise I will keep.

She sent one more wire to her father, then hurried back to the orphanage to gather the flock, who had been in preparation the past two days for the journey. The small entourage left Saint Louis around eight in the morning. Jesse, Doog, and Margaret Ann walked behind the wagon and were soon struggling to keep up. Aaron and Payne sat on the narrow wagon seat, manhandling the reins. The newly purchased covered wagon rolled cumbersomely over the soggy ground. The children were forced to step lively as the wheels on the large prairie schooner sluiced through deepening ruts. It wasn't a fit day for man or beast to be about, but Susanne prayed the weather would clear by early afternoon.

"Keep moving, children. The rain will surely let up soon!" Susanne glanced anxiously over her shoulder when Aaron urged the oxen up a steep incline. The creak of harness and leather filled the air as the massive animals labored to pull their heavy load.

Harlon rode ahead on a mule he'd purchased, hat pulled low on his forehead in an effort to shield his face from the rain. Corliss rode in the wagon and tried to entertain the younger children. Now and again she popped her head out to keep an eye on the ones walking.

Because the weather was warm, the children had been instructed to tie their shoes together and hang them over their shoulders to prevent them from wearing out the leather on the long journey. Susanne couldn't afford to buy new shoes this winter, so not one complaint was heard.

Phebia rode next to Payne on the wagon seat, hugging her doll, Marybelle, to her chest to protect it from the pelting rain. "Me want to go hooooome." She had begun sobbing almost the moment they'd left the city limits. "Me getting all wet!"

Susanne momentarily climbed into the wagon and tried to explain that they couldn't go home—they *had* no home—but to Phebia's three-year-old mind, the explanation was useless. The child had already wearied of the journey.

The oxen topped a rise in the early afternoon, and Aaron halted the wagon to allow sufficient time for the smaller children to catch up. Susanne rested against the back of the wagon bed, studying the rain-soaked horizon and trying to shake the depression that had been with her since waking that morning. Overhead the sky threatened more rain.

They'd been traveling for more than four hours, and she was certain they had covered only a few miles. No matter how hard she tried to convince herself that she could do it, the long trip loomed bleak ahead of her. *When the rain lets up, we'll be able to move faster*, she reasoned. Gray clouds hung low, shrouding the earth with a pewter mist. Suddenly the sky opened up and poured.

Harlon galloped up beside the wagon and had to shout to be heard above the torrential downpour. "I be thinkin' it might be a good time to stop for dinner!"

"I think you're right!" Susanne called back, thankful for any reprieve.

"There's a grove of sycamores 'bout a quarter mile on up the road. Looks like as good a place as any to make camp."

"I'll follow you!" Susanne was taking her turn driving the team, and she fought to keep the animals moving as lightning streaked wildly across the sky, followed by earth-rattling thunder. Phebia screamed. Marybelle's straw-colored hair wilted in the rain.

"Phebia, darling, Marybelle will be fine." Susanne chanced a quick pat on Phebia's knee before she was forced to turn her attention back to the team.

Her sympathy only served to remind Phebia of how thoroughly miserable she was, and she bawled even more loudly.

Susanne herself was close to crying a few minutes later when she heard the back wagon wheel lurch, then slip deeper and deeper into a quagmire.

Corliss poked her head through the canvas opening. "What's going on?"

"The wheel—I think it's stuck!"

Susanne stood in the midst of the cloudburst, hands on her hips, surveying the wheel that was hopelessly mired to the hub. Phebia screamed harder. There wasn't a thread of dry clothing left on any of them, and if Susanne could have gotten her hands on Cass Claxton at that moment, she—well, her behavior wouldn't be Christlike.

Cass traveled fast and light. His horse covered the ground in smooth, even strides despite the worsening weather. Within fifteen minutes of the time he'd received Beau's message, he was on his way. His mind raced with the possibilities that might await him when he reached Cherry Grove. Beau was ill? Something had happened to his wife, Charity? Surely it wasn't their little girl, Mary Kathleen. . . . She had been a healthy, rosy-cheeked infant when Cass had last seen her, but that had been more than six years ago. Had something happened to her— or maybe to the twins, Jase and Jenny?

He flanked the stallion harder; worry lines creased his face. Something had happened to Ma . . . or Willa, the family housekeeper . . . or his older brother and his wife, Cole and Wynne.

Forgive me, Lord. . . . I should have kept in closer touch with the family. He'd become a loner; he knew it. But when a man was single it was hard to stay in touch with people. Particularly when a good portion of his time had been taken up with making money and taking care of his business. He'd been a fool to put personal wealth ahead of family ties. How long had it been since he'd seen most of them? Four, maybe five years.

The horse topped a rise, and he abruptly reined the stallion to a halt. The animal was already winded, and Cass realized he was pushing too hard. Running the horse to death was not only cruel and senseless, but would cost him more delay. He rested against the pommel of the saddle, allowing the horse to catch its breath and cool down. His eyes skimmed the valley below, focusing on a covered wagon in the near distance, contortedly leaning to the left side. Several figures milled about in apparent confusion while a couple of young lads tried to unhitch a cow and a goat that were tied behind the wagon. A large chicken crate remained fastened to the side of the wagon, its occupants flapping their wings and cackling loudly in the confusion.

Pioneer family in trouble, Cass concluded. He sat watching what appeared to be an elderly man and woman, along with a younger woman, struggling to free the wheel from a muddy confinement. He could see now that there were children—a whole slew of them—adjacent to the mud hole that imprisoned the spoke wheel.

After studying the situation for a few minutes, Cass decided the wheel was going to be impossible to free the way they were going about it. He shifted uneasily in the saddle, grappling with his conscience. His first instinct was to swing around the wagon and be on his way. It wasn't his problem. If he stopped to help, he could be delayed for an hour or longer, and he could hardly afford the wasted time. However, he could plainly see that at the rate they were going, the family would be stuck until the sun came out and the road dried.

And some of those kids sounded real unhappy. The desperate wail of a small child sobbing her heart out drifted on the wind.

He yanked his hat lower, hoping to overcome his conscience. He'd never claimed to be a Good Samaritan . . . but he was a decent sort, and he knew he couldn't just ride by and ignore the situation, much as he'd like to.

Ma would wring him dry if she ever heard that he'd ignored a soul in trouble.

Sighing, he picked up the reins, wishing at times that he'd been raised a heathen. It would have made his choice easier. He clucked to his horse, figuring he might as well ride down there and get it over with so he could be on his way.

As he approached the wagon, he quickly recognized Susanne McCord, and he felt his expression go from open to incredulous. No. It wasn't possible. Not *her*.

Rain spilled in rivulets off the brim of his hat. He sat on his horse and stared down at her. It was uncanny how this woman turned up to haunt him! He didn't know why the good Lord continued to throw her in his path, but here she was, her wagon bogged down in a muddy slough, while nine children stood helplessly beside the road, looking to him as if he had just come off a mountain with stone tablets in his arms.

"What are you doing here?"

"I think I could ask the same." Susanne turned to look back at the wheel. She stood ankle-deep in mud. "How fortunate we are that you've come along."

Cass coldly met her look. "I fail to see anything fortunate about it." He wouldn't put it past the wench to have set him up again, but she couldn't have known that he would be traveling this particular road at this particular hour.

She brushed a strand of damp hair out of her eyes, apparently ignoring his brusque tone. "You can see we are in a good deal of trouble. Would you be so kind as to lend a hand?"

"Ha!"

She blushed, casting an apprehensive glance toward the older couple, who were so engrossed with the problem at hand that they didn't appear to have heard the exchange. "There's no need for sarcasm," she reproached. "We are in need of a good strong back, and yours should do nicely."

Cass was about to tell her what she could do with that idea when he turned sharply at the sound of the elderly man groaning with misery. The fellow strained against the large pole he was manipulating in a vain effort to pry the wheel loose.

"Harlon, your heart!" his wife called.

Cass glanced back at Susanne, struggling with his conscience.

The littlest girl burst into renewed tears, setting up a wail that would raise the dead. "Me sooo wet and hungrrry!"

She held a doll; its flaxen hair trailed through the mud as the child dragged it by the feet when she made a beeline toward Susanne. The little girl buried her face in Susanne's rain-soaked skirt and howled.

"Please, Cass. We *need* your help. There are other people involved here, not just me," Susanne pleaded. Several of the other children tried to comfort the sobbing toddler.

Swinging out of the saddle, Cass shot Susanne a pointed look that he hoped clearly said *Just so you understand, I'm only doing this for them.* He motioned for the two oldest boys to step up.

Over the next few hours differences were set aside and the group worked as a team to free the trapped wheel.

Harlon wanted to help but couldn't, so he and Corliss were put in charge of feeding the younger children their noonday meal.

Susanne proved to be more of a hindrance than a help. Cass gruffly ordered her to step aside when he and the boys heaved and tugged on the stubborn wheel. In an open effort to appease him, she would obediently step away, but moments later she would be back in the thick of the action, working alongside the men.

At one point he found her arms locked tightly around his midsection when the oxen, Aaron, Payne, Doog, Cass, and she formed a human chain of brute strength.

Midafternoon, exhausted and knowing that the animals

needed rest, Cass called a halt to work. Wearily the entourage sank down to the saturated ground to eat the fatback and cold biscuits Corliss pressed into their hands. Since the downpour refused to let up, anything more substantial was impossible to fix.

The children milled around, making the best of the situation, but Cass and Susanne chose to eat their food in a withdrawn and uncommunicative silence.

Handing Cass a third biscuit, Susanne finally decided to make an attempt at civility. "I'm sorry there's no hot coffee."

Cass accepted the peace offering, but she could see that his mind was still on freeing the wheel. "I've lost a good four hours," he muttered.

"Oh?" Susanne bit into her second biscuit. "Are you going somewhere important?"

Cass turned to give her a baleful stare. Rain spilled from the brim of his hat in torrents. "Now why would you think of that? Isn't this the sort of weather any man in his right mind would go out riding in for the pleasure of it?"

She shrugged.

"Obviously, I'm going somewhere."

She took a bite of bread. "What a coincidence that we should happen to run into each other this way."

"Yeah, what a coincidence," he returned dryly.

"It was a stroke of good luck for us, but I'm sure we'll be able to free the wheel soon and then be on our separate ways."

She lifted her brow inquiringly. "Where was it you said you were going?"

He swallowed the last of his biscuit and stood up. "I didn't say."

"Oh." It was apparent that he didn't care to elaborate, and Susanne didn't push the issue.

He shoved off to address the wheel.

Struggling to her feet, Susanne smiled brightly. "I'll be there in a minute!"

It was late afternoon before they managed to free the wheel. The old wagon lurched forward, and Harlon, Corliss, and the children shouted with glee. Payne and Aaron stood back with big grins spread across their youthful faces. Only the whites of their eyes and teeth showed through the thick layers of muck caked on their noses and faces.

Doog suddenly bent, scooped up a handful of mud, and flung it at Jesse. The day's tensions eased as quickly as they had come, and soon the ensuing mud war caught everyone in its spontaneity.

Susanne glanced warily at Cass, who looked no better than she, and abruptly they joined in the fun.

Susanne thought the mud balls Cass hurled at her had entirely too much velocity to them, but she stood her ground and returned fire in a wholehearted attempt to go him one better.

The participants were a pitiful sight to behold when a truce was finally called. Even Corliss and Harlon were covered with mud, having been innocently caught in the cross fire.

"You look funnnny." Phebia pointed at Susanne, who gagged and spit out a clump of mud.

"Land sakes, I never saw such goings-on!" Corliss complained. She rounded up the smaller kids, shooing them to the back of the wagon where a bar of lye soap and the water barrel awaited.

Cass followed the crowd, and Susanne made belated introductions. She didn't go into detail about her and Cass's prior history, saying only that they'd met before.

Once he was presentable, Cass walked away from the boisterous group and headed for his horse.

CHAPTER 4

Susanne glanced up from scrubbing mud out of Lucy's hair and saw that Cass was leaving. "Margaret, come help Lucy, sweetie," she murmured under her breath. "There's something I need to do."

Cass frowned when she strode purposefully toward him. He reined the stallion in the opposite direction, but she was faster than his intent. Her hand snaked out and grabbed the bridle, impeding his departure.

"I want to talk to you," she stated flatly.

"Sorry. I've already wasted a whole day."

"I seriously doubt you'll consider what I have to say a waste of your time," she promised.

"Anything you have to say I'd consider a waste of my time, Miss McCord." He cut the reins to the left, and she was forced to step aside.

"Make that *Mrs.* Claxton," she corrected. "Mrs. Cass Claxton," she repeated a little louder when he showed no signs of staying.

The words—fighting words—stopped his departure cold. He reined up.

She saw his back muscles tighten, almost as if he knew what was coming next. Without turning around, he spoke in a voice so ominous that it should have made her think twice about what she was about to do.

"Mrs. Cass Claxton—now what's that supposed to mean?"

"If you'll stop being in such an all-fired hurry to get away from me, I'll tell you what that means."

Cass turned his horse and walked the animal back to where she stood. He sat staring at her for a moment; then he slowly dismounted. His blue eyes fixed on hers with a soundless warning. "All right, what are you up to this time?"

"I need your help, Cass. Badly. That's what I've been trying to tell you." She swallowed and dropped her gaze.

The disgusted sound that came from the back of his throat was not encouraging. "Don't you *ever* let up?"

She took a step, her voice now brimming with underlying urgency. "I will let up; I promise. If you'll help me this one last time I will never bother you again."

He bent forward, tipping his hat politely. "Can't do it, lady. Sorry. I got troubles of my own."

So. He was going to hold to his stubborn, mulish pride. All right. She didn't want to match his heartless tactics, but he left no other choice. She lifted her eyes to meet his. "You have more trouble than you think."

"What did you mean by that 'Mrs. Cass Claxton' remark?" he repeated, and she took small comfort in the fear that now started to creep into his self-satisfied expression. He could bluff all he wanted; she knew the truth—ugly as it might be.

His expression dropped from forced tolerance to looking tempted to draw his gun on her, so she decided to divert the blow. She preferred not to antagonize him, but she knew that was impossible. Her mere existence annoyed him. "You're on your way to Cherry Grove, aren't you?"

For one imperceptible instant she thought she saw his mouth slacken with disbelief. "No."

"You're not telling the truth."

"Okay. Suppose I am on my way there?" This time he swung out of the saddle, apparently ready to stand his ground.

"I need you to take the children and me to Cherry Grove with you," Susanne said before she lost her nerve.

"Over my dead body."

She smothered the urge to strike out. Instead, she kept her tone pleasant. "Mr. Claxton, if I could have arranged that I would have long ago. I think, for your benefit—and for that of your French lady friend—you'd best consider what I have to say."

Cass shifted his weight impatiently. "Laure? What does Laure have to do with me taking you, two elderly people, and nine children to Cherry Grove, Kansas?"

"Listen, and listen well, Mr. Claxton. *If* you escort us there, then I in return will hand you signed annulment papers dissolving our marriage."

"I should have a copy somewhere, shouldn't I?"

She smiled. "I don't think so; I never applied. Did you?"

"Me? I thought you'd file—" He stiffened. "I *told* you to take care of it."

"You *told* me a lot of things, sir."

His eyes narrowed. "Are you telling me that our 'marriage' is still—?" The news apparently rendered him temporarily scrambling for a scathing denial.

"I believe you heard me correctly."

Coherent thoughts appeared to fail him. "Just what makes you so cocksure I'm even going to Kansas?"

She quickly focused on her hands. "I'm . . . not sure you are. . . . I just assume you might be, since I know you have kin there. You said no sane man would be pleasure riding in weather like this."

"Look, Susanne." She felt mildly relieved that he was at least using her name now. "I am not taking you or anyone else to Cherry Grove. I'm going to travel hard and fast, and I can't be dragging twelve other people along with me."

"We'll keep up," she promised. "Just help us drive the team, and make sure we're not attacked by marauders or wolves or the like."

"Now how am I supposed to do that?"

"You can," she said, firmly believing that even though he was a miserable excuse for a human being, his knowledge of the land was invaluable. "The boys and Harlon will keep us in fresh meat and water, and I promise we won't ask anything of you if it isn't necessary."

"Just that I get twelve people to Cherry Grove without incident."

Susanne didn't like to think of it that way, but that was the general drift. "Yes."

He grinned. "Well, now. How about this? The day you hand me the signed annulment papers will be the day we'll discuss my getting you to Cherry Grove with your pretty little head intact."

"I can't give you the papers this moment because I don't

have them!" *Oh, dear Lord! I'm slipping. Grant me patience. Grace. Strike me deaf so I can't hear his taunts.*

Cass turned back to mount the horse. "Then consider the subject closed."

She reached out and grabbed the bridle. Their gazes locked in silent duel. "Just to Cherry Grove, then you're free of me. Forever."

His eyes darkened. "And if I don't agree to your blackmail?"

She shrugged. "I'm in no hurry to remarry. Are you?" The silent message rang out like a bell. She could hold out on the annulment, never sign the papers even if he filed, contest the annulment in court, do a hundred and thousand things to make his life miserable. She wouldn't, of course, but at the moment the unspoken threat was the only remaining weapon in her arsenal.

She waited for his reaction. When it finally came, it was nothing close to what she had expected.

He simply stared at her, a muscle working tightly in his left jaw.

"Cass?" She edged forward, extending her hand to him, aware that the matter distressed him. "I promise, I will give you the annulment. . . . Please don't think I enjoy using underhanded tactics . . . but you must see that my situation is impossible without your help—"

"Susanne, I wish I could believe you."

She deserved that. Reestablishing trust wouldn't be easy, and she had treated him abominably.

"I will do better, Cass. I won't even come around you. The children are my only concern."

"We've been married for six years?"

She nodded hesitantly. "Yes—on paper only. But that needn't

upset you. If you're on your way to Cherry Grove, then what can it hurt if we ride along? I think we could make it fine on our own, but Harlon needs an experienced man to see us through the wilds." She bit her tongue, wanting to add "and I can think of no other man with your *vast* experience" but she knew he would construe the remark to mean women—which is how it was meant to be taken. So she refrained. "I promise you, the very day we reach Cherry Grove I will file for the annulment. There won't be any trouble in having the mock marriage set aside."

Guilt that she would take God's solemn ceremony so lightly flooded her, but she had asked for and received forgiveness. She swallowed. "After that, why, you'll never see me again."

His eyes shifted to the covered wagon swarming with children, then on to Corliss and Harlon, who were sitting in the wagon looking as though they were about to draw their last breath. She waited, wondering if he was a man strong enough to put pride aside in lieu of common sense.

"If I say no, you will lie and say the vows had been consummated. Your father, Judge Leviticus McCord, will make doubly sure that the marriage was duly recorded in order to protect his daughter's sterling reputation."

"I've changed, Cass. I wouldn't do that. But I would fight to prevent the annulment long as I could." He couldn't know that she was telling the truth; she had a bad history of falsehoods and willful nature. But she meant every word.

He laughed. But not from humor. She recognized ugly disbelief, and she knew she had earned his lack of respect.

"Will you help us?" She waited for the answer, not sure what she would do if he refused her. There were no more tricks in her arsenal.

Cass shook his head wordlessly. Then, shooting her a look that could have sent a strong man to his knees, he mounted the stallion.

"Aren't you going to say anything?" she asked.

He calmly turned the horse toward the wagon. "The moment we get there, Susanne. I want those signed papers in my hand the same day."

Relief flooded her. She nodded. "You have my word."

He snorted.

Thank You, God. I know I don't deserve this grace after the underhanded way I've made him help. But this promise I will fulfill. One day after arriving in Cherry Grove, barring any technicalities, Cass will have his freedom.

She didn't have the slightest idea why the thought should make her so sad.

"You think them border ruffians will attack us and steal our wagon?"

Cass slowly cracked an eye open and stared into a pair of solemn gray ones. "I thought you were supposed to be fetching wood."

"I was." Jesse gestured toward a small pile of limbs and twigs lying at Cass's feet. "Now what about them outlaws?"

"What about 'em?" A fly buzzed in a lazy circle above Cass's head as he lowered the brim of his hat to shade his eyes from the glare of the midday sun. The past two weeks had been gruesome. Rain. Heat. Kids. Everywhere he looked a kid came into view. Susanne kept her promise to stay away from him, and the old folks went to bed so early he barely knew they were around. For a while the kids had steered clear of him. Phebia still wouldn't have anything to do with him, and Aaron and Payne had walked around him like a coiled rattler. Jesse had been the first to open up, and the others had followed.

"They gonna kill us?" Jesse asked.

"I don't imagine so."

"How do you know?"

Cass glanced at Susanne, who was standing in the stream doing wash. "Because they're never around when you need them."

Susanne overheard the remark. She wrung out a shirt and laid it across a flat rock to dry. Sunday was a day of rest—if washing, cooking, and standing guard over the camp while the men went hunting was considered rest.

The night before, they had been blessed to find a grove of tall pines adjacent to a clear-running stream to make camp. After morning chores were finished they gathered for Bible study. Harlon, who enjoyed leading, had a tendency to name his lessons. He announced his chosen Scripture, Romans 12. "Today we're going to be studying How to Behave like a Christian."

Susanne stiffened at the first verse, aware that Cass was

watching her as Harlon's voice boomed out, adding emphasis she felt was entirely uncalled for. "'Let love be without hypocrisy.'"

The words fell upon her heart like stones as he continued. "'Be kindly affectionate to one another with brotherly love.'"

She had lied to force Cass into marrying her and then tricked him into accompanying them on this dangerous journey, taking him away from his comfortable home and his business. She certainly hadn't been kind to Cass. Hadn't been acting like a very good Christian either. *I'll do better,* she vowed silently. After all, she should live her beliefs before the children.

Harlon wound up his Scripture reading. "'Rejoicing in hope, patient in tribulation, continuing steadfastly in prayer, distributing to the needs of the saints, given to hospitality.'"

Susanne sighed. Why was it so difficult to do what was right and so easy to do wrong? And rejoicing in hope? Her troubles were too overwhelming, too enduring, to leave much room for rejoicing.

Cass shot her a sardonic glance from beneath the brim of his hat, and every bit of her remorse vanished. Susanne glanced at the children gathered around them and hardened her heart. She would make it up to him after he delivered her charges to Cherry Grove. They were her first priority. Cass was a grown man. He could take care of himself. The children couldn't.

After Bible study, they gathered around the fire, where Corliss had a kettle of stew simmering. Susanne helped dip up the fragrant mix of meat and vegetables simmered in home-canned tomatoes.

"Mr. Cass?" Margaret Ann stared up at him, her eyes inquiring. "What's a hypocrite?"

Cass hesitated; then a note of malice crept into his voice. "Why don't you ask Miss McCord?"

Susanne felt the heat rise in her cheeks. "I assume you caught the part about distributing to the needs of the saints and being given to hospitality? It seems you've been a trifle slack in those areas." After all, if he'd agreed to let her have the house he owned they wouldn't be traveling overland to Kansas.

Cass quirked an eyebrow. "Ah, but I've never considered you a saint."

Susanne opened her mouth to give the unspeakable cad a lesson when Corliss intervened. "Will the two of you please remember this is the Lord's Day? I'll not have any childish squabbling; you hear me?"

"Yes, ma'am," Cass muttered, looking disconcerted.

Susanne pressed her lips together, suppressing the words threatening to spill out. The title of Harlon's Bible study shamed her. Behave like a Christian. She sighed. *I'm sorry, Lord. Forgive me again.*

Why did she let Cass upset her like this? She picked up the ladle and started dishing out seconds. The mischievous gleam in Cass Claxton's eyes didn't do anything to improve her disposition.

After lunch, the children wandered off to fish and swim, openly enjoying their reprieve from the long days. Actually they'd made good time, considering the obstacles a group of their size confronted daily. She and Cass had avoided each other. The kids knew something was wrong, but not one had mentioned the strange conduct.

Corliss and Harlon noticed the animosity between Cass and her, but they were polite enough to ignore it. Susanne knew

Harlon was too relieved to hear that Cass had agreed to travel with them to ever question why.

She had wondered how the children and Cass would get along. Sometimes she still worried that he might lose his temper with them, but she thought he'd shown a surprising amount of forbearance for their constant chatter and endless curiosity.

Aaron and Payne were clearly in awe of this man who seemed to know everything. The two boys were never far from Cass's vicinity, even though they rarely tried to get his attention.

Phebia was the only one who still kept herself at bay. Cass had made several attempts to win her trust, but the three-year-old remained skeptical when it came to the tall, dark-haired stranger who had come so suddenly into their lives.

All in all, the days were beginning to settle into a routine, and Susanne was thankful. She began to think her worries were groundless, that the trip might pass without incident. And Cass would be out of her life forever.

She pretended to be absorbed in her work while she listened to the conversation taking place a few feet from her.

"Bryon, leave my gun alone."

Bryon's inquisitive fingers persistently crept over to explore the shiny Colt revolver Cass wore strapped to his right leg. The weapon was an enduring source of interest to the boys, who were familiar only with the old-fashioned muzzle-loading rifle Harlon kept in the wagon for protection.

Moments later Susanne heard Cass warn Bryon again; the child's curious fingers had started to creep toward the pistol a second time. Even Doog and Jesse were eyeing the weapon with a determined look in their eyes.

"Can't you see Mr. Cass is trying to sleep?" Payne admonished the smaller boys. He leaned against the trunk of a tree whittling a new whistle—for Joseph, Susanne guessed. "Why don't you go find something to do?"

"Don't want to," Bryon said.

"Then let's take a nap," Aaron threatened.

"Don't want to!"

Four-year-old Joseph walked up and straddled Cass's chest. "Don't want to either!" he joined in.

Cass sighed and sat up, lifting Joseph from his chest.

Corliss looked up from her mending and sharply admonished, "You children, git! Let Mr. Cass rest!"

"It's all right, Corliss. I promised Harlon I'd help fix the broken harness," Cass said.

"Now that you're awake, will you show us your gun?" Bryon persisted.

Susanne had to turn her head to keep from laughing out loud.

Even Margaret and Lucy looked up when they saw that Cass was going to oblige. Dropping the articles of clothing they'd been scrubbing, they scampered quickly from the stream when the shiny gun came out of its holster.

Cass squatted down on his haunches, and the children gathered around him. Only Phebia, clutching her doll, chose to stand to one side and watch instead of participate.

His strong baritone gentled. "A gun can either save your life or take it. You have to learn to respect whatever kind of weapon you decide to carry. This particular pistol is what they call a percussion revolver." He checked the empty chamber before he handed it butt first to Aaron.

The young man's hands trembled with excitement when he took the gun and examined it closely.

"The thing about a percussion revolver is its firepower," Cass continued. "Like a breech-loading weapon, a revolver can be loaded and fired rapidly. You can put six shots in the cylinder of a percussion firearm and fire it in a matter of seconds. That's quite an improvement over the time it takes to fill a muzzle loader with powder and ball and cap it."

Doog, Jesse, and Bryon pressed closer, eager for a turn to hold the gun.

Aaron reluctantly passed the pistol to Payne for his inspection.

"Mr. Cass," Margaret Ann said primly, "a gun is necessary, but isn't it also dangerous in the hands of an inexperienced shooter?"

Cass flashed a crooked grin at her. "Very good, Margaret. Like anything else, you have to take the bad with the good. There's a possibility of the revolver discharging several chambers at once. The flashback of hot powder and gases from the gap of the barrel and cylinder could seriously injure a man—or woman."

Lucy flinched and moved closer to Cass, draping her arm protectively around his neck. "Throw it away," she insisted. "Me don't want you hurt! I wuv you!"

Susanne wasn't surprised to hear Lucy's flourishing declaration of love. Clearly she'd been enamored of Cass from the moment he'd joined them. Cass had that effect on women.

"*I* don't want you hurt. I *love* you. " Susanne automatically corrected the child's English and wrung out a muslin petticoat.

At the sound of her voice all heads shot up. Chatter ceased.

Susanne glanced up, startled to see that they were staring at her. Her cheeks grew hot when she noticed Cass's eyes fixed on her. He met her flustered gaze and he grinned. She realized the cad was *amused* by her innocent blunder! They'd mistaken her statement for a declaration, not a simple correction.

Even Corliss had misunderstood. She sat gaping at Susanne, needle and thread suspended in midair.

"Land sakes! You all know what I *meant.*" Susanne dropped her head sheepishly and focused her full attention on the collar of Harlon's flannel shirt. How one man got so dirty was beyond her!

The children's eyes turned back to the pistol, but Susanne's unsettled feeling lingered. She noticed that though Cass continued to talk to the children, his eyes repeatedly strayed back to her. And the man was still grinning!

She ignored the sudden butterfly swarm in the pit of her stomach, grimly conceding that, try as she may, she was finding it increasingly hard to ignore the fact that he was an exceptionally appealing man.

Susanne wasn't aware of just how serious her attraction had grown until she stepped out of the wagon a couple of mornings later and saw Cass stripped to the waist, shaving.

She stood frozen in the shadow of the canvas, staring at him as he lifted his chin, eyed himself in the small mirror tacked to the tree, and drew the straight-edged razor across his cheekbone.

The sight of his bare chest covered with a mat of curly, dark brown hair made her look away in guilt. Other than her father's, Susanne had never seen a man's chest—and most assuredly Leviticus McCord's chest looked *nothing* like the solid ridge of muscle she now found herself staring at again.

She shook away the disturbing image, ashamed of herself. She should be about her work, not ogling a man, but her eyes refused to budge from the tightly corded muscles that rippled along his arms when he leaned closer to the mirror, carefully shaving his upper lip and then around the long, dark sideburns.

Laure Revuneau popped unexpectedly into her mind, and she felt a stirring that was very close to jealousy. How often had Cass embraced the lovely Frenchwoman?

Susanne was startled to find that the question intrigued and annoyed her; she deliberately set her feet in motion.

It didn't matter how many women had been in her husband's life. He'd made it clear to Susanne that *she* would never be one of them, no matter how badly she was beginning to wish that she'd started out on a better footing with him.

She rounded the corner of the wagon, pretending not to notice his presence as she filled the coffeepot and swung it over the fire.

Corliss appeared, and they exchanged morning greetings. The older woman flapped the skirt of her apron and made clucking sounds as she gathered the six white laying hens and one rooster that she released from the chicken coop each night. The chickens seemed to sense when it was time to move on. They flew into the portable coop without a backward glance.

Giving both women a perfunctory look, Cass said good morning. Phebia came around the corner, dragging Marybelle by her heels.

"Poor Marybelle's going to have a knot on her head," Cass observed when Phebia came to a stop beside him. She stood silently staring up at him.

He set the razor aside, reached for a towel, and wiped the stray remnants of shaving cream off his face. "Something I can do for you this morning, Miss Phebia?"

Susanne was amazed at the way he handled the child's continuing reticence, allowing her ample time to warm to him. He would make a wonderful father, she realized and was astonished at her observation. A few short weeks ago she wouldn't have wished Cass Claxton on her worst enemy, let alone an innocent child.

Phebia remained silent, but a few moments later Susanne saw her tug at Cass's trouser leg.

He glanced down, and the little girl cautiously handed the rag doll to him. After a brief examination, Cass noted out loud that Marybelle was missing an eye. He reached for his shirt, slipped it on, and acknowledged soberly, "This looks serious."

Motioning for Susanne, who had been listening to the exchange while she'd dropped slices of bacon into a large iron skillet, he ordered briskly, "Nurse McCord. Prepare for surgery."

Playing along with his theatrical manner, Susanne dramatically passed the fork to Corliss and went to the wagon to fetch her sewing box.

Moments later Marybelle lay on a large, flat rock, her one remaining eye staring sightlessly up at the mock medical team.

Nurse McCord located a new eye (that almost matched the old button), and the doctor set to work. Phebia watched with rounded eyes when Cass's surprising nimble fingers drew thread in and out of Marybelle's tender cotton face. "This should only take a few minutes," he told the anxious mother.

Operation completed, the patient rested comfortably—with one green and one blue eye.

"How did you do that?" Susanne whispered. "My father couldn't sew a button on his shirt."

He grinned. "Sewn up so many cattle, horses, and dogs it comes second nature."

Before Susanne could pronounce the patient fit, Phebia scooped the doll into her arms and squeezed her tightly.

Cass reached for his hat and adjusted it on his head, grinning at the elfin three-year-old. "You know, Phebia, if you carry Marybelle in your arms instead of letting her face drag the ground, she'll be likely to keep her eyes longer."

Nodding, the child started to skip happily away when she suddenly paused and turned around. Slowly she walked back to Cass. Crooking one finger, she motioned for him to lean down.

Phebia is going to kiss him! Susanne observed. The child had come so far from the day they found her on the orphanage doorstep.

Cass obligingly crouched to her level, and the child's brown eyes somberly met his blue ones.

Suddenly Phebia's forefinger and thumb darted out, clamped onto his nose like a vise, and twisted.

"Phebia!" Susanne dropped her sewing basket and bolted to break the child's grip. Wrestling the child's steely hold, she demanded that she stop.

Cass wobbled back and forth, trying to retain his balance. Finally Phebia gave his nose one final jerk, then calmly released it, stuck her thumb in her mouth, and skipped away to join the other kids.

Cass fell backward onto the ground and lay there for a moment.

"Oh, Cass!" Susanne knelt beside him, brushing dirt off his shirt. "Did she hurt you?"

"Yes!" He rubbed his nose, which was now a glaring red. "I've fought with men twice my size and come out in better shape." He stared up at a laughing Susanne. "What's so funny? The kid nearly took my nose off!"

"I think that's Phebia's way of accepting you," she offered. She covered her mouth, suppressing a giggle.

"Accepting me!" His fingers examined his smarting nose for broken cartilage. "I'll have to blow my nose out of my ear from now on. She's maimed me for life."

Susanne gave him a helping hand, which he grasped, and she pulled him to his feet, determined to ignore the way her heart jumped when their hands touched.

"You know something?" he asked, slapping dust from his pants with his hat.

Susanne worked hard to maintain a sober face. His nose was fairly glowing. "What?" Had his eyes always been that blue? They were beautifully expressive—even when angry.

"The kid reminds me of you."

The likeness hit her the wrong way. Had she been expecting a compliment? From him? That was as likely as snow in August. She whirled and marched back to the fire. She wasn't about to pursue the remark, because no matter what she did, he managed to find fault with her. She'd gone out of her way to be nice to him lately, but he hadn't bothered to say one kind word to her.

"Don't walk away from me while I'm talking."

"When you say something worth hearing, I'll listen," she tossed over her shoulder.

Which she felt sure wasn't imminent.

CHAPTER 5

Trouble, Cass decided, was his middle name. And he'd been right to hold off on marriage and having kids. God had not equipped him to be a family man. The next morning, he reluctantly agreed to keep an eye on Phebia while Susanne, Corliss, and the other children went off to pick the last of the wild berries.

While he shaved, Phebia played with Marybelle around his feet. He had to sidestep twice before he could convince her that she should go feed Marybelle a late breakfast and get out of his way.

To his relief, the child bought the idea and raced to get a biscuit from the supply box. She sat on a nearby rock, taking intermittent bites and then squashing crumbs into Marybelle's unyielding mouth while Cass finished shaving in peace.

He was wiping soap from his face when he heard Phebia let out a scream that raised the hairs on the back of his neck.

He whirled. "What's wrong?"

"Caw-doo. Me want caw-doo!"

Cass stared back at her blankly. "Caw-doo?"

She nodded succinctly.

"Caw-doo, caw-doo," Cass murmured. He glanced around the camp, wondering what in the Sam Hill *caw-doo* meant.

"Caw-doo!" Phebia demanded, her tone turning more belligerent.

"Caw-doo . . ." Cass was getting frantic. A thought came to him, and his heart nearly stopped. Kneeling beside the rock where Phebia perched, he whispered hesitantly, "Did you do something in your britches?"

Cass hoped to high heaven that wasn't the case. He'd never had to deal with anything like that before, and he wasn't sure he could.

Her eyes narrowed, and her face puffed with indignation. She shook her head and cried out, "Caw-doo!"

"Okay. Caw-doo." Relieved, Cass started grabbing anything in sight, trying to figure out what she wanted.

He held up her bonnet.

She shook her head. No.

He held up the remainder of the biscuit she'd been eating. "No!"

A bar of soap.

"No!"

A towel.

"No! *Caw-doo!*"

"Why don't you sit there and suck your thumb until Susanne gets back?" he offered, knowing that he shouldn't be encouraging her to continue a habit they'd all been trying to help her break, but he was stumped.

Phebia stood up and stamped her foot, clearly outraged by his stupidity. *"Caw-doo!"*

Cass felt sweat starting to trickle down his back.

After several more futile attempts, he sat down on the rock beside her, admitting defeat. "Phebia, I'm sorry, but I don't know what you want."

He glanced up, relieved to see Aaron rounding a corner carrying a bucket mounded with berries.

"Hi."

"Aaron, you got any idea what *caw-doo* means?" Cass asked.

"Water."

Cass looked up, startled. "Water?"

"That's what she calls water." Aaron grinned at Phebia. "You want a drink of water, squirt?"

Phebia eagerly nodded. "Me want caw-doo!"

Cass watched while Aaron led her to the water bucket and reached for the dipper.

Caw-doo, Cass thought irritably. *Imagine that.* He could have sworn it would be something you'd step in, not drink.

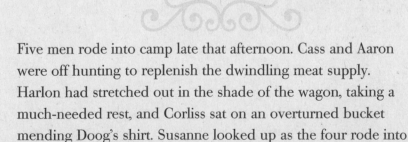

Five men rode into camp late that afternoon. Cass and Aaron were off hunting to replenish the dwindling meat supply. Harlon had stretched out in the shade of the wagon, taking a much-needed rest, and Corliss sat on an overturned bucket mending Doog's shirt. Susanne looked up as the four rode into the small clearing, and she knew in an instant this could be trouble. They were a ragtag bunch—none too clean and unshaven. Three wore overalls with the sleeves of their red long johns serving as shirts. Battered felt hats crowned their heads, and each one packed a sidearm and had a rifle in the saddle boot.

The way they eyed her left Susanne feeling uneasy. She was used to more respect, even from Cass. However, she knew better than to show a sign of weakness. Her chin lifted, and she waited for the men to state their business.

"Ma'am." The biggest one tipped his hat. His undersized, shrewd eyes, almost eclipsed by the broad expanse of his hat, squinted back at her.

Susanne nodded and gripped the wooden spoon she'd been using to stir a batch of corn bread. Who were these ruffians, and what did they want? She spared a glance at the encroaching tree line, wishing Cass would return. From the corner of her eye she saw Harlon sitting up and slowly edging closer to his rifle.

"Bull Hanson here," the big man said. "We've been traveling quite a spell. Don't guess you'd be able to spare a hot meal?"

Susanne swallowed. She did not want these men spending any time in the camp, but she could hardly say no. The unwritten code of the trail required that she offer them hospitality. She had a feeling nothing she could say would make any difference anyway.

Aware too much time was passing with no answers from her, she hastened to reply. "Of course. Supper will be ready in an hour or so, which will give you time to take care of your horses."

A second man, the lower half of his thin face covered with ragged stubble, edged his horse forward. His gaze skimmed the camp. "You all traveling alone?"

Susanne shifted her grip on the spoon. "My husband and oldest son are hunting. They should be back any moment."

"That so?" The thin man grinned. His eyes raked her. "Now why would he go off and leave a pretty little thing like you all alone?"

"I'm not alone." Susanne indicated Harlon and Corliss and the children.

"Seems like something's missing," the man said. "Like maybe that husband of yours is just a story you tell people?"

"That's not true." Susanne heard the catch in her voice. *Oh, Cass, come back. Hurry.*

A shot sounded, followed by a second one, and the big man, Bull Hanson, lifted his head to listen.

Relief swept Susanne. "That's him now. He'll be back to camp soon, likely bringing fresh meat for supper."

The third man, cleaner than the others, young but with an air of competence about him, gathered up the reins, turning his horse. "Reckon we'd best ride on, Bull."

The big man appeared to consider the thought before shaking his head. "No. That stew smells powerful good. I believe we'll stay."

He dismounted and the others followed suit, tying their horses to saplings and gathering around the fire. Susanne went about her work, aware of five pairs of male eyes following her every move.

Corliss gathered the children into the shelter of the wagon; Harlon stayed close to his rifle. Every passing moment seemed like an hour.

Cass, where are you? I need you.

But even if he came back, he'd be outnumbered and walking in unaware of the scruffy company. There must be some way she could warn him, but her mind refused to cooperate.

Cass approached camp carrying the young doe Aaron had shot. He'd fired simultaneously but his bullet missed. The kid had taken a lucky shot and dropped the deer. His first, judging from the big grin he wore like a badge. A break in the trees allowed Cass a full view of camp. He stopped, eying the five men seated around the fire, their attention centered on Susanne. He motioned for Aaron to wait.

The boy's eyes grew wide when he saw the visitors. His voice dropped to a stage whisper. "What are you going to do?"

"I don't know." Cass lowered the deer to the ground, looking over the situation. After a minute, he motioned to Aaron. "You come in from the south. I'll work my way around and approach from the north. Don't move a muscle until you hear me whistle."

Aaron nodded and Cass moved away, walking quietly. When he was in position, he whistled, low but clear. He noticed the way the men tensed, covertly looking around the campsite. Probably outlaws. Copycat scum spawned by admiration for the James boys and the Younger clan.

Once even Cass had admired Frank and Jesse James, believing them to be victims fighting for their rights. Over the years his view had changed when he came to realize the truth. Frank and Jesse might have started out with noble intentions, but they had turned into renegades, outlaws who would rather steal than work.

He eyed the five who stood around the fire. Dirty, spiritually corrupt men, preying on the weak. The Jameses and Youngers had a touch of class. This bunch wasn't in their league. Probably a good thing he and Aaron hadn't been in camp when they'd arrived. At least this way they had an element of surprise in their favor.

Cass stepped from the concealing brush and advanced toward the campfire. Five pairs of eyes watched him, the men's expressions calculating. Susanne looked relieved, and Harlon relaxed perceivably. Cass looked past the men, nodding as Aaron strode from the thicket, rifle held in a casual yet thoroughly businesslike manner.

The big man made a small gesture and the others settled back, their expressions becoming less watchful. Cass strode into camp, moving easily, rifle at the ready. "Afternoon."

The leader stepped forward and extended his hand. "Hanson's my name. Bull Hanson. Your missus invited us to stay for supper." He glanced at Aaron. "Fine-looking son you got there."

Cass shifted his attention to Susanne, noting the flush staining her cheeks, but her eyes met his readily enough. He guessed she'd run a bluff. This was one time he appreciated her spunk.

"Sure thing." He shook Hanson's hand. First man he'd met who was as tall and imposing as Sar. "Glad to have company. Payne, you and Jesse help Aaron carry the deer in and we'll get it dressed."

He passed Susanne on his way to the wagon and dropped his hand on her shoulder in a possessive manner, eyeing Bull Hanson as he did so. The faces of the outlaws remained neutral, revealing nothing. Cass had a bad feeling about the company. Had this band managed to stumble in on them, or had they been trailing a lone wagon, waiting until Susanne and the children were left with only Harlon to defend them? Starting tomorrow he was teaching the three older boys to use a gun.

The boys carried the deer into camp, and Cass strung it up

from the branch of a white oak tree, preparing to remove the skin. One of the strangers, the cleanest one, came over to watch. His brown hair was in need of a haircut, but his hazel eyes were steady and nonthreatening. Nothing was said for a few minutes, and then the stranger took out a knife and stepped in closer. Cass tensed, waiting for what would come next.

The man grinned. "Slim Watkins here. Just trying to help."

"Help's always welcome." Cass slit the skin down the inside of one leg. "You from these parts?"

"I'm from a lot of places," Slim said. "Some of them I can even go back to."

Cass smiled. "We're just passing through ourselves."

"A word of advice," Slim said. He stepped closer. "You see that scrawny dude eyeing your wife? Watch out for him. He'd as soon shoot you in the back as look at you."

"Can't see why he'd do that." Cass's stomach tightened at the thought. He'd noticed the thin man with the wolfish grin, but figured Bull could keep his men in line.

"Oh, Joe Killen doesn't need a reason. He just plain likes to hurt people. See one like that once in a while."

"Seen some in the war," Cass admitted. "Never cared for the type."

"Me neither. You fought in the war? Which side?"

"The South."

"I'm a Johnny Reb myself," Slim said.

Cass knew the war could bind men together in a way that had nothing to do with where a man came from or what kind of work he did. He knew Beau and Cole felt the same way. The men they had fought with were like family.

"I don't think you'll have a problem with this bunch." Slim

helped pull the hide loose from the carcass. "But if Joe or Bull starts something I'll weigh in on your side. Just wanted you to know."

"Why would you do that?"

"I draw the line at some things." His eyes wandered back to the fire site.

"Then why would you ride with scum?" Cass deftly slit open the deer, removing the organs and placing them into a bucket Slim held.

"I'm thinking seriously of parting ways. My mama didn't bring me up to run with the likes of Bull and Joe."

"A man needs to stay close to his raising," Cass agreed. "I got a good mama myself. Been too long since I've seen her." Before he went back to Saint Louis he planned to drop by River Run and check on Ma and Willa—eat some of Willa's chicken and dumplings.

"Yeah." Slim watched as Cass sliced the fresh meat, getting it ready for the fire. "Think I'll be riding back to the Missouri Bootheel before much longer. There's not much future in outlawing."

"Never much wanted to die with my boots on," Cass agreed. "I'll take a feather bed and my family anytime."

Slim hefted the pan of fresh meat. "I'll take this to your wife."

"Any chance of you all riding out after supper?" Cass asked.

"Can't say what Bull might do." Slim turned and walked back to the campfire. Cass watched him go, wondering if the young stranger was being truthful or if he was trying to pull a fast one. Get them relaxed and off guard so Bull could move in and catch them by surprise. That wasn't going to happen.

He finished dressing out the meat and carried it to the fire, where Corliss and Harlon would take care of it. Susanne already had thick steaks sizzling over the flames. The scent of cooking meat blended with the smell of simmering stew and a skillet of baked corn bread. No wonder the band of outlaws chose to stay for supper.

One by one the men got up from supper, stretching. Slim carried his dishes to a fallen log where Corliss bent over a pan of soapy water, doing cleanup. "That sure was a fine meal, ma'am. Believe it was one of the finest I've eaten in a spell."

Susanne heard his remark and decided if all the men were like him she wouldn't mind having them around so much. She didn't like the way the skinny one, Joe, looked at her. Several times she'd seen him watching Cass with a calculating gleam in his eyes, as if wondering if he could take him. She wouldn't put it past the outlaw to shoot a man in the back if he thought he could get away with it. That's why she had slipped into the wagon and gotten her own derringer—the one that she had inherited from Aunt Estelle. Her aunt had been a woman of many talents, one of which was the ability to use a pistol—and the determination to use it if necessary. Susanne hoped she had the same resolve.

Lord, I wouldn't shoot a man unless it was absolutely necessary; You know that. But if these men made one move toward hurting a member of her party it would become necessary in a hurry.

The men looked as though they were settled in for the night, something Cass didn't want. He moved over to stand beside the rifle he'd left leaning against the wagon, one hand lingering close to the butt of the pistol hanging at his waist. "So you got far to ride tonight?"

Bull Hanson looked up, suddenly alert. His eyes took in Cass's vigilant stance, Harlon standing at the end of the wagon bed, rifle close by. Aaron leaned against a tree to the right of them, weapon dangling from the crook of his arm. Bull's teeth clamped on his lower lip for a minute as he apparently weighed his options.

"Thought we might spend the night here. Heard there was a group of renegades working this area. You folks might be in the need of a little protection."

"Oh, I think we can handle ourselves just fine," Cass told him. "Wouldn't want to delay your ride."

Slim rose to stand a little to the left. "We might ought to ride on, Bull. Got a way to go."

Bull looked at him, considering. "You buying into this?"

"No. Just think it might be the smart thing to do. Looks like these folks can take care of themselves."

The outlaw's eyes narrowed. "Maybe. Like you say, Cass here and old Harlon look pretty capable." He slowly got to his feet. "Time to saddle up, boys."

"Now, let's not be in any hurry," Joe said. "Seems like this here's a good place to spend the night. Lots of services, if you get what I mean."

Cass was quite certain that he understood what the man had in mind, and if he dared put a hand on Susanne, he was going to need an army of doctors to put him back together again.

Bull turned slowly and faced Joe. The man took a step backward. "I said, let's ride. Unless you got a different idea?"

"No, let's ride." Joe backed toward his horse. Cass let his hand rest on his pistol. He planned to make it clear the men had outstayed their welcome. The outlaws mounted up and slowly rode out, the silence so deep the only sound was the creaking of saddle leather. At the edge of the clearing Slim twisted in the saddle and lifted his hand in farewell. Cass nodded an acknowledgment. He hoped the young man followed through on his intentions and left the gang.

Cass motioned for Harlon and Aaron to stay on alert. He wouldn't put it past the outlaws to circle around and come back. It looked like he was going to stand guard tonight.

Susanne helped Corliss get the children ready for bed.

Phebia resisted all efforts, claiming she needed to stay awake to take care of Marybelle. "Her's afraid of the dark. And those ole men might come back."

"Then you need to take her to bed with you and cover up her head so she won't be afraid. And Cass won't let 'those ole men' hurt you, darling."

The child's indignation rose. "Her can't breathe with her head covered up."

"I see. Well, really, I do believe Marybelle will be just fine if you hold her tight and tell her a bedtime story."

"Me don't know any stories. You tell her story."

"Not tonight. I still have work to do. I'll be in plain sight if you need anything."

Phebia sighed and held the doll up against Susanne's face. "Kiss Marmarbelle good night."

Susanne obediently kissed the doll and then dropped a second kiss on the little girl's forehead. "Sleep tight. Don't worry; God will keep you and Marybelle safe."

Phebia nodded. "God and my Cass."

Susanne smiled. "Mr. Cass will watch over you too." They bowed their heads and Phebia made her petition to God.

The child then turned on her side, arm curved over Marybelle, and stuck her thumb in her mouth. Would they never break her of that habit? Apparently not. Phebia had a mind of her own.

Susanne finished cleaning up the campsite and leaned back against the wagon bed. Harlon and Corliss must be asleep, judging from the duet of snores coming from behind the canvas covering. A loud snuffling hoot from Harlon, and a lighter fluttering gasp from his wife.

She thought about the older couple, how they looked after each other on the trail. More than once she had caught them holding hands, and Harlon often looked at Corliss as if she was still the most beautiful woman in the world. Sometimes she envied the couple the love they shared.

A silvery moon rose overhead, throwing patches of light over the clearing, turning shadows into black pools of darkness.

Susanne felt restless. The band of renegades had frightened her more than she liked to admit. If they had been traveling without Cass it could have been very different. She was so thankful he had agreed to stay with them, and to do him justice, he was keeping his part of the bargain. The children adored him. Harlon deferred to him on every decision, and Corliss flat-out catered to him, but unfortunately, he made it clear he had no time for Susanne McCord.

She wandered across the clearing, drifting closer to the deep shadows beneath a large oak tree. A hushed whisper reached her ears. "If you're going to walk around out here, at least have enough sense to stay in the shadow."

She stopped, pulse racing. "Cass?"

"You're lucky it's me. What would you do if Bull Hanson or Joe Killen was waiting out here?"

"I thought you were asleep." She edge into the tree line, trying to spot him.

"I would be if I could be sure we weren't going to have unexpected company."

"You think they might come back?"

"It's a possibility or I wouldn't be out here. Do I know they will return? No, but I'm not taking the risk."

Pausing, her eyes adjusted and she located him. "You'd protect me?" She felt joy rising like a bubble in her chest. He cared enough to protect her?

"I'd have to. Otherwise I'd have to take care of these kids by myself."

She tried to determine if there was a smile in his voice and decided probably not. Cass Claxton didn't do any smiling when she was around. "I see. You don't care what happens to me."

"I didn't say that. I wouldn't turn a dog over to those men."

He was comparing her to a dog? How charming. And infuriating. She moved close enough she could smell the smoke from the campfire on his clothing. *Let's see what Mr. Claxton is made of.*

"You care nothing at all for me?" She breathed the words into the night, for his ears alone. She didn't believe him; somewhere deep in his heart he had to care a little.

"Is there a reason why I should?"

His words had a rough edge that she didn't think came from anger. Being unable to see him heightened her senses. Hearing his words without seeing his face gave a different impression, and she had a feeling Cass Claxton wasn't as immune to her as he tried to pretend.

"Why shouldn't you? We're traveling together, and for the first time we have the opportunity to get acquainted. Why not relax and enjoy each other's company."

"I'm not sure I want to get acquainted, but exactly what do you have in mind?"

"Why, nothing in particular." She faltered. "But technically, we are married—"

"Only technically."

"Only technically," she grudgingly agreed. "But we should at least pretend to get along. For the children's sake."

"I'm not good at pretending. And I don't want you for a friend. Every time I get close to you I end up with more trouble."

"You surely can't blame me because those men rode into camp. What do you think I could have done to stop them?"

"There was nothing you could do, but if they come back it will be because of you."

She hesitated, stunned by what he was saying. Why hadn't

she thought of that before? Those men wouldn't come back to harm the children or kill Cass and Harlon. If they came back, it would be for her. The thought made her sick to her stomach. She reached out to touch him, needing the comfort of his presence. The feel of his arm beneath her hand, the muscular strength of him, sent a tingle of awareness through her.

He tensed and she moved away. "I'm sorry. I didn't intend to disturb you."

"I'm not disturbed."

Susanne felt a new element inserting itself into their presence. Something she hadn't wanted or welcomed. When had she stopped thinking of Cass as someone she could use and begun seeing him as an attractive man she would like to know better? How could she have fallen prey to this man? The moment that he could free himself of her he would be gone, and she would never see him again. The last thing she needed was a lifetime of unrequited love.

She turned to go and stumbled over a root, pitching forward. Arms closed around her. She leaned against his chest, struggling against the sensations racing through her mind. This was Cass Claxton. She hated him. She loved him. She was . . . confused.

His face was only a few inches from hers. She could feel his breath against her hair. Slowly, sweetly, he turned her and their lips met. She closed her eyes, drifting. Her arms reached up to encircle his neck as a wild sweetness surged through her until she was floating in a rising tide of joy.

He released her, gently but firmly removing her arms from around his neck. "I think you'd best turn in for the night."

Susanne drew away, stung by his rejection. For a moment

she stared at him; then shame sent her reeling. What had happened to her? Had she thrown pride out the window where this man was concerned?

"Yes, of course," she murmured. She stepped back, moving away from him until she left the shelter of the shadows, edging out into the clear, cold light of the moon. Her fingers brushed her lips, marveling at his taste.

"Good night, Mr. Claxton." Her voice trembled.

"Miss McCord."

She walked away, torn between shame and exhilaration. Had she really behaved in such a wanton manner? After a moment she decided that she had. Oh, dear. She was so frightened at her feelings.

Terrified that she would lose her heart to this man and never regain it.

CHAPTER 6

Cass had spent a restless time standing guard. He still wasn't sure they'd seen the last of the outlaws—especially the one called Bull—but he could be wrong. He had a feeling the man could be as mean as sin when he took a notion, and he had no real desire to tangle with him.

Susanne, still clearly peeved about last night's chance encounter, avoided him. Watching her, he could tell her anger simmered barely beneath the surface as she went about breaking camp.

He decided to ignore her. He had slept only a couple of hours, and his disposition wasn't the best this morning. He had too much on his mind to worry about an ill-tempered woman. Beau's telegram still concerned him; how much trouble was his brother in and what kind of trouble? At the back of his mind he wrestled with the blooming attraction he felt for Susanne and the way she'd felt in his arms. Memories of the kiss they'd shared plagued him. The woman meant trouble with a capital *T*. He had to steer clear of her or risk getting more deeply involved.

He wouldn't be caught up in another situation with this aggravating female, no matter how much she egged him on. If he wanted that annulment—and he surely did—Susanne McCord was off-limits.

When Susanne sailed around the corner carrying a pan of dirty dishwater, Cass was crouched beside the wagon checking the left front axle.

The sight of him set her off again. Arrogant, self-centered cad. The way he'd kissed her, taken advantage of her innocence. She preferred not to remember the way her knees had gone weak as a newborn kitten and her pulse had fluttered like a trapped butterfly. She had been caught off guard. She would never intentionally let a man like Cass Claxton kiss her.

Determined to avoid another scene with him, she whirled and started off in the opposite direction, but suddenly her footsteps slowed. Cass was preoccupied with the wheel, apparently unaware that she was even in the vicinity. So like him. Pursing her lips, she struggled against the overpowering urge to fling the greasy water at him.

You've changed, Susanne. You don't behave like a hooligan anymore.

Still, it would serve him right for treating her the way he had last night—though she knew if she followed her impulse, it would be tantamount to waving a red flag at a salivating bull.

But he *deserved* every nasty, revolting, repulsive, obnoxious ounce of water in this pan.

Before she fully realized it, she had tiptoed closer to the wagon. When she was within firing range, she straightened and reared back to take aim. Cass stood up and turned to face her as the water flew out of the pan, headed straight in his direction.

His features went momentarily blank before what she was doing registered. His eyes widened with incredulity, and he dodged to one side in a vain attempt to avoid the onslaught, but his defense came too late. The dishwater hit its target squarely on the bull's-eye, leaving soggy bits of bacon rinds dangling limply from the front of his drenched shirt.

Jerking herself upright, Susanne could see that he was livid. She braced herself for the eruption that wasn't long in coming.

"You . . . you . . . what did you do *that* for?" he bellowed.

She looked at him with round-eyed innocence. "Oh, my, I'm so sorry. I didn't see you."

He wiped greasy water from his eyes. "Don't try to pull that. You didn't see me? Like thunder you didn't! You always throw dishwater on the axle?"

A chunk of garbage dangled from his shoulder. He angrily flicked it aside.

She smiled smugly. "This morning I did." She shrugged, ignoring the blistering looks he sent her way. "Guess we'd better be getting a move on."

Susanne turned, aware that he was peevishly fanning the front of his shirt, mumbling things under his breath she was sure a lady wasn't supposed to hear.

"Sure has started off to be a fine day so far," she observed.

Cass was still eyeing her when she sauntered away, swinging the empty dishpan in her right hand.

Midmorning the wind kicked up. Aaron drove the team while Corliss rode on the seat next to him. Susanne walked behind with the children.

Harlon wasn't feeling well this morning—summer complaint, he thought—so about an hour ago he'd climbed into the back of the wagon to catch a short nap.

Susanne kept falling behind to oversee Lucy, Bryon, Joseph, Phebia, and Margaret Ann when they paused to gather armloads of wildflowers that grew along the roadway.

They'd forded a small creek a while back, the water shallow enough that the children waded across, splashing and laughing. Susanne watched their fun, thinking how life on the trail had changed them. Days spent in the sun had given the children a tanned, healthy look, so different from the city pallor. Eyes alert, cheeks rosy, full of energy, they followed the wagon, running as much as they walked, shouting out each new discovery from birds' nests to the pretty pebbles Phebia stuffed in her dress pockets.

Margaret Ann walked beside Susanne, leading Lucy by the hand. "Are we getting close to Kansas?"

"I'm afraid it's still a long way yet. Are you tired of living on the trail?"

"Oh no."

Susanne smiled at the dignified tone of voice. If women ever got the vote, as some claimed they eventually would, Margaret could very well be the first woman president and she'd do just fine.

Now the child looked up with a serene expression. "I wish we could go on forever like this. It's so enjoyable."

"Enjoyable in what way?"

Margaret Ann shrugged. "You know what it was like back in Saint Louis, worried about money all the time. We don't need money on the trail."

Ah, the innocence of children. Yes, they were surviving, mostly because of the fresh meat the men brought in, but they were running short of other staples. They would have to restock once they reached Westport. Susanne prayed daily that their meager supply of money would be sufficient. Aunt Estelle's voice echoed in her mind. *The night is always darkest before dawn. Hope in the Lord.*

Well, there must be one spectacular, blazing dawn headed this way, because to her mind the night was about as dark as it could get. *Hope in the Lord.* Easy to say, difficult to do when everything was going wrong. She shook her head, wondering what it would be like to have such an unwavering faith as her aunt had lived by, so that no matter what happened, you could rejoice in hope.

Susanne sighed. It must be something that came with spiritual maturity; apparently she was still growing.

"Miss McCord?"

"Yes, Margaret Ann?"

"I feel closer to God on the trail than I do in church. Is that a sin?"

"No, dear. I feel the same way. Churches are built by men, but nature is God's creation."

"Then why do we go to church?"

"Because it is a commandment—we are not to forsake the gathering together to worship—and because we want to praise and worship the Lord."

"I see. So it is all right to worship God in church and outside too."

Susanne hugged Margaret Ann. She was such an adorable child. "It's always right to worship God, darling, wherever we may be."

Margaret Ann sighed, relief evident on her features. "I'm glad to get that settled. Now I need to check on Phebia. She tends to be unruly sometimes."

"She does at that." Susanne watched as Margaret Ann scampered away to check on the younger girl. How could anyone have abandoned a special child like Margaret Ann? But then all the children were special. She loved every one of them as though they were her very own. A soft sigh escaped her. Would she ever have children of her own? Would she ever find a man that she could fall deeply and hopelessly in love with? Enough to marry—truly marry and spend the rest of her life loving?

Susanne kept a wary eye on Cass. From the smoldering glances he sent in her direction she supposed he was still angry. Why did she do her best to torment him? No wonder he despised her so. Her conscience nagged her. *God, I'm such a contrary soul. Can't You give me a few redeeming qualities?*

She thought of Cass's outraged expression and gave a muffled laugh. All right. Maybe she was past help. God was no doubt ready to wash His hands of her. Cass certainly was. She needed to be nicer to him. No more taunting or teasing. She would be as dignified as Margaret Ann.

A tall order, one Susanne doubted she could deliver.

Cass rode a good distance to the rear, keeping a close eye on the group. He'd seen nothing to indicate that renegades were still in the area, but that didn't mean they weren't there. Although the Civil War had been over for several years, the violence spawned by the conflict had never gone away. Frank and Jesse James, the Youngers, and others had inspired a number of gangs who would rather prey on the helpless than work for a living. But for now, the small group was making steady progress. Threat of trouble seemed remote for the time being. He took a moment to count his blessings. Health. Life—many a man had lost his during the war. Family. *Father, I have nothing to complain about— just praise for Your grace. I thank You for safekeeping and returning me home to my family. Lord, I guess what I'm trying to say is that I thank You for everything.*

He caught a glimpse of Susanne and thought about the way she could rankle him without trying. *Well, almost everything,* he amended.

The wind continued to pick up, and he found his attention drawn more to Susanne's skirt than to anything else. The heavy gusts would snatch up the flimsy cotton and toss it as high as her head, providing Cass with a glimpse of white pantalets.

What was wrong with the woman? Didn't she have any sense

of modesty? They were traveling through strange territory, and not everyone they met could be trusted. The surrounding tree-covered hills and hollows could hide a dozen renegade groups bent on causing trouble. He couldn't be expected to fight them all.

Keeping Susanne under control was harder than herding coyotes. Get her out of one mess and she fell into one even worse.

He nudged his horse's flanks and quickly rode up beside her. "Are you aware your pantalets are showing?"

Susanne glanced up startled. "What?"

"Every time the wind blows, your pantalets show."

She drew back defensively. "I beg your pardon! What business is it of yours?"

"None at all, I'm just the fool who'll have to rescue you if some stranger decides he likes what he sees. If you can't think of your own safety, you might at least think of the others."

He could feel the heat of her anger when she glared up at him. "I've told you several times I can take care of myself."

"Sure you can. Ever heard of sewing buckshot in your hem to keep your skirt from flying over your head?"

Her chin lifted with a stubborn set. "I have not heard of sewing buckshot in my skirt to keep it from flying over my head," she mimicked.

"Woman, you're driving me over the edge."

"It wouldn't be a very long journey, now would it?"

All right now. He'd had enough. Cass leaned down and scooped her up, hauling her into the saddle in front of him. Almost immediately he recognized his mistake.

"*What* do you think you're doing? Put me down this

instant!" she demanded. The children stopped walking and stood watching the skirmish in wide-eyed fascination.

She twisted to confront him. Their faces were inches apart when she took a deep, self-righteous breath and said in a disgusted rebuke, "You should be *ashamed* of yourself!"

He grinned, aware that she knew he'd been angry when she had doused him with dishwater. Payback time had arrived. "That will be the day!"

"You . . . you heathen!" She struggled to free herself, and he gripped her tightly to keep from dropping her. Now that he had her, what was he going to do with her? An idea occurred to him and he liked it. It was time he taught this contrary woman a lesson.

"You might as well pipe down," he warned. "If you don't have the good sense to keep yourself covered, then I suppose I'll be forced to see that you do."

"What do you mean, *covered*! I was covered! I can't help it if your heathenish thoughts—"

Cass cut her off. "Payne, you see to Jesse and Doog. They're wandering too far ahead." He hit his horse on the flank and it trotted off, with Susanne loudly protesting.

"This is an outrage, and I demand that you *set* me down this instant! What do you think you're doing?"

"You think you can do such a good job of taking care of yourself; I'm going to give you the chance to try."

She stiffened in his arms, looking suddenly afraid. He squelched a stir of compassion. Somehow he had to make her understand the seriousness of their situation. Hadn't the woman learned anything in the past six years?

"What are you talking about?"

He noted with satisfaction that although she made an obvious effort to sound in control, her voice had a slight tremor.

"I thought I'd set you down out here on your lonesome and let you walk back."

Her eyes narrowed to viperous slits. "You wouldn't dare."

"Oh, wouldn't I? Maybe you'll get lucky and not be forced to fight off big Bull Hanson. I'm betting he could pull you into the saddle even easier than I did."

Her eyes widened at the implication of his words. "Cass. You're just teasing; aren't you?"

"Why should I tease about something like this? Besides, you have it coming after that trick with the dishwater."

He was surprised to see a shamed expression cross her face. She took a deep breath and looked past him, avoiding eye contact. "I'm sorry I wasn't more observant. There's no excuse for my behavior, and I apologize.'

"The fact that I'm about to set you afoot doesn't have anything to do with your heartfelt apology, does it?"

"No, it doesn't." She pressed her lips tightly together and sighed. "I'll try to be nice to you from now on."

"Susanne, you don't know the first thing about being nice." Deciding they'd come far enough to teach her a lesson, he turned the horse and rode back to camp.

But as he expected, her show of repentance didn't last long. "You conceited, disrespectful *worm*! You don't have the slightest idea what I'm like."

Cass put spurs to the horse. "I know all I want to know."

"I've said I was sorry for that, and if you were any kind of gentleman you would accept my apology."

"I'll accept your so-called apology the day you hand me the annulment papers."

"You'll get your papers as soon as you deliver us safely to Cherry Grove." After a few moments of silence she said, "There isn't anything I like about you."

He grinned, knowing he was about to infuriate her further. "You didn't complain when I kissed you."

He heard her soft intake of breath and chuckled. Her hand shot out to smack his leg, but he quickly thwarted the move and halted the horse beside the wagon.

"Put me down!" she gritted through clenched teeth.

"Well, anything you say, darling."

He released her and she sailed off the horse, hitting the ground with a solid thud.

"Cass Claxton!" she wailed.

Cass sat on the horse, grinning, waiting to see what she would do.

All of the unexpected commotion caused Corliss to stick her head out of the back of the wagon. "Everything all right back here?"

"Everything's fine, Corliss. Miss McCord insisted on walking." Cass tipped his hat at Susanne. "Don't tire yourself, darlin'."

Corliss looked blank for a moment, then shrugged and dropped the curtain back in place, as if to say whatever was going on, she didn't want any part of it.

Lucy grasped onto Margaret Ann's hand, looking as if she might burst into tears at any moment. Susanne calmly picked herself up out of the dirt and stalked toward the wagon.

Cass watched her walk away, thinking he might have been a

little rough on her. He didn't know what it was, but something about Susanne McCord brought out the worst in him. Lilly Claxton had not raised him to treat a woman with anything less than respect.

But then Ma hadn't met Susanne.

Late that afternoon the wagon topped a rise, and they spotted a small caravan traveling about a mile ahead. Susanne counted the wagons out loud: "One, two, three, four, five."

"And fifteen to twenty head of cattle," Cass observed.

"You think they'll let us join them?" Susanne asked. Cass's warnings were beginning to sink in, and she'd feel a lot safer with reinforcements.

He took off his hat. "I'll ride ahead and see if they'd mind if we hook up with them."

"Seems like the smart thing to do," Harlon agreed. "We'll wait here until we get a proper invite."

Thirty minutes later Cass returned bearing the good news: they were welcome to join the wagon train.

That night, six wagons camped in a pasture after getting permission from the owner. They formed the customary pear-shaped corral, the pole of each wagon pointing outward, and the hub of the fore wheel of the next wagon set close to the hind wheel of the wagon just ahead of it. The exact placement of the wagons formed an enclosure large enough to pen the animals belonging to the train. It also provided a defensive arrangement that made an attack unlikely. The chances were slim that a group this large would run into trouble in Missouri or eastern Kansas, but the danger was greater in Oklahoma, where the rest of the train was headed.

The women quickly formed a comfortable relationship. When the children had been safely tucked in that night, they sat around the fire, stitching handiwork and exchanging small talk. The men enjoyed their pipes and cigars while they discussed the weather and whether they were likely to encounter hostile Indians farther west.

Ladies openly expressed concern about savages when they crossed into Oklahoma, though most agreed the threat was small. With the casual friendliness of the trail they accepted Susanne into their midst, showing interest in her new quilt pattern. Their companionship was bittersweet because Susanne knew the friendships she made here would be short-term. They would be leaving the wagon train when it reached Westport. She and her family would travel on to Kansas, while the others would journey south into Oklahoma.

She glanced up from the quilt she was piecing when she heard Cass excuse himself, saying that he was going to turn in early.

Ernest Parker's teenage daughter, Ernestine, sprang to her feet to say good night. It was evident from the look in the young beauty's eyes that she'd developed a full-blown case of puppy love for the blue-eyed, curly-headed stranger, who promptly rewarded her with a smile guaranteed to melt any woman's heart.

Susanne watched Cass get to his feet to say good night with mixed feelings. The events of that afternoon still lingered with her. He'd been hateful today, but in her heart she knew she had deserved it. What had gotten into her? From the moment they'd met she'd gone out of her way to provoke him. Even worse, although she didn't understand her emotions, a part of her wanted them to be friends—even more than friends. She had to admit no other man had ever touched her life in quite the same way, making her feel so aware, so vibrantly alive . . . so in need of . . . something. Love? she wondered.

She'd had to remind herself twice this evening that she would be three times a fool if she were to let herself fall in love with Cass Claxton. He was a rogue and a rascal who'd treated her as badly as she'd treated him.

When they reached Cherry Grove and she handed him the annulment papers, that would be the last thing he'd ever want from her. She was confident that she would never see him again. She knew that he had every reason to want her out of his life, but the realization didn't make her growing feelings for him any easier to accept.

Why do I do the things I do? she silently agonized. *Why couldn't I have been the perfect lady, one who would have captured his heart instead of his ire? A soft-spoken Christian lady.*

Now it was too late to hope he would ever see her as anything but the headstrong, stubborn girl he thought her to be. In her heart she couldn't blame him for despising her. By an act of defiance and deceit, she still shared his name, but it would be a woman like Laure Revuneau who would eventually win his heart.

Dear God, how do I make amends? Perhaps he could forgive if given the chance. You forgave me—even died on a cross for me.

But Cass was not God. He came close in the children's eyes, but still he was not their Maker.

It shamed her to know that Ernestine Parker's lovesick gaze was not the only one that followed Cass's tall form when he strode toward the wagon. Susanne was ready to admit, at least to herself, that she was falling in love with the very man she'd so foolishly forced to marry her.

And there was nothing she could do to hold it back.

The following morning Lucius Waterman's voice rang out a warning: "Steep hill comin' up!" His words echoed down the line.

Susanne eased the team to a halt when Cass rode up beside their wagon.

"Better let Aaron take the reins. Looks like there could be trouble," he said.

Susanne lifted her hand to shade her eyes from the hot sun and squinted up at him. "Can he handle the team?" Aaron was wiry and slight of build, although he insisted he was as strong as two grown men put together.

"He can handle it." Cass assessed the hill. "It's a bad one, though—steep, with little room for error."

"What will you do?"

A frown creased his forehead, and she knew he was trying to determine the safest angle of descent. As far as she could see, there didn't seem to be one. Having the wagon fall and break beyond repair while being windlassed down the steep grade wasn't something she cared to think about.

Susanne climbed down from the wagon, and Cass

dismounted and stood beside her. He removed his hat and ran his sleeve over his forehead. "Get the children together and keep them at a safe distance," he said quietly. "Tell Harlon and Corliss they'll have to walk down the hill. I don't want anyone near this wagon except Aaron and me."

Susanne's eyes lifted to meet his. "It's bad, isn't it?"

"Just do as I say," he repeated softly. He adjusted his hat back on his head.

"Then I'll drive."

"Do as I say, Susanne. Aaron and I will take care of the wagon. You and the children stay back."

Knowing it was useless to argue, Susanne went in search of the children while Cass drew Aaron aside. She could see the two talking, and her heart filled with pride. It was almost as if he *were* her husband, teaching their son one of life's lessons. Then a terrible sense of dread filled her. If either one of them should be seriously injured, she didn't think she could bear it.

The train sprang into activity. Women called out to children, and men started unloading some of the heavier pieces off the wagons and setting them beside the road.

When two of the women realized they were parting with family heirlooms, they started weeping and begging their husbands for compassion. Stern-faced, the men kept about their work, though one kept apologizing and assuring his wife that he was only doing what had to be done.

Since Susanne and Corliss had brought nothing but the bare necessities, the McCord wagon was ordered to the head of the line.

"Payne, you and Jesse scout around for the biggest log you can find," Cass called as he knelt to check the left front axle. The axle was low on lubricant. "Doog, tell Susanne I need the bottom side of a bacon slab."

"Yessir!" Doog scampered off and Harlon hurried over to help. By the time Doog returned with the requested bacon rind, Harlon and Cass had taken off the white oak wheel. Cass took the bacon fat and carefully wrapped it around the axle hub. Moments later the wheel slipped back into place.

"Think that'll work?" Harlon asked.

"It should."

"Mr. Claxton?" Ernestine Parker stood at Cass's heels, her eyes wide with worry. "You do be careful, you hear?"

Cass winked, and a flush stained the girl's cheeks. "I plan to do that, Ernestine."

Payne and Jesse returned, dragging the biggest log they could handle.

Reaching for the ax, Cass told Payne to grab the long hemp rope lashed to the back of the wagon and follow him. They tied the log to the back of the wagon to act as a brake. Cass eyed it, doubts forming in his mind. He surely hoped this worked. If it didn't he and Aaron were in for a rough ride.

When he was confident that everything was in order, Cass swung into the wagon beside Aaron. He removed his hat and wiped his forehead on his shirtsleeve. "Well, I can think of things I'd rather be doing."

Aaron swallowed, his Adam's apple bobbing. "Yes, sir. Me too."

Cass turned to face him, a slow grin forming. He'd developed a real affection for the boy. "I suppose you know how to stay on a woman's better side?"

Aaron frowned before a sheepish grin formed on his youthful features. "Well . . . uh . . . there are a couple of things I've been meaning to have you clear up for me."

Cass chuckled. "Son, there's a couple of things I still don't know."

Aaron's grin widened. "Yessir!"

"You've noticed that pretty little Ernestine Parker, haven't you?"

Aaron's Adam's apple bobbed again, and he flushed a deeper red. "Yessir . . . a little."

"A little, huh?"

"Yessir . . . a little."

Cass grinned, deciding the boy was relaxed enough to start. "You about ready to get this wagon down the hill?"

"Yessir!" There was a slight tremble in the youth's voice, but Cass saw that his hands were steady when he picked up the reins.

"Then let's get this over with so the women can stop their fidgeting."

"Yessir."

"I want you to take it real easy. Keep the reins good and tight, and ease the animals down real slow. The tree will act as a drag, but it's up to you to see that the animals don't get away."

"I can do that, sir."

Cass clasped one of Aaron's thin shoulders confidently. "I'm counting on you."

He swung down from the wagon and turned to give a sharp

whistle, signaling that they were ready to take the first wagon down. The other members of the train stopped what they were doing and came to watch.

"I'll need a couple of volunteers," Cass called out. He pulled on a pair of leather gloves.

Matt Johnson and Lewis Brown stepped up. Young men with strong, sturdy backs.

Glancing around to see where Susanne and the children were, Cass found them standing off to the side, looking worried. Susanne tried to smile when her eyes sought Aaron. Cass realized the boy was young to have so much responsibility thrust upon his shoulders, but kids grew up fast on the trail.

Sweat stained the back of Aaron's shirt. He gripped the reins so tightly that his knuckles turned white.

Cass took his place at the back of the wagon. "Okay, son, let's—"

"Cass!" Susanne shouted.

Cass glanced up. "What?"

"Please . . . be careful!"

He nodded curtly, surprised that, for a change, she wasn't cheering him on to trip downhill and be trampled by a herd of longhorn.

"Let 'em roll!" he shouted.

The wheels on the wagon began to turn. Cass, Matt, and Lewis latched on to a rope that trailed behind the tree, letting their weight act as an additional drag.

The crowd of onlookers collectively watched when the wagon began to laboriously descend, easing down the incline. The hill wasn't long, just steep.

Aaron gripped the reins, fixing his eyes straight ahead. Sweat poured down the sides of his dust-streaked face. Cass could hear him urging the animals in low, soothing tones to take it easy.

The harness creaked and the brakes protested. The team strained to move the now contrary wagon. Overhead, clouds blocked the sun as a threat of rain sprang up.

Cass watched the sky, praying that a thunderstorm wouldn't break out before they'd gotten all of the wagons safely down the hill. *God, we could use help here.* He dug his heels in, trying to keep his feet under him when the wagon threatened to career down the steep slope.

Susanne held her breath, trying to ignore the tight band of fear suddenly gripping her middle. Her heart was in her throat, her eyes riveted on Cass. She could see the muscles in his arms bunching tightly when he strained against the rope. The wagon dragged him and the others like rag dolls down the hillside.

She wished she could take his place, that she was the one in danger, not him. It wasn't fair that he could be injured—or perhaps killed—trying to help her.

The wagon picked up speed, rolling faster. Men's anxious shouts echoed through the countryside. Aaron threw all of his weight against the reins, trying to force the animals to slow down. A fierce gust of wind nearly took the canvas off the wagon when the first clap of thunder sounded.

Susanne closed her eyes and prayed in a frenzied litany.

"Don't let them be hurt, don't let them be hurt, don't let them be hurt. . . ."

Minutes seemed like hours; the heat closed in around her. She felt light-headed and faint, and the children's excited voices seemed to come to her from far away.

Suddenly a whoop went up, and she felt her knees buckle with fear.

"They made it!"

Her eyes flew open. Tears of relief streamed down her cheeks when she saw that the wagon was safely at the bottom of the hill. She could see Cass—his clothes filthy now, but blessedly safe and sound—calmly untying the rope in preparation for the next wagon.

A flurry of clamoring feet swept her along in their wake as the children rushed down the hill to meet him.

Margaret Ann and Lucy descended on Cass like a whirlwind, throwing their arms around his waist, nearly dragging him to the ground in their exuberance.

Aaron hopped from the wagon, his face flushed with victory and his wide grin assuring the others that he was going to be hard to live with for a while.

Ernestine, who'd been headed for Cass, stopped and blushed prettily when Aaron turned his smile in her direction. He winked—a gesture he'd picked up from watching Cass—and the teenage girl's face turned a deep crimson.

"Bet that was fun, huh?" Doog prodded Cass, his eyes conveying his deep longing to be old enough to do such an exciting thing.

"Never had so much fun," Cass teased. He tried to control the girls, who bounced around his feet like grasshoppers.

Margaret Ann demanded a hug, then Lucy, then Phebia, and of course, Marybelle. Cass knelt down to oblige the ladies, though he pretended to be wary of Phebia. Susanne grinned. The little imp still had an unnerving way of latching on to his nose when he least expected it.

Susanne arrived when Cass finished the hugs and stood up. Giving a cry of relief, she threw herself into his arms. "Oh . . . I thought you were going to be killed."

His arm tightened around her as naturally as if he'd held her a hundred times before. "Me? I'm invincible—haven't I mentioned that?"

She grasped the back of his head and hugged him with all her might.

Susanne hadn't realized what she was going to do. She hadn't planned to show the depth of her feelings, but now she realized she was glad she'd done it. And she would die if he cast her aside in front of the children.

After a long moment, he gently set her aside, his eyes filled with amusement. A grin started at the corners of his mouth when he surely recognized the alarm growing in her eyes. "Why, Miss McCord," he challenged softly, "I didn't know you cared."

"I . . . I didn't know either," she confessed.

His amusement disappeared, and the blue of his eyes darkened when he contemplated the meaning of her admission. "Well, well, what do you know about that."

She held her breath when he looked at her. It was as if he were seeing her for the first time.

Their gazes continued to silently assess each other. She prayed that he would be kind, that he wouldn't openly reject her. *Please, God, don't let him reject me this time. Not this time.*

He glanced down at the children and winked; then, gathering Susanne in his arms, he hugged her warmly. "Thank you, Miss McCord. Sure do appreciate your concern."

For a moment she was caught by surprise, but then she enjoyed the unexpected. His arms felt exactly as she thought they would: superbly masculine, exciting—wonderful.

She sighed and stood on tiptoe, her arms encircling his neck more tightly. "Thank *you*," she whispered into his ear.

If it hadn't been for the children, she would have shamelessly stayed in his arms forever. But the sound of embarrassed giggles broke the spell.

Cass eased out of the embrace as quickly as it had begun. "Storm's about to break. I've got the other wagons to see to," he said gruffly.

A new, headier thrill shot through Susanne when she realized that he was as shaken by the embrace as she was. "Yes, of course," she murmured.

He turned to the children, who were still chortling. "If you children don't have anything better to do than stand around giggling at the old folks, I'll find something to occupy your time," he warned.

Squealing, they scampered in all directions.

Susanne watched Cass walk back up the hill, her heart overflowing with love.

The storm's already broken, Mr. Claxton, she thought with a grin. *You just don't know it yet.*

CHAPTER 7

The wagons stopped at the brink of a swift-moving creek
Monday morning. Matt Johnson rode his big bay out into the
stream, trying to gauge the depth. "I think it's all right," he
yelled back to the ones waiting on the bank. "Hold upstream
and aim for that gravel bar. Should be a good place to pull out."

Cass watched as the other wagons eased into the water one
by one. The force of the water and the loose gravel in the
streambed caused the Waterman wagon to shift sideways, but
Lucius Waterman cracked his bullwhip and the oxen changed
course, struggling to the bank.

Aaron sat on the wagon seat, holding the reins. Cass rode up
beside him. "You ready for this?"

The young man nodded. "I'm ready."

"All right. You see where that wagon went wrong? Aim about
six feet upstream from where Lucius crossed and I think you'll
be fine." Susanne, Corliss, and the children rode inside the
wagon. This stream was too deep and too fast to wade across.

Aaron nodded, and when his turn came he drove out into the

water as steady and sure as if he'd been doing it all his life. Cass smiled. He was right proud of the boy. He'd do to ride the river with. As a matter of fact, every one of these kids was first-rate. A man would be proud to claim any of them as his own.

After the wagon was safely across, Harlon rode his sorrel out into the water, sitting easy. A good man, Cass thought. The elderly gentleman had done what he could to pull his weight on this trip. Made a real hand.

Cass caught his breath when the horse slipped and went down, taking Harlon with him. Before Cass could reach the struggling horse and man, the animal rolled onto its side and Harlon disappeared under the water. Corliss screamed and jumped from the back of the wagon to race to the edge of the bank, wringing her hands.

When Cass approached, the horse struggled to its feet and surged toward the shore. Payne jumped to catch the bridle, bringing the animal under control. Swinging out of the saddle, Cass fought to keep his balance against the strong flow. The reins slipped out of his hands, and his animal took advantage of its freedom to head for shore.

Harlon surfaced and tried to regain his footing, slipped, and went under again. Cass lunged, catching hold of his shirt. He hauled upward, bringing the older man's head above the water.

Payne waded toward them, slipped on a rock, and fell with a mighty splash. Immediately he was back on his feet, plowing toward them. Between them they got Harlon upright, but he floundered, a deadweight. Cass grabbed him under one arm and motioned for Payne to do the same. Struggling, one slow step after the other, they managed to drag the older man to shore.

They dropped him on the rocky shingle, and Corliss pushed

them aside to kneel beside her husband. "Oh, Harlon. You're hurt," she gasped.

Harlon coughed, spitting up water. "Think my leg's broke, and I nigh drowned. Guess Cass and the boy saved my life."

Cass coughed, spit water on the ground, and then said, "I think Payne saved us both. I wasn't having much luck getting you on your feet."

He knelt and examined the older man's leg. "It's broke all right. I can set it, but it's going to hurt."

"Hurts now," Harlon said. "Might as well go ahead and get it over with."

"Aaron, you and Payne get me Susanne's quilting frame. It will do as splints."

"My quilting frame?"

He looked up to find Susanne standing beside him. "You got a problem with that?"

"No. Of course not. I suppose you'll need something to bind it to his leg? I'll rip up an old petticoat."

When the items arrived, Cass took the frame from Aaron and carefully measured the wood. "Cut it right here. Okay?" He indicated the length.

"Sure." The two boys went to work and shortly handed Cass the narrow, sturdy pieces of pine.

"All right now, Harlon, we're going to pull that leg back in place and splint it. Bear with us." He pulled, with Aaron holding the older man by the shoulders. The leg gradually eased into position, and Cass quickly bound the splints in place. Harlon hadn't made a sound, but he had gripped Corliss's work-worn hand so tightly that she had winced. With Cass on one side and

Aaron and Susanne on the other, they carried the injured man to the wagon and made him comfortable.

Cass patted Harlon's shoulder. "I'll be back to check on you later. You need anything, have Corliss call and we'll come running." He glanced at Corliss. "Do we have any whiskey on hand?"

She shook her head. "Nary a drop."

Sweat dripped off Harlon's forehead. "Sure glad you were here, Cass. I owe you one for this."

"You don't owe me a thing. You're going to have some real pain."

"It can't get much worse," Harlon said with an attempt at a smile. Cass walked over to take the reins of his horse from Doog.

"Is Harlon going to be all right?" The boy asked, his youthful features pale.

"He should be fine. These things happen. He'll mend." Cass prayed that he was right and not misleading the boy. Harlon was aging and his bones would take time to heal.

Doog grinned and scampered off to join the others.

Cass took his position at the rear of the train, thinking of Harlon. It was a common trail accident. Apart from his concern for the old fellow's recovery, he realized that the accident meant there would be one less hand to help with the work.

It could take months—or longer—before Harlon would be on his feet again, but he was lucky to have come out of it with his life.

They had been on the trail for five weeks, and Cherry Grove was a little more than a hundred miles away. Cass was confident that he could get by; Aaron and Payne were old enough to accept extra responsibilities.

The October mornings had a nip to them now. He knew it wouldn't be long before Indian summer gave way to howling winter winds. They should reach their destination long before that, so he wasn't concerned.

After supper that evening he walked to the back of the wagon to visit Harlon, who lay on a mattress looking peaked, with his foot propped up on a pillow. Cass could see the older man was suffering. "Can I do anything for you? If you need it, just name it." He wasn't a man to drink, but he knew whiskey's medicinal purposes, and if Harlon needed something he'd try to oblige.

"Thanks, son, but I can't think of a thing I need."

Cass perched atop a bundle in the wagon and leaned back against the frame.

"I'm much obliged to you for settin' the leg," Harlon said. "I told Corliss I don't know what we'd have done if you hadn't been here to help us."

"You don't need to thank me. I was glad to help."

"You've been a real godsend to Susanne—well, to all of us. I hope you know that."

Cass appreciated the praise but found he was uncomfortable with it. "Susanne's a strong woman. She'd have made it with or without my help."

Harlon's eyes twinkled. "She's not as strong as you might think, boy."

Cass fell silent; he guessed Harlon could sense he would prefer to drop the subject, because he glanced resentfully at the splinted leg. "I could just kick myself for breakin' this gol-burned thing! I'm as helpless as a turtle on its back," he complained.

Cass smiled. "You'll heal."

"Well, I shore hope so. I don't want to be no trouble to anyone." He reached for his pipe and smoked in silence for a while. Someone in the train strummed a guitar, the sound adding to the peace of the evening.

"Gettin' colder," Harlon observed.

"Yes—change is in the air."

Susanne's and Margaret Ann's voices approached the wagon.

"Margaret Ann," Susanne was saying, "before you go to bed I want you to run over and ask how old Mrs. Medsker is this evening."

"Yes, ma'am," Margaret Ann replied and skipped off to do as she was told. Cass heard her return within minutes. "Mrs. Medsker said she didn't think it was any of your doin's how old she is," Margaret repeated.

Cass grinned when he heard Susanne's sharp intake of breath before she skirted Margaret off to Winoka Medsker's wagon to explain the misunderstanding.

"How come a nice-looking chap like you never took a wife?" Harlon asked. "Seems to me that a man your age ought to have his own children's mistakes to chuckle about."

Cass shifted uncomfortably at the question. "The right woman's never come along."

"Maybe you haven't looked in the right place," Harlon said, and Cass wondered if he was thinking about Susanne.

"Harlon, I'd like to talk to you about something."

"Certainly."

"I guess I'm asking your advice."

"All right."

"Bull Hanson and his men have been following us for days. They dropped out of sight for a while, but they're back now."

Harlon glanced up, a frown on his brow. "Is that right?"

"What do you think he wants?"

Harlon drew on his pipe thoughtfully. "Hard to say."

"I've been wondering whether I should let it pass or pay a visit to Mr. Hanson one of these evenings."

"I don't know, son. The man 'pears as ornery as a caged skunk to me."

"I don't want him scaring the women."

"No, we couldn't put up with that."

"What do you think I should do?"

"Well, I think I'd wait him out. If he shows any sign of trouble, you can deal with him then. There's no use raisin' a stink if he's merely travelin' the trail with us."

"I guess you're right." Still, Cass didn't like the close quarters; it made him edgy.

"Keep a close eye on him."

"I plan to."

Harlon drew on his pipe again, sending a plume of smoke rolling out of the wagon. "You don't suppose the women have noticed him?"

"I don't think so. Susanne would have mentioned it if she had."

As much as Susanne irritated him, Cass didn't want her subjected to a man like Bull Hanson.

Harlon sighed. "Well, maybe we're just borrowin' trouble."

Cass's gaze followed Susanne when she and Margaret Ann emerged from the Medskers' wagon. He didn't know why he found the outlaw's presence so disturbing, but he did.

"Yeah, maybe we are."

But even Aaron mentioned Bull Hanson's continuing presence a few days later. His young features were stoic as he watched Cass saddle up. "Have you noticed Hanson and his thugs have been following us for days now?"

"I've noticed."

"What do you think he wants?"

Cass shrugged.

"You think he has his eye on Miss McCord?"

Jerking the cinch tighter, Cass frowned. "I think if he's fond of wildcats he's on the right trail." He swung in the saddle and adjusted his hat low on his forehead.

"You're not worried about him?"

"Not in the least."

Aaron grinned. "I guess you know how to handle the likes of Bull Hanson. He's awfully big, though."

"A man's size doesn't mean that much." Cass winked. "It's his will that counts."

Aaron nodded. "Mind if I ride behind your saddle this morning?"

"You're not driving the wagon?"

"No, sir. Miss McCord said she was going to."

"Climb aboard."

The horse trotted through camp; Cass spotted Susanne rolling up the night's bedding and storing it in gutta-percha sacks.

Their gazes met, and he tipped his hat mockingly.

She stuck her tongue out at him.

"Miss McCord's a right fine-looking woman, isn't she?" Aaron remarked when Cass spurred the horse into a gallop.

"I suppose she'd do in a pinch," Cass allowed. If a man was desperate, which he was not.

Early that afternoon the train of wagons stopped to water the stock in a wide brook. Indian summer had turned hot as a smoking pistol. The cool, clear water felt heavenly, and the weary travelers splashed the liquid on suntanned arms and faces. The children's delighted squeals could be heard for more than an hour as they laughed and played in the bubbling water. When they were loading to leave, a new wagon rolled in.

"Oh, brother!" Susanne muttered irritably when she saw that the old buckboard was decked with an outrageously gaudy yellow-fringed awning.

A wagonload of fallen angels.

Protective mothers hurriedly gathered the children and herded them into the wagons in an effort to shield their young eyes from the unsavory sight. Husbands followed suit, but not without one or two curious glances at the new arrivals.

However, the less-than-cordial welcome didn't dampen the spirits of the scantily dressed women. The women piled out of their buckboard and headed straight for the water.

Within minutes they were cooling in the stream, oblivious to the resentful looks fired in their direction. There wasn't actually a beauty in the lot, but that didn't seem to discourage the men's rapt attention.

Susanne kept a close eye on Cass. He and Aaron sat on the horse with their eyes glued to the spectacle going on before them.

Even Payne's and Jesse's eyes were rounder than usual. They peered around the corner of the wagon, gawking. Corliss hollered for them to *git*, and their heads quickly disappeared.

A buxom redhead focused on Cass. She gave a come-hither smile, displaying her dazzling white teeth and full cherry red lips. "Hello there, handsome. Nice camping place you got here." She reached into the pocket of her dress and pulled out two thin cigars. She lit one and offered the other to Cass. His mouth curved into a lazy smile, and he leaned down and took it from her. He put it, unlit, between his teeth.

It was clear to Susanne that the redhead had snagged his undivided attention.

"Afternoon, ma'am. Mighty warm today."

"Yes, it is," she agreed in a sultry Texas drawl.

"You ladies traveling far?"

"Far 'nuff." She lowered her lids demurely. "Where you-all goin'?"

"Kansas."

"Sure 'nuff? Why, I have a dear old grandma who lives in Wichita."

"That so?"

"Sure 'nuff. Are you by any chance going to Wichita?"

Cass shook his. "No, ma'am, afraid not."

"Well, that's too bad. . . . Listen, sugar, we'll be stopping not far down the road tonight. Maybe you'd like to drop by, so I could give you a letter to mail to my dear, sweet grandma once you reach Kansas."

Susanne had heard enough. She reached for the bullwhip under the wagon seat, stood up, whirled it around her head a couple of times, and let it fly.

Cass heard the deafening crack of the whip about the same time his cigar splintered into oblivion.

Stunned, he lifted his blank gaze to encounter Susanne's snapping eyes. Bits of tobacco fragments swirled in the air.

"It's time we were on our way," she snapped.

The butt of his cigar dropped from his lips and rolled down the front of his shirt before it dawned on him what had happened. His face turned crimson, and for the first time in his life he was speechless. Had she swung that whip? By grab, she had. Swung that bullwhip at him! Cut the cigar in half. No woman had ever treated Cass Claxton in such a manner. And he wasn't in a mood to take it now.

He clenched his jaw, feeling the veins standing out in his temple. *Lord, why did You make this woman so blamed ornery?* Rile her and no man was safe in her vicinity! He swung off his horse, intent on teaching her a lesson. Before he could move, Margaret Ann blocked his path.

"Mr. Cass. Think what you're doing."

He peered down at her. "What?"

"I believe you might mean bodily harm to Miss McCord. Is that right?"

"You better believe it."

"Do you think force ever solves anything?"

He drew a deep breath. Wasn't it too bad Miss Have-my-own-way-or-bust McCord didn't have one-tenth the common sense of this child? The world would be a far better place.

"Well?" Margaret Ann's direct gaze brought him to his senses.

"Probably not." But it sure would help him to let off a load of steam. He heaved a sigh and reluctantly climbed back on his horse, feeling he had been taken to the woodshed by this moppet. Fine thing when kids started taking their elders down a notch.

Susanne wielded the whip a second time, and the wagon lurched forward. The other drivers followed suit, and the train started moving.

Once they were out on the trail she glanced back to see if Cass and Aaron were following. She was relieved to see that they were, although they were trailing at a distance.

"Guess I showed that Jezebel that she best not mess with my husband and expect to get away with it," she muttered tightly under her breath. She swung the whip again and sent it blazing over the oxen's heads. Oh, her temper had gotten the better of her; she'd gone too far this time. Cass would be mad as a hornet and yell at her or worse for embarrassing him in front of the whole wagon train, but he'd deserved it.

A grin escaped her when she recalled the horrified look on his face when he'd realized what she'd done.

But he sure 'nuff had it coming, Lord.

Camp was quieter than usual that night. Since Mort Harrison had the first watch, he was preparing to take up his post. Meanwhile, Buck Brewster sat beneath a tree, playing his violin— a sweet, lilting refrain that floated pleasantly through the wagons.

Cass lay on his bedroll, looking up at the stars. It was a clear night, and the heavens were ablaze with God's handiwork.

Aaron and Payne had rolled up beside him, and he sensed that the two boys had something on their minds. He could wait until they were ready to say whatever it was that was bothering them.

"You got a pa?" Aaron asked.

"My pa died a short while after I was born," Cass said. "My mother raised me with the help of an older brother."

"I think mine's dead too," Payne admitted. "I can't be sure though. Been on my own for as long as I can remember."

"Sure would be nice to have a pa to talk to—or maybe a ma," Aaron mused.

"Mothers are nice," Cass admitted, remembering his own mother and how long it had been since he'd last seen her.

A few minutes passed before Aaron finally broached the subject Cass figured was uppermost in his mind.

"Cass . . . those women we saw today . . ." He sat up and his voice trailed off.

Cass squelched the urge to laugh. These boys were on the verge of manhood. They didn't have a pa to confide in, so he guessed he'd been chosen to answer their questions. "What about them?"

"Well—" Aaron cleared his throat—"they weren't nice women, were they?"

"Probably not."

Aaron was quiet for a moment, and Payne sat up. "A man's not supposed to have nothing to do with that kind of woman . . . is he?"

"I guess it depends on the man. Some men take their pleasure where they find it, but a steady, God-fearing man would prefer to find a good woman and settle down and raise a family."

"The Good Book says that kind of behavior is evil," Payne reminded.

Cass nodded and added quietly, "The Good Book also says 'Judge not, that you be not judged.'"

"Have you ever been . . . acquainted with one of those women?" Aaron asked.

Cass sat up and stared at the stars, wishing the conversation were a little easier to handle. "Rule number one: a gentleman never kisses and tells."

"Even if he's been kissing with one of them women?"

Cass eyed Payne dryly and considered the question. "Especially if he's been kissing one of those women. How do you know so much about 'those women'?"

Payne flushed. "Well . . . I saw this book one time. . . ." He stopped and a sheepish grin formed.

Cass nodded. Youngsters were curious, but he needed to explain the difference in women. "There's nothing that can compare with a decent, God-fearing woman. Like the Bible says, a good woman is worth more than rubies."

"Rubies?" Payne asked. "They're worth a lot of money, aren't they?"

Aaron sounded puzzled. "What's it mean, she's worth more than rubies? You can't put a dollar amount on a person."

"No, you can't," Cass agreed. "It means that having a woman who loves the Lord and tries to do right standing beside you is a blessing straight out of heaven."

"Well, maybe, but—," Payne began.

But Cass interrupted. "You can trust a woman like that with your life. She'll be there when you need her, work with you, pray with you, and raise your children to be God-fearing adults."

Cass thought of the way Susanne had tricked him into marriage and felt his ire rising. He tamped down on his anger. Right now he had to make the boys see the difference between a sober, decent, God-loving woman and the other kind.

"I have a mother who loves God and raised her boys to do the same. I've wandered off the straight and narrow a few times, but my mother's teaching always brought me back. That's the way it is with the right kind of woman. No matter how much you're tempted to do wrong, you'll never want to disappoint the woman who loves you and believes in you."

"Well, I suppose the kind of woman you're talking about is all right," Payne said. "But it seems to me the other kind is more exciting."

"That's where you're wrong," Cass said. "The kind of woman you'll want to tie up with will smell like wildflowers after a rain; she'll have skin as soft as cotton, and her hair will feel like French silk when you run your fingers through it. She'll be gentle by nature, and she'll have a way of making a man feel eager to come home at night."

"What about the other ones?" Payne asked. "I already know what I'm *supposed* to want."

"Well, the Bible says the wrong woman will lead a man to destruction. You have to realize there are some 'bad' females. Some are misguided, and some do what they have to do to survive. I treat all women with respect, and I'd suggest you do the same. When you meet up with a woman, you treat her like a lady, no matter what other people think of her. If a man trifles with a woman, then walks away, he's nothing but a piece of trash."

The three lay back to stare at the stars. Silence surrounded them.

"What kind of woman do you think Miss McCord is?" Payne asked.

"Payne, she's a good woman!" Aaron gasped. "Isn't that so, Cass?"

"I would imagine."

"Don't you know?"

Cass realized he didn't know anything about Susanne, other than she was like a burr under his saddle most of the time. What sort of woman was she? he wondered. Beautiful, yes, he couldn't deny that. Over the last six years, she'd turned into a lovely woman, charming when she wanted to be, and a blessed saint when it came to dealing with children.

"I think I'll just try out a few of the other kind before I look for a nice woman," Payne decided. "Seems like that'd be the practical thing to do."

Cass winced. "What part of this conversation were you not listening too?"

He made a mental note to take Payne aside for a more detailed discussion of the subject. It appeared that the boy had missed a point somewhere.

"Well, how are you gonna know who's what?" Payne asked, clearly confused. "Miss McCord—she's real pretty and I think she's nice, but how am I going to know unless I try out a lot of women?"

"Gentlemen—" Cass rolled to his feet, thinking he'd ride back along the trail and see if Bull and his men were camped anywhere in the general vicinity—"it's getting late."

Aaron looked up and winked. "But Miss McCord's pretty hard to overlook, ain't she?"

Cass chose to ignore the question. "Go to sleep. I think I'll take a ride."

"I've been thinking," Aaron said. "There ain't *no* woman gonna hog-tie and brand me; not if I can help it!"

Yeah, Cass thought. *You've got a lot to learn about women, son.* He'd once felt the same way until he met up with an angry father and a shotgun-toting sheriff. And he'd been paying for it ever since.

Cass paused to speak to a young woman who sat in a large rocking chair just outside one of the wagons. She was trying to soothe her fretful infant, who'd been ill for days.

"How's the baby tonight?" he asked.

"I think she feels a mite hotter than she did earlier." Mardean Gibson's wan smile gave mute testimony to the strain she was under.

Cass touched the baby's forehead, and his brow furrowed with concern. "Do you need another bucket of cool water?"

"No, thank you. Boyd said he'd fetch me one when he got up." Boyd and Mardean had been taking turns sitting up nights with the infant. Cass felt sorry for the young couple. Still teenagers, they were barely more than children themselves.

"I'll hold your baby if you'd like to rest a spell," he offered.

Mardean gazed tenderly at the sleeping child on her lap. "I'm beholden to you, Mr. Claxton, but I want to stay with her," she said softly.

Giving Mardean's shoulder a friendly squeeze, Cass smiled. "If you need anything, you let me know."

Her face brightened momentarily. "Thank you. I surely do appreciate your kindness."

Susanne had just pulled the pins from her hair and was about to give it a thorough brushing when she saw Cass come walking back through camp. She was surprised to see that he was still awake.

The fires had burned low, and Buck Brewster was slipping his fiddle into its case, preparing to retire for the night.

Susanne watched the exchange with Mardean, and a feeling of envy engulfed her.

What she would give to have Cass speak to *her* with such compassion, such concern, such caring. . . . Her thoughts wavered. She watched him walk to where his horse was grazing.

Now where did he think he was going at this hour? He picked up his saddle and slung it over his shoulder. Suddenly she was sure she could guess. He had to be going to visit those women.

He was going to see that redhead, she thought. And the two of them were not going to spend their time composing a letter to dear old grandma in Wichita!

Scalding tears sprang to her eyes, and she swiped them away angrily. She tried to tell herself that she didn't care. But she did care, desperately.

Somewhere a legal document had been recorded verifying the hasty marriage. She wouldn't even try to fool herself into believing that a mere piece of paper could prevent him from seeing other women, but not in her presence. She would not allow him to disgrace her by running off in the middle of the night to cavort with one of those women of easy virtue.

She walked toward the wagon, conceding that her logic might be flawed. After all, no one on the train knew that she and Cass were married, so he could hardly disgrace her in their eyes.

But *she* knew they were married. And the thought of his spending time with another woman when he'd avoided her—his own wife—like the plague set her blood boiling.

How dare he even contemplate such a thing? No decent, godly man would dream of visiting one of those . . . those . . . women. Didn't he know the Good Book frowned on such behavior?

She paused, hands clenched into fists, and did some serious thinking. The Bible warned against being unequally yoked with an unbeliever. She struggled to remember whether Cass had ever talked about his spiritual beliefs. Was he a Christian? If so, didn't he know what he was thinking of doing was wrong? Better for her to punish him than to let him set his feet on the road to destruction and risk God's wrath. Why, she would be doing him a favor by stopping him.

Then it hit her. Sometime during the past weeks, she had unconsciously begun to think of Cass as her property—her man. Now she asked herself if a woman didn't have a right to protect what was hers, even though what was hers had never wanted to become hers in the first place. She frowned. That sounded complicated, but she knew exactly what she meant.

She reached the wagon, and her hand fumbled under the seat for the bullwhip while she kept her eyes trained on Cass. He was acting as if he were simply about the business of saddling his horse for an innocent moonlight ride. Well, she was about to change his destination.

Cass had one foot in the stirrup when he momentarily paused. Cocking his head to one side, he thought he could detect the sound of a whip oscillating in midair.

The meaning of the ominous whir suddenly sank in, and he braced himself for what he knew was coming.

The soft *wisp, wisp, wisp* grew louder.

"Susanne, you'd better think twice," he warned, glancing over his shoulder.

She stood behind him in her nightgown, covered by an enveloping wrap, whirling the whip above her head. "Where are you going?"

"That's none of your business."

"Oh yes, it is."

Wisp, wisp, wisp, wisp.

"Susanne—"

"You're not going to that woman." A menacing crack split the air, and Cass clamped his eyes shut and gripped the pommel tightly as he felt the back of his shirt split in half. He sucked in his breath, waiting to feel his blood gush, but he gradually realized that she hadn't touched his flesh—a fact, he decided, that had most likely saved her life!

"Don't push me, Cass. I can draw blood," she warned in a tight voice.

"What's this all about?" he demanded, stunned to realize that for once his voice sounded thready instead of cocksure.

"You are not going to that woman."

"What woman?"

"*That* woman!"

"*What* woman? I wasn't going to meet a woman—I was going for a ride!"

He didn't know why he was bothering to inform her of where he was or was not going. She didn't own him. He started to turn around and tell her so when the whip cracked again.

This time it sliced through his sleeve and separated the fabric cleanly from his shoulder.

"Don't lie to me! You were going to see that woman!"

Cass had had enough. He whirled and lunged at her, catching her around the waist. She jerked back, and he reached for the whip. Susanne fought like an enraged cat, clawing and scratching. She punched him in the chest with her free hand while the other held the whip out of reach. It was an unequal contest, and his strength easily overpowered hers. They fell to the ground, and he landed on top of her, hearing the breath go out of her with a whoosh.

"Get off me, you big oaf!" she gasped.

He sat up and, with a strength born of pure rage, snapped the whip in two and threw it as far as he could send it.

"I have another one!" she said. She didn't make any effort to sit up, and he guessed he'd knocked the wind out of her.

He glared at her. "Miss McCord," he said in a voice so ominous that even he felt the hair rise on his arms. He wouldn't strike her, would he? "You are sorely getting on my nerves, woman."

"You were going to that . . . that woman," she accused. For some strange reason she sounded as if she was about cry.

"I was not—and what if I was? You have no right to be telling me what I can do! I'm doing what I said I'd do. I said I would get you, the children, Harlon, and Corliss to Cherry Grove safely, and I'm trying my level best to do that. Now, woman, you've browbeaten me, badgered me, bullwhipped me, and bad-mouthed me about all I'm going to stand for. You're going to stop. Do you understand?"

"I am your wife!"

His jaw dropped. He couldn't believe she'd said that. "My wife?"

"Your wife . . . I am, you know—no matter how hard you try to deny it!"

"I don't want you to be my wife! I've told you that a hundred times."

"But that doesn't change the fact that we *are* husband and wife," she argued. "And the Good Book says a man and woman should cleave together."

"Hold on. What's *cleave* mean?"

"I don't know—it's beside the point. They're to stay together—and you're not even trying to obey the Word."

"Let me get this straight. You're suggesting that just because of some idiotic, meaningless ceremony that took place in the middle of a road six years ago, I should actually consider myself married to you?"

"Well . . . yes." Their eyes were still locked. "I . . . I wouldn't object—truth is, I'd be honored."

"Me and you?" he repeated, feeling as if she had just asked him to step before a firing squad.

"Don't sound so shocked. We could be . . . married."

Cass slumped, resting his face in his hands. For a moment he thought he was going to break down and cry like a baby. Then he started to see the humor in this situation. His body heaved with barely suppressed hilarity.

Susanne stiffened, her eyes blazing with fury. "What is so funny?"

"You!"

She struggled to sit up. "I fail to see how my offering to be your wife should be so hilarious."

His hand snaked out, grasping her shoulder. "Now wait a

minute." Slowly he eased her back to the ground. "I didn't say I wouldn't accept your offer."

"You would?" She didn't sound so sure of herself.

He managed to keep a straight face, knowing that to consider her offer seriously would bring more trouble than it was worth. This woman was a spitfire, a wildcat, and the biggest obstacle he'd ever tried to overcome. She was a beautiful albatross who also happened to be his wife, albeit in name only. And he had a vested interest in making sure it remained in name only.

She took a deep breath. "So now what?"

The moonlight turned her hair to silver. A faint fragrance of woodsmoke from the campfire tinged the air. Cass found himself remembering how soft her lips had been, the way she had fit in his arms the day they lowered the wagons down the hill. Susanne McCord . . . Claxton. For a minute he was tempted, and then common sense intervened. She might be pretty, but he still had half a mind.

"You can go where you like; I'm going for a walk. Without you."

She clenched her fists. "You're rejecting me *again*?"

"That's right. You're nothing but trouble, and if I ever get free of you, I'm going to be mighty particular the next time around."

"You . . . you . . . ," she spluttered.

"And you want to know what makes me the maddest?" He could feel the slow burn of anger rekindle. "The fact that you think I'd have anything to do with one of those women. I might not be perfect in the eyes of God, but I do make an effort."

She stared up at him, mouth open. "But I thought . . ."

"Thought what?"

"Laure . . . Miss Revuneau . . ."

"Laure Revuneau is a decent woman, active in her church and involved in mission work. What gives you the right to insult her?"

"Well . . . I . . ."

"At least she's never tricked a man into marrying her, or taken a bullwhip to one."

"Well—you don't know that!"

"Good night, Miss McCord. Sleep well." He turned and walked off, wondering where she kept the other whip. Finding it and destroying it would be his next move.

CHAPTER 8

The following morning when Susanne rounded the wagon, she found Mardean sitting in the rocker, cradling her infant to her bosom.

Tears rolled silently down the girl's cheeks when Susanne knelt beside her. She reached out to smooth a stray lock that had fallen across the young mother's forehead. The girl looked exhausted. "Mardean . . . is the baby worse this morning?"

Mardean lifted her red-rimmed eyes, and Susanne saw in them the depth of human misery: Mardean's child was gone. She rocked back and forth, quietly holding her infant's lifeless form.

Sometime during the night, her baby had passed away.

Susanne didn't know how things could get much worse. Why did the world have to be so complicated?

A bright sun shone overhead, birds chirped, and the squirrels chattered noisily in the trees. It didn't seem a proper day for a burial.

The small group stood around the shallow grave as Lucius Waterman spoke the words of interment. His voice was solemn when he opened his worn Bible and read from Matthew 19:14: "But Jesus said, 'Let the little children come to Me, and do not forbid them, for of such is the kingdom of heaven.'"

Lucius glanced at the bereaved young couple. "Nothing can replace the loss of this sweet infant, or ease the pain you are feeling right now. This suffering is too new, too fresh to easily endure. But I want you to know that the loss of this baby wasn't a punishment for your sins. God didn't take your baby to cause you grief.

"There'll be other babies, and you'll love them and care for them, but you'll never forget this one, your firstborn. Now I want you to hear me out. When it seems you miss her so much you can't go on, you close your eyes and picture this sweet child healthy and happy, running through fields of flowers, the wind fresh and cool against her face, the sound of laughter and music filling the air.

"Then I want you to remember your child isn't lost to you. She's there, in heaven, waiting, and someday you'll meet her in a joyful reunion in the presence of Almighty God."

Susanne stood between Cass and her own brood, wondering how she would cope with such loss. Was her own faith strong enough to see her through the tragic ordeal? She felt it was; but then why did she despair when it came to Cass? She'd asked the Lord to intervene, to help her make amends. Now she, like Mardean, must trust that He loved His children and heard their cries.

The children that stood quietly beside her were not her own, yet she loved them all as dearly as if she'd carried them in her womb. Her heart went out to the young grieving father, Boyd. He stood tall with his arm around Mardean, who openly sobbed. Susanne could see that he was trying to be brave, even as his own grief streamed from the corners of his eyes.

Lucius spoke words of comfort and encouragement as Boyd and Mardean, along with their friends, listened in silence.

Susanne could feel a kindness in all of them, a deep understanding. The grim reaper often lurked on the trail; not a soul here was unaware of the dangers that could befall them.

Lucius closed the Bible and took stock of the small group. "Let us pray." Lifting his gaze upward, he began in a reassuring voice, "Father, we know not why You have called Sari Gibson home today, nor do we question Your will. Grant her parents the strength they will need to see them through their loss. Lend us the strength to give comfort and sustain Boyd and Mardean through the dark days ahead. God, we pray that You grant mercy to us all. Amen."

Four men stepped forward. Susanne could hear the scraping of the shovels. She knew each thrust of dirt would lay bare Mardean's heart.

The service broke up; others broke camp, allowing the grieving parents the last remaining moments with their child.

Susanne could see the young couple standing next to the mound of fresh dirt, holding tightly to each other.

She wondered if she would ever experience the kind of love Boyd felt for Mardean. If a tragedy befell her, to whom could she go for comfort? *I know I could go to You, Father, but I desperately need someone human to hold me. Lord, I feel so alone.*

Her eyes searched for Cass. She found him busy hitching the team to the Gibsons' wagon, and she suddenly needed the assurance that he was nearby.

Gathering the last of their supplies, she stowed them in their wagon, then ambled over to where he was working.

Perched on the tongue of the wagon, she watched him adjust a piece of harness. He didn't seem to notice her, but she was strongly aware of the way the sun glinted on his hair, the way his appearance had changed from the rather dandified city man to a tanned, rugged man of the saddle.

Phebia ran up, crying. She'd smashed her thumb—the sucking one. With solemn eyes, she silently extended her injury to Cass.

"I don't think it's serious, but I'll bandage it," he reassured her.

Minutes later Phebia skipped happily away, dragging Marybelle by the hair, her injured thumb encased in a huge, snow-white bandage.

"Maybe now she'll stop sucking the thing," Cass remarked when he turned his attention back to the harness.

"She seems to rely on you more and more in all her crises."

Cass shrugged. "She's a good kid."

Susanne sighed and clasped her hands in her lap. "Real sad about the Gibson baby, isn't it?"

He glanced her way, but he kept working. "It is."

"I'll never get used to the thought of death." Her eyes misted when they wandered back to Boyd and Mardean. "I know we shouldn't question God's will, but you wonder why He would want to take a baby."

"God didn't promise there'd be no pain here on earth. Losing a child is one of the hardest things a man or woman has to accept."

She looked at him. "You sound as if you've had firsthand experience."

"A few years back my brother lost both his wife and the child she was carrying." Cass jerked the leather straps together. "The loss almost killed him."

"I'm sorry."

"Meant to be. After a year or so he married a little gal named Charity, and from what I hear, he couldn't be happier. God has a way of turning loss into victory if we allow Him."

"Would that be Beau?" she asked softly, trying to ignore his words. She'd never gotten accustomed to losing. In fact, she had devoted a large part of her life to making sure she didn't lose. She didn't even like to think about loss. She'd met Beau Claxton years ago when she'd gone to the Burks' cabin to ask Cass to take her back to Saint Louis. That night with the others sleeping soundly, she had hatched a plot to force Cass to marry her and take her with him when he left. An act she now realized hadn't worked out exactly the way she had planned.

"It was Beau," Cass acknowledged.

"Do you have other family?"

"An older brother, Cole. And my mother. They live in Missouri. And Trey McAllister. He fought with my brothers in the war and since has become almost like family."

"No sisters?"

"No sisters."

She was pleased to discover that they could carry on a normal conversation without fussing. It felt good for a change. Maybe they were making progress, she thought wistfully, realizing that it would probably last only long enough for her to finish her next statement.

"Cass?"

He glanced up. "Yes."

"There's something you need to know."

"All right." He didn't seem overly curious, and she realized nothing she could say would surprise him. She guessed he'd learned to expect the worst from her.

"I sent you the telegram from Beau."

Cass never looked up. "Doesn't surprise me," he said quietly. "Knowing you, I've sort of suspected it. Seemed like you were too certain of my destination for our meeting to be purely coincidence. I'm just relieved to learn that Beau isn't in trouble. That did worry me considerable."

She blinked, stunned by his benign acceptance. "You're not angry?"

He looked at her this time, long and hard. "Would it do any good if I was?"

"No." She lowered her gaze to study her hands. "I know it was an awful thing to do."

"You seldom do anything that's nice where I'm concerned."

She looked away again. "I know."

"Exactly why do you do these things, Susanne?" he asked. "What drives you to be so ornery?"

"I don't know. . . . I suppose because nobody ever cared enough to stop me."

"Your folks never taught you the wisdom of asking for favors instead of bullying your way through life?"

"They tried; certainly Aunt Estelle taught me right from wrong. But after Mama died, Daddy was so wrapped up in his grief that he went off into his own little world. Seemed to me the only way I could get his attention was to throw fits, make demands, and act perfectly outrageous. When I found out that he wasn't going to come out of his shell long enough to do anything about it, then I suppose I just got worse." Maybe that was when she had started making sure no one ever ignored her again. Now, looking back, she could see her behavior must have appeared to be childish and out of control to others.

She lifted her gaze, aware her eyes were bright with unshed tears. "What my father didn't realize was that I was hurting too. When I lost Mama, I didn't know where to turn or what to do. It isn't right to make a fourteen-year-old face death all alone. I needed him, Cass, but he wasn't there. Then he up and moved us to Cherry Grove to begin a new life. I didn't know anyone at all. I was sure that my world had come to an end."

"Did you ever let your father know you felt this way?"

"No." She sighed. "He wouldn't have understood. He's a good man, but he hasn't the faintest idea of how to deal with a child."

"So you were lonely and miserable, and you decided to trick me into marrying you and taking you back to Saint Louis."

"I see now how terrible that was, but at the time I thought it was my only hope. I was sure that if I could just return to my aunt, then everything in my life would be all right again." She sighed, glad to have her weighty confession finally out in the open. "I always felt loved and wanted by Aunt Estelle. I guess she had a way of making everyone feel that way."

Cass stopped what he was doing and stepped over to tilt her chin up to meet his gaze. "Susanne, I'm going to tell you something, so listen to me. You don't bully people into loving you. You earn people's love by being honest and decent, by being a woman of your word. That gets their attention every time."

"Maybe it isn't attention I want," she whispered. "Maybe I want to be loved the way Boyd loves Mardean."

"I know of nine children who think you've hung the moon."

"I know . . . but sometimes I despair that no man will ever love me," she added softly.

"That's foolish."

She smiled, feeling tears sting her eyes. "Maybe I want to be loved by a man like you."

Their eyes met, and she wasn't sure of what she read in his gaze . . . pity . . . sympathy . . . maybe something entirely new. Could it be a grudging realization that she wasn't as bad as he'd thought she was?

"Then I suggest you give a man like me a reason to love you," he said simply.

They studied each other, his expression void of emotion. She was unprepared for the surge of affection he triggered in her. Could he see how deeply she loved him? She wasn't sure she wanted that. Right now she was too confused in her thinking about Cass Claxton. One minute she wanted him so badly she wanted to cry and the next she was plotting ways to get even.

"Mr. Cass! Mr. Cass!"

They looked up to see Jesse dashing headlong in their direction.

Cass frowned. "What is it, Jess?"

"Doog . . ." Jesse was panting so hard he could barely get his breath. "Doog . . . fell . . . over a cliff."

"A cliff?" Startled, Susanne sprang up from the tongue of the wagon. "Where? When?"

"Just now. Down by the river. Hurry."

Cass paused long enough to grab a rope; then the three raced through camp, shouting for extra hands to help with the rescue.

Corliss poked her head out of the canvas flap of their wagon. "What's going on now?"

"Doog . . . he's fallen over a cliff!" Susanne shouted.

"Land o' mighty!" The flap fell back into place. "I'll be there soon as I find my shoes."

The growing assembly fought their way through dense briars and thickets, tearing off the prickly vines that angrily snatched at their clothing. A stitch formed in Susanne's side, but she ran on, her shorter legs barely able to keep up with Cass's long strides.

They ran for what seemed like a long time before Jesse skidded to a halt. He pointed to a patch of brush. "There," he panted. "Just behind those bushes."

Motioning to the others to stay put, Cass moved to peer past the heavy thicket. The abrupt drop-off on the other side shocked him. Moving farther, he stood on the edge of a near-vertical drop of fifty feet that ended on the rocks of a dry riverbed.

"Doog! Where are you?"

"Down here," came the weak, frightened reply.

Cass leaned even farther over the edge and spotted Doug about halfway to the bottom. He had one arm wrapped around a small cedar tree that jutted from the side of the cliff. Cass saw immediately that the tree was all that was keeping Doog from the perpendicular drop below him.

"Are you all right?"

"My arm hurts."

"Is he all right?" Susanne crowded closer.

"I think so," Cass yelled over his shoulder. "Stay back."

Cass glanced up to see Ernest Parker and Boyd Gibson already tying a loop on the end of a rope. He was stunned to see Boyd, but here he was, temporarily putting grief aside to help another.

Mardean stood behind Susanne, placing a gentle hand on her shoulder. She had just buried her own child, but she was here, lending silent support.

"Doog, I'm going to lower a rope. I want you to grab it and tie it around your waist," Cass ordered.

"I can't. . . . My arm's all funny looking, and it hurts real bad!"

"Is it broken?"

"I don't know. . . . Maybe."

Cass pushed to his feet, his eyes gauging the firmness of the soil at the cliff's edge. He didn't want to dislodge rocks that would harm Doog. He turned back to Susanne. "I'm going down there."

"Oh, Cass. Be careful."

They quickly tied a loop into a second rope and dropped it around Cass's waist. Ernest, Lucius, Boyd, Matt Johnson, and Lewis Brown took hold of the opposite end. Laurence Medley, Mardean's father, stood by to help oversee the operation.

"We're ready anytime you are."

Cass realized he might be putting his life in their hands. He removed his hat and handed it to Susanne. "Here, make yourself useful and hold this for me."

"Please—" Susanne's eyes locked helplessly with his— "please . . . I'm so worried."

He grinned. "You worry too much."

Her lower lip trembled, and his smile faded. "I'll be all right . . . okay?"

She nodded wordlessly.

In a completely uncharacteristic gesture—at least toward her—he reached out and tugged her nose playfully, then turned to face the four waiting men. "Gentlemen, I hope you have strong grips."

Moments later the men carefully lowered Cass over the cliff.

Susanne couldn't bear to watch. She turned and buried her face against Martha Waterman's shoulder.

The cliff was almost vertical and was composed of loose shale rock that made climbing up impossible. Cass moved as carefully as he could, but dirt and rocks still rained down on Doog.

"You still all right, Doog?"

"Yessir."

"Any particular reason you picked today to walk off a cliff?" Cass asked, trying to keep the boy's mind off his problem.

He was about ten feet above Doog when the rope went slack for an instant and then tightened again. A fine sweat broke across his forehead. He paused, braced his feet against the wall, and tightened his grip. "Everything all right up there?" he yelled.

"Sorry. We've got you now."

Doog's voice trembled. "I was just chasin' a rabbit, and I was runnin' real hard. . . ."

Cass eased down another few feet until he was level with the boy. "We're going to get you back up on top."

"Good."

"You scared?"

"A little . . . What about you?"

"A little. Your arm hurting you?"

"Yessir. Is Miss McCord up there?"

"Yes, she is."

"I'll bet she's scart, huh?"

"She looked a mite peaked. Hold on while I figure out how to get you tied into this rope."

"Okay. Mr. Cass?"

"Yeah?"

"Better hurry. Them snakes are making me kinda nervous," Doog admitted.

"Snakes?" Cass paused, his heart sinking.

Doog nodded his head toward the cliff on the other side from Cass. "There's two big old rattlers layin' on a ledge just over there a few feet. One's just kinda layin' there lookin' at me."

Oh, Lord—say it isn't so. Cass wasn't afraid of snakes, but he didn't necessarily cherish the thought of having a tea party with two of them while dangling at the end of a rope.

He could see them when he leaned away from the cliff face and looked past Doog. Sure enough, they were big ones, lying there sunning themselves.

"Listen, Doog. Stay perfectly still. Don't move a muscle." Cass deliberately kept his tone neutral, hoping to keep the boy from knowing what they were up against.

"My arm hurts."

For a moment Cass had forgotten about the child's injured arm. "All right . . . let me think for a minute." He could feel sweat trickling down his back; his eyes focused on the snakes. This was not going to be his day—he could feel it.

"Cass, are you all right?" Susanne's anxious voice came to him from far up the cliff.

"We're doing fine!" he called back.

One of the snakes opened its mouth and moved from a full coil into an S shape. Cass's skin crawled.

"Just fine," Cass repeated softly, hoping to believe it. *God? You watching? Fine doesn't exactly cover it, but I guess You know that.*

"Are rattlers likely to attack?" Doog asked when he noticed Cass's reaction to them.

"Not usually, son."

"But sometimes?"

Cass kept his tone impartial. The last thing he needed was for Doog to spook and try to scramble away from the reptiles. "Doog, how much does your arm hurt? If I put this loop around your waist it will slide up into your armpits when they start to pull you up. Can you stand that?"

Doog kept glancing back at the snakes. "I'm not sure. Can they pull both of us up at once?"

Cass did some quick mental calculations. The boy was light; maybe sixty pounds. He was uneasy about the strength of the men and the rope if they had to go up together.

"Susanne!"

"Yes!"

"Tell Lucius we may have to come up on the same rope. Ask him if he thinks they can handle us both."

Seconds later her voice echoed, "They say they can if they have to."

Doog looked at the snakes again and gave a start. "Mr. Cass, they're moving. I think they're coming this way."

"Don't move. Just don't move."

Still dangling from the rope, Cass slowly tried to edge past the boy and get between him and the snakes. His movement seemed to awaken the one who had looked to be asleep the whole time.

"Bad idea," he said to himself.

Doog looked down as if he thought he might try to escape by letting go of the tree.

"Don't look down," Cass cautioned softly. "We can't go down. We've got to go up."

The boy obediently lifted his eyes. "I'm scart," he whispered. "Real scart, Mr. Cass."

"I know. You're going to have to climb over to this side of the tree and get on my back. They can pull us both up at the same time."

Cass looked closely at the boy's face, trying to gauge his ability to do what was being asked of him.

Doog swallowed. "I'll try." He shifted his feet, trying to find a solid spot that would support his weight for the move.

Out of the corner of his eye, Cass saw one of the snakes was moving their way. He didn't seem angry and he wasn't rattling, but he was on the move.

I've got to buy us some time. Disregarding his earlier "don't move" strategy, Cass scrambled to the other side of Doog. Bracing his left foot against the cliff face, he placed his right boot squarely in the snake's path. Then he waited.

Sure enough, the snake crawled onto the toe of his boot. When it was about one-third of the way across the boot, Cass kicked out and the snake sailed through the air to the rocks below.

"Now, Doog, before the other one wakes up, get up here and hang on to my back, just like a piggyback ride." With an urgency born of fear, the boy did as he was told.

Holding on to the rope with his left hand, Cass reached his right hand around his back under Doog's seat to help support the boy's weight.

"Now pull!" he yelled. "Pull for all you're worth."

Immediately he felt the tug of the rope as those on top went to work. Doog was making a small whimpering sound, not unlike a scared puppy. He was trying hard not to cry, and Cass had a quick thought of admiration for the lad's courage.

Cass felt sweat stream down the sides of his face. Doog's good arm threatened to choke him. Then the pulling stopped.

What's going on up there? he thought. That's exactly what he would have yelled if he could have gotten any sound by Doog's arm.

Then he heard some confused yelling, and the pulling started again.

"Hold on, Cass," Susanne yelled. "Hold on."

Slowly they were pulled upward. Cass tried to get some toeholds in the cliff face and help the men above, but the loose shale kept flipping away. Someone yelled, "Quit all that flopping around down there. You're making it harder!"

So he held on tighter than ever and hoped they would reach the top before he blacked out from lack of oxygen.

Doog kept repeating, "Please, God, don't let us fall. Please, God, don't let us fall." Cass found his prayers in unison with the boy's.

After what seemed like hours, they were high enough that strong hands reached out and took Doog from Cass's back. Cass scrambled up another foot or so and lay with his upper body on the ground and his feet still dangling over the precipice.

After a few minutes of rest he stood up. Doog was on his knees a few feet away, trying to catch his breath and compose himself. Susanne was kneeling in front of him, trying to assess the seriousness of the injury to his arm.

Cass walked over to the boy and whispered in his ear, "I don't see any need to let Miss McCord and the others know about our little friends down there. It would only upset them. Women are real funny about snakes, you know, so why don't we just keep this between us men?"

Doog nodded without raising his head. "From now on I'm gonna be real funny about 'em too."

When Susanne looked up and saw him, Cass thought she might stand up and give him a big hug. Instead she kept worrying over Doog.

Corliss ran her hands over the boy's upper body and diagnosed his injuries: a sprained shoulder and a bruised arm. She prescribed a sling and a period of rest. Doog, who was openly distressed by all the fuss that the womenfolk were making, tried to wriggle from her grasp and edge toward the other boys.

Ernestine Parker fawned over Cass, patting his arm. "I declare, you're so *brave*, Mr. Claxton. I could never have gone down into that terrible old creekbed."

He smiled down at her. She was a pretty girl—would make some lucky boy a good wife in a few years. "It wasn't all that bad." He thought of the snakes and suppressed a shudder. No, it had been bad. Real bad.

"Are you all right?" Susanne asked. She laid her hand on his sleeve.

"I'm fine. Nothing to get upset over." Cass and Doog exchanged a conspiratorial glance and both grinned.

Susanne's eyes took note of Cass's sweat-stained clothing, and she shook her head. "I'll bet it was terrible down there."

He shrugged.

Phebia marched over and immediately demanded that he remove the bandage from her thumb. Since it had only been for show anyway, he complied.

"Good!" She popped the thumb back into her mouth.

"Folks, we best be gettin' on the trail," Lucius warned. "We've lost nigh onto four hours today."

The group wandered off toward their camp, talking among themselves about all the strange happenings the morning had brought.

The children clustered around Cass and Susanne when they started walking. Cass casually placed his arm around Susanne's waist; Corliss fell into step, carrying Phebia and Marybelle.

Doog was loudly extolling his adventure to the other boys, omitting the part about the snakes, though Cass could tell it pained him to leave it out. Without that part, it sounded as if he'd simply fallen off a little hill and Cass had come down to fetch him.

Cass smiled down at Susanne as they walked along, enjoying the lovely fall day, thinking that they looked like a real family as the twelve of them sauntered down the road together.

A real family.

What was he thinking?

CHAPTER 9

Sunday morning, members of the wagon train gathered for an early morning service. Preservice talk among the men centered on hunting and the weather.

Lucius stood before the group holding his Bible. "Our text today is taken from the thirty-first chapter of Psalms. 'Be of good courage, and He shall strengthen your heart, all you who hope in the Lord.'"

Lucius looked out over the small congregation. "*'Be of good courage.'* Let those words take root in your heart. Life is hard; bad things happen to good people. Sometimes we don't know where to turn next, but our God is a merciful God who longs to bless His people if we give Him a chance.

"Don't let trouble bow you down and cause you to take your eyes off the goal. Be of good courage and God will give you strength—His strength—for everyone who hopes in the Lord."

As Susanne listened to the familiar words, it seemed Lucius spoke directly to her. She felt she gained a message from God—

and Aunt Estelle—to have hope in the Lord. Sad that she often lost sight of that hope. *Father, help me to remember that whatever happens, You are there. Give me Your courage and strength, Lord, because I sure don't have any of my own.*

Susanne had seen firsthand how God had blessed her aunt and the work she had done at the orphanage. He hadn't stopped loving the children because they had left Saint Louis. He would take them safely to Cherry Grove. She had to trust.

Jay Lassiter strummed his guitar, while Buck joined in with his fiddle. Voices rose in singing "Amazing Grace." Susanne added her soprano. She could hear Corliss's rich alto, and surprisingly, Cass contributed a fine baritone.

After services the members scattered to their midday meal. Corliss had outdone herself with fricasseed squirrels and a rich hickory-nut pie. Susanne knew she would miss the bounty of the Missouri countryside when they left the hills behind to enter Kansas. The prairie had its blessings too, but she had come to know and love the Ozarks.

After dinner, Cass took the older boys with him, saying that he would enjoy the company. Susanne and Corliss and the younger children carried the dirty clothes to a small stream, taking advantage of the layover to catch up on laundry. Wash days never occurred on Sunday back in Saint Louis, but life on the trail was different. Here you did what you could when you could. It was also the only time they could catch up on the week's gossip without the men being around to scowl at them. They chattered like magpies as they went about their work sudsing and wringing out garments.

Susanne helped Corliss with most of the laundry, but shortly before two she announced that she and Phebia were returning to camp to begin the baking.

Corliss absently waved her off, never missing a lick in telling her story about how Jesse had put a frog in Bryon's bedroll two nights ago, describing the howl the five-year-old had sent up.

After feeding Phebia a biscuit and a cup of milk, Susanne put her down for a nap. Almost everyone had drifted out of camp by the time she turned her attention to bread making. She had just dumped several cups of flour into a large wooden bowl when she heard footsteps approaching. She glanced up and was startled to see Joe Killen, one of the renegades who had stopped at their camp a few weeks earlier.

The man stood looking at her, a grin spreading across his dirty features. He tipped his hat politely. "Afternoon, ma'am."

Susanne stepped back when his foul smell assaulted her.

"Mr. Killen . . . what are you doing here?"

His eyes traveled over her and her skin crawled. "I thought you might be sparin' me a cup of coffee, ma'am."

"Well . . . I suppose I can." She didn't like the idea of this man around while Cass was gone, but she didn't want to be rude. She moved to the large pot hanging above the fire, poured coffee into a tin cup, and handed it to him.

His fingers brushed hers when he took the cup. "Thank you, ma'am. I'm right beholden to you."

Susanne nodded and quickly stepped away. She was dismayed to see him amble over and settle himself comfortably upon a rock a few feet away from where she'd planned to work.

Deciding she could do little about it, she concentrated on mixing the dough.

"Right purty weather we're havin'." He took a sip from the cup.

She nodded, fixing her eyes on her work.

"Sure was sorry 'bout the old man a-breakin' his leg. At his age it'll take a spell to heal."

Reaching for the salt, Susanne felt lightning in the pit of her stomach. How would he know Harlon had broken his leg—unless, of course, he'd been following them?

"Where is the rest of your party, Mr. Killen?"

"Jest call me Joe, honey."

She let a warning light enter her eyes when she turned and evenly met his gaze. "My name is Mrs. Claxton."

"I know what your name is." His insolent gaze skimmed her.

"Then use it when you speak to me."

Joe grinned. "I like a woman with spunk. Makes the game worthwhile."

She didn't answer and he added, "Bull and the other fellers are camped down the road a ways."

"I'm surprised. It was my understanding that you had business elsewhere. I would think you could travel much faster than we can."

"Oh, we ain't in no hurry," Joe said. "Just kinda like to take our time and enjoy the scenery—you know what I mean?"

Susanne knew.

"Where's your man today, Mrs. Claxton?" His tone remained friendly, but Cass's earlier warning about the outlaws made Susanne leery. She wondered how far away he was.

"Are you referring to Mr. Claxton?" she returned coolly.

"Yeah, Mr. Claxton. Where he be off to on such a fine day?"

"He's hunting nearby."

"That so?" Killen peered at her over the rim of his cup, and he took another swallow. "You know, if I had me a fine-lookin' woman sech as you, I'd be sending them young bucks off to do my huntin'."

The implication in his voice hung heavily between them.

Susanne continued her work, determined to ignore him. Surely he would move on.

"I suppose the old man is around?"

"Harlon's . . . resting in the wagon." Susanne didn't want him to think that she was alone, without protection, so she quickly added, "He's here in case there's any trouble."

Killen glanced toward the wagon some thirty feet away. "Is that a fact? 'Course, there ain't much an old feller with a broken leg can do, now is there?"

"Not much," Harlon's voice agreed. The barrel of his gun slid out the back of the wagon and leveled at the center of the outlaw's chest. "But ol' Myrt here can sure get her point across!"

The tin cup clattered to the ground. Killen sprang to his feet, jumping back when the hot coffee seared the material of his shirt. "Here now, I was just makin' conversation. T'ain't no call to be getting' all riled up!"

"You git on out of here, Joe Killen. We don't take to the likes of you comin' around botherin' our womenfolk." Harlon kept the gun trained on his target.

By now Jesse, Doog, and Joseph had returned to camp for dinner. They stood watching the tense exchange with wide-eyed curiosity.

The outlaw sent an uncertain look in Susanne's direction.

"He means what he says, Mr. Killen. You'd best be moving on."

A look of sheer hatred flared unchecked in the renegade's eyes. "All right, but you'll be regrettin' this, missy," he yielded in a voice so tight that Susanne barely caught the message. He whirled and stalked off.

The boys raced to Susanne, their eyes aglow with excitement. "What'd he want, Miss McCord?" Doog asked.

Susanne drew the boy close, distractedly giving him an assuring squeeze. "Nothing, Doog . . . just a cup of coffee."

But Susanne knew what he had wanted, and the realization sent a cold chill down her spine. The man was evil, and so was his ugly pack waiting just beyond the shadows.

She turned to the wagon and said, "God bless you, Harlon. God bless you!"

The men had a good hunting day. Even Laurence Medley killed a small doe. That night there was fresh venison steak for all.

After supper Cass took Aaron and Payne down to the river to wash. The three whooped and yelled as they plunged headlong into the icy water. The shock nearly snatched their breath away. They waded to the bank to lather themselves with the bar of soap Susanne had supplied.

Jesse and Doog sat nearby, skipping rocks on the water.

"Don't see any sense in washing again," Doog complained. "We just bathed last night, so we got a whole week to go before we need to put ourselves through that again."

The sun was sitting behind a row of towering sycamore, casting a mellow glow on the red and gold leaves shimmering with vivid splashes of color. The air already had a sharp bite to it, and being wet didn't help matters. Cass washed faster.

"How many rabbits did ya kill today, Payne?" Doog wanted to know.

"'Bout six, I guess."

"How 'bout you, Mr. Cass?"

"Twelve rabbits and four squirrels."

"Man!" Doog exclaimed. "I'll be glad when I get old enough to go hunting. Fact is, I'll be glad when I get old enough to do anything."

"What did you boys find to do to keep out of trouble?" Cass asked.

"Nothin'. We just sat down here and threw rocks in the river whilst we listened to them women cacklin' like a bunch of ole settin' hens." The boys giggled.

"Hear anything interesting?"

The two looked at each other sourly. "Not a thing."

Socially acceptable again, the men waded out of the water, shivering. They toweled off and put on clean clothes.

"That outlaw came to camp today," Doog announced.

Cass's hands suddenly paused in buttoning his shirt. "Bull Hanson?"

"Nah, that other one, Joe Killen. Boy, he is nasty dirty!" Jesse made a disgusted face.

"What'd he want?"

"Miss McCord said he just wanted a cup of coffee," Jesse relayed.

"But Harlon had to turn the gun on him," Doog said.

Cass finished dressing and sat down to pull on his boots, digesting the news. He hadn't talked to Harlon tonight. The older man was asleep during supper. Since his leg was keeping him up nights, Corliss hadn't wanted to disturb him.

"Why did Harlon turn the gun on him?" Cass asked.

Doog was about to skip another rock when he let his arm slip back to his side. "Don't know . . . 'cept I think maybe he wasn't bein' real mannerly to Miss McCord."

Cass stood up, suddenly hot with anger.

Aaron reached to restrain Cass with his right arm. "Best check with Harlon afore you get all riled. Doog's stories aren't too reliable at times."

"They are so!" Doog turned to Jesse. "Didn't that ole outlaw come to camp today?"

Jesse lifted his eyes to Cass. "He did, Mr. Cass. Honest."

"Aaron, look after things here," Cass said. "I have business to tend to."

"I'm coming with you." Aaron stepped forward, meeting Cass's eyes.

"I appreciate your offer, but I can take care of this matter myself."

"I know you can, but there be four of them. I figure that's two apiece."

Cass grinned. "You think you can handle two?"

Aaron drew his unimpressive stature to its full height. "Yessir."

"Then I guess you and I better go teach a low-down piece of nothing a few manners."

"Can I go too?" Payne was on his feet in a flash.

"I need you here," Cass said as the five walked back to camp. "With Harlon down, I have to leave a man here to help the women."

"Oh . . . all right," Payne said. "But I'd rather go with you."

"Staying here is important. Someone has to look after the women, and, like I said, it needs to be a man."

Payne's chest puffed with pride. "I can handle it."

"Gentlemen, I think we'd better keep this under our hats," Cass advised as they drew closer to the site. "The women will get all fussy if they know where we're going."

The boys nodded, conveying the silent pledge to keep the mission quiet.

"Man, I don't like girls!" Doog complained. "They're always taking the fun out of everything."

Cass sympathetically clamped his hand on the boy's shoulder. "Try to hold that thought, son."

Susanne glanced up when her men walked into the clearing. She felt such warmth when she thought of how the boys idolized Cass. It was apparent that Aaron respected and loved him deeply, and she wondered what the boy would do once they reached Cherry Grove and Cass left.

She watched Cass and Aaron break away and pause to talk with Harlon for a moment. Seconds later, the two emerged from the wagon, matching strides on their way to saddle the horses.

Realizing they were about to leave again, Susanne abandoned the dishwashing to run to catch up with them.

"Cass!"

He paused and turned at the sound of her voice.

"Where are you going?"

"Aaron and I have a little business to conduct," he said easily, his tone too quiet to suit her.

She frowned. "Business—tonight?"

"We won't be gone long."

She looked doubtfully from Cass to Aaron. "You be careful. . . ."

Cass nodded. "We plan to."

She turned and started away, then paused, reaching out to clasp his arm.

Cass looked at Aaron and grinned. He pulled Susanne close for a reassuring hug. "You're worrying again."

"I can't help it. It seems to me you're storying about where you're going." She had an uneasy feeling that Cass was keeping something from her.

He drew back innocently. "Me? Story to you?"

"Don't you look so innocent, Cass Claxton!" She brought her hands to her hips. "You'd story to me in a minute." She turned to Aaron. "Is he storying to me?"

Aaron shrugged and gave her a sheepish grin.

Chuckling, Cass drew her back into his arms. He gave her another hug before he turned her in the direction of camp. "Go wash your dishes, woman."

Susanne still had a niggling feeling in the pit of her stomach that something wasn't right as she watched him walk away.

Exactly *what* it was she wasn't sure, but she had a feeling it wouldn't take her long to find out.

The moon was high when Cass and Aaron returned to camp. Susanne thought she'd never seen two more disreputable-looking characters in all her days.

Their clothes were filthy, their shirts torn at the shoulders, and both were sporting the biggest, blackest shiners she had ever seen.

They got off their horses and turned to face her, their expressions guilty. She saw that each had a pumpkin tucked under his arm.

"You've been fighting!" she accused, drawing her wrapper closer against the night chill. She'd lain awake for hours, listening for their return.

"Fighting?" Cass shot a knowing glance at Aaron, and they both grinned. "We have not. We've been picking pumpkins." He gallantly extended his bounty to her.

"I hope you didn't steal these."

"Nope, we sort of—well, they were lying around and we took them," Cass said.

Corliss's head emerged from the back of the wagon. Seeing Aaron's sorry condition, she squired him off to patch him up. That left Cass in Susanne's care.

"I have never seen such going-ons!" Susanne usually borrowed one of Corliss's standard sayings when she didn't know what else to say. Quietly she set the pumpkin aside and stepped over to help Cass at the improvised washstand.

He good-naturedly shrugged her away, insisting that he didn't need any help.

Susanne decided that whatever he'd been doing, it had left him in a good mood. He was buoyant and elated, completely unconcerned that she'd been up most of the night, worrying herself half to death.

After pouring water into the enamel basin, she reached for a bar of soap.

"If you've been out all this time consorting with that woman . . . ," she began, remembering the redhead who'd been itching to get her hands on Cass. If that woman continued to fool with her husband . . . She couldn't finish the thought. "I can't believe you'd subject Aaron to such—"

"Redhead, redhead! Is that all you can think about?" Cass complained. "Do you honestly think I'd let a woman do *this* to me?" The flying cloth garbled his words.

Susanne wrung out the cloth and started scrubbing his face much as she would have scrubbed Phebia's. "I don't know what to think of you! And I didn't say anything about a redhead—you did!"

"Ouch! That hurts!"

"You'd better not have taken Aaron out to teach him things he shouldn't know!"

"Aaron is sixteen years old. What he doesn't know he should be learning." She heard his swift intake of breath when the soap found an open wound. "Will you stop it? I can wash my own face!"

"What *have* you been doing, Cass?"

"I told you; I had business to take care of."

"And you involved Aaron in your rowdy shenanigans?"

"He's a great kid." Cass's voice held nothing but respect for Aaron, the boy that no one had wanted.

Susanne didn't know what the two had been up to, and it didn't seem likely she was going to find out. But there was no way on earth she believed they'd been out picking pumpkins.

"You should be ashamed of yourself!"

Cass sighed. "You're not going to let up on me, are you? All right, I'm ashamed of myself."

"You are not!"

"I know it, but I figure you're not going to pipe down until I say that I am."

Irritated, Susanne dabbed white salve on his cuts, silently admitting that she'd been more scared than angry. From all appearances they had been fighting. She felt a smile threatening when she wondered how their opponents must look. "It's a wonder you weren't shot."

"Not a chance. I'm smarter than that."

She helped him out of the soiled shirt, handed him the washcloth, and went to get a clean shirt from his pack. By the time she returned he looked more presentable. She handed him the clean garment and walked to the dying fire to pour a cup of coffee.

Frost had settled on the ground; a bright harvest moon hung overhead. The midnight hour gleamed as bright as day. Susanne turned and finally smiled, noting the relief on his face when he accepted the silent truce. She handed him the tin cup. "Drink this. It'll help to warm you."

He slipped into his coat, his gaze locking with hers. "Thanks. Why not stay and share a cup with me?"

She was surprised by the invitation. It was the first time he'd asked her to join him—for any reason—and she fought the urge to read more into his unexpected request than simple gratitude.

"Thank you. I would enjoy a walk." She busied herself pouring a second cup of coffee as he walked over to pick up his bedroll. Moments later they left camp so that they wouldn't disturb the sleeping children.

Side by side, they walked until they came to a grassy knoll, where Cass paused.

Susanne helped unfold the blanket. "Nights are getting cooler," she remarked. They sat down and settled their coffee cups on the ground.

"Another month and the snow will be flying. Would you like my coat?"

"I'm warm enough, thank you."

They sat for a moment in compatible silence, sipping the coffee.

Susanne spoke first. "Killen paid a visit to camp this afternoon."

"That right? What'd he want?"

She frowned, thinking about the vile man and his crude remarks. "He asked for a cup of coffee, but I think he was up to no good. Harlon had to ask him to leave."

"Oh?"

"Aren't you a little surprised he's still around?"

"No."

"You don't think he intends to cause trouble?" She thought about mentioning the insinuations Killen had leveled at her, but she knew if she did it would only add to Cass's troubles, so she left out details about the visit. She was confident that Harlon had properly discouraged the man from coming around again.

Cass sipped his coffee. "I'm not worried about Joe Killen, and there's no need for you to be either."

"Well—" Susanne was confident that Cass could handle whatever trouble the Killen man could cause—"I'd sure be happier to know that he was a hundred miles on down the road."

They shared the silence again.

When Susanne thought of something to say, she had to cover her mouth to stifle her giggles.

Cass drew his brows into an affronted frown. "What's so funny?"

"You . . . you look like you tangled with a wildcat!" *And lost,* she added silently.

A muscle quivered in his jaw, and she could tell that he was trying to restrain his amusement. "You think it's funny, huh?"

Her eyes gleamed with merriment. "Yes . . . I never knew a jack-o'-lantern could be so ferocious!"

He shrugged, gazing up at the moon. "Go ahead and laugh."

Had she upset him? She didn't think so. "Thank you, I believe I will!"

Susanne broke into a renewed round of mirth, and by the time she was near tears, Cass had decided to join her. He knew that he looked a sight, but it had been worth it. He and Aaron had taught Joe Killen a lesson tonight that the man would never forget.

He wasn't about to tell her where he'd been because if she found out that he'd gone to take care of the man who insulted her, she'd assume he'd done it as a favor to her—which he hadn't. Anyway, he didn't think he had. He was pretty sure he'd wanted the outlaw out of his own hair. He'd been relieved to see that Slim Watkins had left the group some time back. He'd liked the man. A thought struck him. How had Aaron known there were only four men in the outlaw camp? He grinned in the darkness. The kid had been spying on them. The boy had grit.

"You remind me of the time Jimmy Lonigan pushed me into a mud hole," Susanne teased. "I declare, I was a mess. My face was caked with mud, my dress was ruined, and the lovely yellow ribbon Mother had tied in my hair that morning looked like a soggy noodle. I was mortified. I pitched a temper tantrum of such magnitude that my teacher was forced to send one of the younger boys rushing out the door to get my mother to come take me home." She laughed merrily. "I refused to go back to school for two weeks, and I'm sure the teacher thought that was too soon."

Cass could imagine her fit; he'd witnessed a few. "What made Jimmy Lonigan want to push you into a mud hole?"

Susanne looked down at him, managing to keep her features deceptively composed. "Why, I just can't imagine! I was such an angel!"

They broke into laughter, and Cass thought it was a nice change from being at each other's throat.

"I remember being embarrassed in front of the whole school

once." Cass gazed across the moonlit meadow as the corners of his mouth lifted with amusement. "My brother Beau had brought a frog to school and stuck it in Elsbeth Wilson's lunch pail. Elsbeth was a real pain. Her folks were rich, so she had more than the rest of us, but she was miserable. She always looked like she'd been eating persimmons. When she opened up her pail, that bullfrog jumped out onto her desk and swelled up with a loud *barrroopt!* You could have heard Elsbeth screaming for miles."

"What did the teacher do?"

"Because I'd laughed the hardest, the teacher thought I'd put the frog in her lunch pail, so she made me sit in the front of the room all afternoon, holding that frog on my lap, apologizing to Elsbeth every few minutes for being 'unsociable and crude.'"

Susanne giggled. "And your brother didn't say a word in your defense?"

"Are you serious? Beau sprang out of his seat, pointed a self-righteous finger in my direction, and hollered that I shouldn't have been so mean and that he was gonna tell Ma on me when we got home!"

They shared another good laugh. When their merriment died off, Cass swiveled to look at her. "I'll bet you were one of those prissy little girls in frilly dresses, with your hair in big blonde curls that hung down to your waist."

She nodded. "Mother insisted on neatness. But Butch Michaels was forever dipping a curl in his inkwell."

"He was probably sweet on you and wanted to get your attention."

"Oh, he got my attention, all right! I gave him a black eye every Monday morning. It got to where he'd run when he saw me coming out the door."

Cass grinned.

"I was pretty terrible most of the time."

"You haven't improved a whole lot since."

Susanne glanced up, and he winked at her.

"Oh, you . . . how would you know what I'm like?" she accused. "You've never taken the time to get to know the real me. You're always blustering around, shouting at me, acting as if I'm about to give *you* a black eye every Monday morning."

"Butch Michaels has my sympathy," he said dourly. "I've experienced a couple of your black eyes."

Susanne knew that he was speaking figuratively, of course. "I'll admit that in the past I gave you reason to feel that way about me, but I wish I could convince you that I've changed, Cass . . . even if I do backslide a bit occasionally."

"A bit? I'd say your lapses are more like rockslides."

"Nevertheless, I am better."

Than what? he wondered. "If that's what you think."

"It's what I know. I'm really not a bad person."

He shrugged. "Who am I to argue? You were the perfect lady the day we met," he conceded dryly. "You recall the incident? I happened to get in your way when we were in Miller's Mercantile—"

"You didn't just happen to step into my way," she corrected. "You deliberately blocked my path."

"But you do recall the incident? You had just bounced fifteen or twenty spools of thread off Edgar Miller's bald head because he didn't have a certain color you wanted."

Susanne blushed. "That was a long time ago."

"The memory is vivid."

"I said I was sorry."

"Since then you've tricked me into marrying you at the point of a shotgun, tricked me into taking you to Cherry Grove, deliberately thrown dishwater on me, and with the aid of a bullwhip, shamed me in front of a whole lot of women. That same night, you turned the whip on me again, nearly peeling the hide off my back because you'd gotten it into your head that I was riding off to meet a redhead—"

"That whip never touched your back!"

His eyes narrowed. "A fact, I might add, that saved your life."

She grinned when he continued. "In the time I've known you, you've browbeaten me, cussed me, spat on me, threatened and coerced me more times than I can count on both hands—now tell me again how you've turned into such a nice person! I'm having a real hard time believing that."

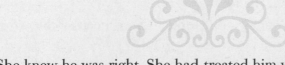

She knew he was right. She had treated him wretchedly. A heartfelt sigh escaped her. "I wish we could start over,"

He fell silent, and she wondered if she had made him angry again. But a moment later he said quite calmly, "Well, I guess there's no law that says we can't."

Her eyes drew to his face, and his steady gaze assured her that she hadn't heard wrong. "Do you mean it?"

"I mean it. I don't enjoy this bickering any more than you do, and for the sake of everyone else, I think we should try to get along with each other. I can't say I'm ever going to forget what you've done, Susanne, because I'm not sure I ever could. I'm the kind of man who likes to control my own destiny—and I sure plan on having the *only* say about who I marry. No woman's ever gonna hog-tie and brand *me*. But I'll concede that people can change, if they want to."

Susanne's heart tripped and thudded at his words. "Thank you," she said softly. "Does that mean you do believe I've changed?"

"That means I'm going to work on it a little harder."

"Thank you . . . because I'm beginning to care for you quite deeply."

"Well, just don't let it get out of hand," he warned.

"What would you say if I told you that I wasn't trying to mislead you the other night? that I really wanted to be your wife?" She knew the question was wanton, shameful, but it popped out anyway.

He slowly lifted the brim of his hat to look at her.

"I do, you know," she said.

He lowered his hat again. "I thought we'd been all through this."

"I understand." She fixed her eyes on the moon, staring hard, determined not to cry. "I don't want to push you into anything. It's just that I get so lonely."

He brushed a stray lock away from her forehead. "I guess I can understand that. You're trying to be everything to everyone. You must feel completely worn down sometimes."

"It's not the children or Corliss and Harlon," she said fiercely. "I love them like they were my own."

"Then what is it?" he asked, and she could have wept at the gentleness in his voice.

"It's just that sometimes I wonder if I'll ever find someone to love me. I want what every woman wants—a home, love, family."

"You have the family," he pointed out.

"In some ways, but you know what I mean."

"I know. I guess most everyone wants the same things. Both of my brothers are married with good wives and children, but somehow settling down never interested me. I might be missing something, but a hunch isn't enough to base a marriage on, Susanne. When a man and woman agree to join their lives together before God, it's serious business."

"Very serious," she whispered. "I used you, Cass. All I could think of was getting away from Cherry Grove. I never thought about what I was doing to you."

Susanne couldn't bear to look at him. All those years when she hadn't seen him, she hadn't given a thought to what her deception had done to him. What if he had married during that time? His marriage would have been a mockery because of her.

"I promise you, Cass; I'll never use you again." And she meant it. Never again would she manipulate him. Never again would she impose her selfishness on him. From this moment on, she would love him as deeply and as wholly as she knew how, even if he never loved her in return.

Cass was strongly aware of the woman at his side. She was desirable; something about her touched him in a way a woman never had. He knew she had changed, and that she would make some man a good wife. He'd never taken to the idea of settling down, being burdened with responsibilities. Life was too sweet, too exciting to swap his carefree existence for the staid, never-ending sameness of married life. It might be all right for Cole and Beau. But not for him.

"I don't think you have to worry. Someday a man will come along and he'll fall head over applecart in love. You're going to have all the things you want. Be patient. Somewhere God has the right person for you."

"But not you."

Did he imagine it, or did he hear a tinge of sorrow? "Not me. I'm selfish, Susanne. Maybe we're too much alike—willing to go to any lengths to win."

"Spoiled? Self-centered? Determined to have our own way?" she ventured.

He shrugged.

"But we've changed, Cass. Neither of us is like that anymore. We've grown up."

"Maybe, but not grown up enough. I've got a hunch we can either one be mighty headstrong when we want to be. Like you with the dishwater."

"And you dropping me off the horse."

He laughed. "I'm sorry about that."

"You are not," she accused. "You enjoyed every minute of it."

"Yeah—I did," he agreed, sobering.

She shifted to look at him again. "If we can't be man and wife, can we be friends?"

"I think we could manage that." He held out his hand and felt hers—warm and fragile—accept the offer. "Friends."

For a disturbing moment he found himself wondering what it *would* be like to take Susanne as his wife. After all, she *had* changed. Or he had.

He quickly discarded the notion. That kind of thinking would surely lead to trouble.

Friends. Susanne tried the word out for size and found it had a nice sound, but it wasn't close to what she wanted. Somehow, in spite of her best intentions, she had fallen in love with Cass Claxton. She had never wanted to feel this sweet longing for his presence, never chosen to have her heart leap at the sound of his voice, never asked for this total misery when she thought of the prospect of never seeing him again once they reached Cherry Grove. She had his answer, though. He preferred the single life to marriage. Especially when it came to being married to her.

He stood up and reached down to pull her to her feet. She stood beside him, feeling small and helpless . . . and lonely. She didn't want another man; she wanted Cass—wanted him with all her heart.

They walked back to camp in silence. Susanne left him to spread out his bedroll with the boys while she went back to her pallet where the girls were sleeping.

Phebia muttered in her sleep, and Margaret Ann rolled over to administer a soothing pat. "There, there, everything's all right."

The child calmed, and Margaret Ann rolled over on her side to look at Susanne. "Miss McCord?"

"Yes, Margaret Ann?"

"Where have you been?"

Susanne swallowed her surprise. She was being questioned by a child? And a child who was at the moment staring at her as if expecting an answer. She decided to tell the truth. "I've been talking to Mr. Cass."

"I see."

For a wild instant, Susanne thought perhaps she did. Then reason prevailed. Margaret Ann was extremely intelligent, but even she had no idea of the relationship between her and Cass.

"Is he going to stay in Cherry Grove with us?"

"No, he isn't."

"I see." Margaret Ann seemed to mull this over. She was silent for the space of five seconds, and Susanne dared to hope the subject was closed. She should have known better.

"Can't you ask him to marry you?"

"I couldn't do that." Mostly because she was already married to him and he couldn't wait to get rid of her, but she couldn't tell Margaret that. She couldn't tell anyone. Her pride would never survive the humiliation.

"I see."

If she says that one more time, Susanne thought, *I will scream.* The child had a decisive, thoughtful way of thinking and speaking that made her offhand remarks sound as though she were the mother and Susanne were the child.

"Why not?"

"Women don't usually do the asking."

"I see. Well, that seems like a very silly rule if you ask me."

Susanne figured she could share a few thoughts on the risks

of asking—or rather forcing—a man to marry you, but she had no desire to dispel the child's dreams.

Thankfully Margaret Ann closed her eyes and ceased talking. Susanne lay back on her bedroll, staring up at the stars. Usually when she saw the night sky she felt overwhelmed by the majesty and glory of God's handiwork. Looking up at the heavens made her feel small and insignificant in comparison. Tonight she barely noticed. All her thoughts were centered on her husband. Why couldn't she have him? After all, they were married. Why should she allow him to just walk away? There had to be a way to hold him.

Please, God, let there be a way. . . .

Cass looked up from inspecting the lead ox's foot to see Margaret Ann approaching. For once she wasn't leading Lucy around, and her expression said she was dead serious about something. Cass felt a prickle of alarm. When this kid got something on her mind, she was hard to shake.

"Good morning, Mr. Cass."

"Morning, Margaret Ann. Sleep well?"

"Very nicely, thank you, but I do believe Miss McCord had a restless night."

"Oh?" He wasn't going to touch the topic.

"I believe she was with you until rather late."

"We took a walk—talked a little." He didn't like being on the defensive. What right did this child have to question him?

"I see."

How could anyone her age pack so much meaning into two words?

"Are you staying with us once we reach Cherry Grove?"

Clay lowered the animal's foot and straightened to face her. "No, I'm not. I'll be returning to my home in Saint Louis. I have business to take care of there."

"We need you." Her eyes were faintly accusing.

"You'll get along fine. Miss McCord will be there and Harlon and Corliss."

"But they're not you."

Cass drew a deep breath. If he didn't answer, maybe she'd go away. He had enough sense to know it wasn't going to be that easy.

She fixed him with a stern gaze that cut right through excuses. "If I asked you to marry Miss McCord, would you?"

He eyed her stoically. "Did she put you up to this?"

"I haven't spoken to her this morning, but it does seem a sensible solution."

"Well, it isn't."

"Why not, pray tell?"

"People marry because they love each other."

"Miss McCord is very lovable."

He shook his head. "Look, Margaret Ann. It doesn't work that way. Miss McCord has her life and I have mine."

Margaret Ann sighed. "Adult reasoning is so lame at times." She turned to leave, and he breathed a sigh of relief, feeling the way he'd felt when he'd been seven and accidentally thrown a rock through the parlor window, breaking the glass and shattering Ma's double-globed lamp with the hand-painted pink roses on it. Margaret Ann's tone of voice reminded him of his mother's when she pointed out how irresponsible it was to throw rocks at glass. Except staying married to Susanne wasn't irresponsible; it was insane.

So why did Margaret's solution make perfect sense?

CHAPTER 10

By the end of the week, the wagons rolled into Westport, Missouri, where Susanne, Harlon, Corliss, the children, and Cass prepared to say good-bye to their new friends before continuing west to Kansas.

Westport was the first major city the travelers had come across since leaving Saint Louis. Even though it wasn't large, the town took the cake in confusion, the trademark of the embarking point for the West.

Three trails left from here: the Oregon, the California, and the Santa Fe. A strange mixture of people thronged the streets, and for the first time they saw Indians. Wild-looking men, bronzed, with long black hair and piercing black eyes.

Phebia had taken one look and the men and declared, "Me don't like Kansas."

"We're not in Kansas yet," Susanne said. The Kansas border was a short way out of town.

"Me don't like it anyway." Phebia poked out her lower lip in a familiar pout.

They stocked up on supplies at Boone's Trading Post, and Cass treated them to a meal at Yocum's Tavern, a place where many of the travelers ended up for one reason or another. At Susanne's request they attended church, choosing Union Church, founded by a Methodist missionary. The Presbyterians, the Christian Reformers, and the Baptists had met here too until they could find suitable locations for their own houses of worship. The brick exterior was handsome and imposing.

Inside they settled on the wooden pews, breathing in the fragrance of beeswax and freshly laundered curtains. Susanne listened to the rustling of ladies' skirts, the soaring notes of the organ, and felt comforted. There was something special about coming together to worship God, whether the worshipers gathered in a stately building or around a campfire. She remembered Jesus' promise: "Where two or three are gathered together in My name, I am there in the midst of them."

It was a morning to enjoy. The children were quiet and well behaved, the music lively and spirited, the sermon inspiring. For a moment Susanne could pretend they were like the other families attending. Anyone looking at them would think they were a husband and wife with a sturdy, growing family.

They shook hands with the minister on the way out and wandered down the street to have Sunday dinner at the Harris Hotel. Corliss and Harlon had elected to stay with the wagon, so as soon as they finished eating they walked back to join them. Susanne felt it had been a glorious morning. The last time they would worship in church until they reached Cherry Grove.

Cass had business acquaintances in Westport, and a prominent man-about-town, Mr. Adrian Holland, came out to the train to meet him. Susanne sat in the shade of the wagon mending Jesse's trousers, which had been torn so many times they appeared to be held together with patches. Cass noticed Holland watching her.

After greetings were exchanged, Cass broached the subject he'd been thinking of since getting into town and hearing the talk. "I hear there's money to be made in Santa Fe shipping."

"Possibly," Holland agreed. "That's if gangs don't attack the train, robbers don't ambush you, wagons don't fall apart, animals don't go lame or die on you, and you don't lose everything trying to ford a river."

Cass grinned. "You're saying there's a risk?"

"A big risk," Holland agreed. "But worth it. You'd need a good wagon master, one you can trust."

"You know one?" Cass asked.

Holland nodded. "Know three, actually. The best is a shyster and you have to watch him. He knows the country, though, and he's never lost a wagon yet."

"So why is he out of work?"

"Because he also likes to fight. Got in a squabble and broke up Yocum's Tavern. Now he's in jail until he can pay for damages, which he can't since he gambled and drank up his last paycheck."

Cass noted the information. When he came back this way

he'd check into the situation. He was always looking for new ways to expand. Santa Fe trading would be a new direction for him. After he completed his business and Holland had left, Cass got up to check on the livestock and met Susanne's disapproving expression.

"Now what?" he asked. She had a way of looking at him with Margaret's discerning eyes.

"Surely you're not going to do business with that dreadful man."

"Holland?" Cass shrugged. "He's a pillar of society, deacon in the church."

"Not him. The one in jail."

"Oh, him." He shrugged again. "The man's a good wagon master. Why not get him out of jail and put him to work? He'd be grateful, and I'd have a good man to get my wagons through. Everyone's happy."

"I suppose so. Making money means a lot to you, doesn't it?"

"Why wouldn't it?"

"I don't know. Why does it? You tell me."

"Well, think of all it can do." He paused, sensing the trap.

"Yes, big houses, fancy clothes, and fancier friends."

He winced at the scorn in her tone. "There's nothing wrong with having a few luxuries."

"I suppose not. And if you're feeling guilty, you can always hold a benefit where everyone who is anyone can eat and dance and gossip and listen while some poor wretch espousing a good cause begs for money."

He heard the bitterness in her voice and knew the source. "Did you get much from the Revuneau benefit?"

"Five hundred dollars. I'm financing the trip with it. But

what I really needed—a home for the children—wasn't even considered. And you know why? Because children like these were considered a nuisance. Until Aunt Estelle took them in they ate out of garbage, stole for food, and slept in doorways. They couldn't be ignored, and your friends wanted them to go away."

He cringed. The rebuke in her voice even sounded like Margaret. He had three houses he could have let her have, and he'd laughed and walked away. Not because he cared about the properties one way or another, but because he hated Susanne McCord. He looked at her now, with her head bent over a boy's ragged britches, hands roughened from hard work. Her hair was drawn back in a roll on the back of her neck, her face tanned brown by the autumn sun. She didn't have Laure Revuneau's exotic flare, but she was lovely, with a grace and sense of dignity that earned his admiration and respect.

Corliss joined them, and Cass walked away, alone with his thoughts. He'd come to know the nine orphans. Might as well admit it—he loved them. Even Phebia, who had an unerring attraction to his nose. It was a wonder the appendage hadn't lengthened by several inches, the way she tweaked it.

He thought of Susanne's compassion for the underdog, and he knew a footloose bachelor interested in money and the power it brought could never be what she needed. Not only could he not be a part of her life, she would be desperately unhappy in his world.

If he claimed her for his wife, she'd have to give up the children, and he knew she would never agree to that. But there was one thing he could do. He would personally underwrite the needs of the orphanage. As long as he had a dollar, Susanne and her brood would never want for food or shelter. Cass expected a warm, sweet burst of satisfaction over the decision. After all, it was the sort of tribute that should warm the cockles of God's heart. But if the Almighty was pleased with his decision, there wasn't any sign of it. In fact, Cass was left with the disturbed impression that his heavenly Father had a few unresolved issues with him yet. He also had a feeling Ma wouldn't be all that happy with him either.

The members of the wagon train gathered for one final evening together. Tomorrow they would be on the trail again—Cass and Susanne and their brood headed for Cherry Grove and the rest on their way to Oklahoma. Susanne knew she would miss Mardean, Winoka Medsker, Lucius Waterman, and Buck Brewster's sweet fiddle music. The group had formed close bonds, and several of the people had become like family to her.

But everyone seemed determined to substitute happy faces for tearful good-byes. After supper, the women brought out the pies and cakes while Buck tuned up his fiddle for dancing.

The camp took on a festive air as the weary travelers set their troubles aside and, as Corliss put it, 'just let their hair down for a spell.'

By midevening Susanne was breathless and rosy cheeked from the strenuous activity. The men had kept the women dancing nearly every jig. Susanne whirled through reels, square dances, and waltzes. Ernest Parker called the squares while Buck and his fiddle skipped through one tune after another. Although she had danced with every man in the group, some more than once, Cass remained on the sidelines. She figured he had forgotten her or was deliberately ignoring her.

She saw Aaron stealing a kiss from Ernestine and made a mental note to talk to him. Well, maybe not. Better have Cass do it. Aaron might take the lecture better from another man. Another *man*? The word caught her attention, but she realized it was correct. Aaron had changed from a shy, awkward boy to a competent young man. The trip had been good for him.

Finally Cass stood in front of her, and she knew she'd been waiting for this moment all night. "Miss McCord, may I say you look right fetchin' tonight," he complimented.

"Oh, I do thank you, kind sir," she returned, matching his airy tone. "Your silver tongue just makes me feel ever so giddy, but I *was* beginning to fear that you were never going to come over and 'fetch' me."

"Been waiting for me, huh?" He threw his head back and laughed. Sobering, he winked and extended his left arm. "Let's take a walk."

Something had changed in their relationship since the night they'd talked. He seemed more at ease with her, less prone to being provoked, more willing to cooperate. "I thought I was going to have to whip Ernestine Parker and take you away from her," she said, accepting his arm.

He winced. "I thought I was going to have to ask you to."

"I believe Aaron's got his eye on her."

Matt Johnson stepped over to claim Susanne. Cass motioned the man away. "Later, Matt."

Smiling, Susanne nestled closer to his side, and they stepped into the deepening shadows.

"Sorry I didn't have time to eat with you and the children," he apologized. The darkness wrapped silky arms around them.

"We missed you, but I'm sure Laurence appreciated help with the broken axle."

"Lucy still cranky?"

Susanne nodded, mechanically carrying on the conversation, but her thoughts wandered.

"Maybe she's just tired of traveling."

"Maybe, but it won't be long now before we're home."

She cuddled against him, happy to be there as long as it would last. Someday he would leave, but tonight he belonged to her.

Her old nature surfaced, nearly choking her. Why should she be forced to give him up? She wouldn't! There had to be a way to convince him to stay with her. He was her legal husband, after all.

Her *legal* husband. That was the problem. As long as their marriage was in name only, Cass would not feel obligated to stay with her. It was really a fairly easy problem to solve . . . but did she dare? It would be far worse than anything she'd done to him so far. Evil. God would turn away in disgust.

"Cass?"

"Hmmm?"

"Do you ever think about me as a woman?"

He appeared to be weighing his answer, and she wondered if she had overstepped her bounds. Finally he said, "If I were to be completely honest, Miss McCord, it would only make your head swell."

She savored a flood of satisfaction. She drew back to gaze into his eyes. "Then you do."

"I never said that."

"But you do." She felt her stomach tie in knots as he gazed back at her.

"All right," he confessed. "I do."

She reached out to trail her fingers tenderly down the side of his face. He moved back as though her touch unnerved him.

"Then don't leave me," she urged in a broken whisper, suddenly wishing she had more control over her emotions. She had been struggling so long to find herself, to know the real Susanne McCord, but it had taken this man to show her that she could be the woman she'd always longed to be. She didn't know how she could bear losing him.

"Susanne, it's settled. I'm not ready to settle down to one woman. . . . I may never be."

"Not even Laure Revuneau?" Susanne knew she was out of line, but she had to know what he felt for Laure.

"Laure?"

"I believe she is hoping for a Christmas wedding, with you."

She felt him tense. "She's free to hope all she wants. "

Her pulse leaped expectantly. "Then you aren't planning to marry Laure?"

He sighed. "My only plans are to return to Saint Louis and attend to my business, which has been sorely neglected of late."

Her eyes met his unashamedly. "I'm going to say something you're not going to like."

"Then don't say it."

"I'm in love with you, Cass—deeply in love."

His face changed and became hard. "Susanne . . . don't do this—"

"I am, Cass. I'm sorry, but I am." She stopped and caught his face in both hands. "I love you and I will never, ever give up hope that someday, no matter what I've done in the past, you will return my love."

"Susanne," he warned, pulling her hands away and drawing her face to his chest, "you're making me nervous."

He was weakening; she could sense it. And wasn't that her plan?

"You always have been a mite skittish," she acknowledged, "but you can't stop me from loving you. You're the best thing that has ever happened to me."

"No, Susanne. It'll do no good for either one of us to think that way. I can't return your love. We bring out the worst in each other."

She wondered who he was trying to convince: her or himself.

She thought of all the times she had rejected other men—easily, cruelly, and without much thought for their feelings. She guessed the good Lord had had His fill of her nonsense and had sent Cass Claxton for her penance.

But if He had, she would gladly accept her punishment and pray that the Lord would see fit to extend it.

Later that night, when everyone was safely tucked in bed, Cass took his bedroll and went in search of a place to sleep. He had watched Susanne move about camp, preparing for bed, and he admitted that he was drawn to her, no matter how hard he fought against the attraction. Her earlier pleading had nearly broken his resolve. No woman had ever had this strange effect on him, but he wasn't cad enough to claim her as his wife, then ride away and leave her.

He spread the blanket on the ground and walked to the creek to wash up. When he returned five minutes later, Susanne—his wife—was lying on the blanket.

He stared down at her, shifting on one foot impatiently. He didn't have the strength to go through this again.

"Hello." Her smile was beguiling and meant nothing but trouble. "Lovely night, isn't it?"

"What are you doing here?"

She shrugged. "Why are you always so cranky?"

He could feel defeat settling in like a noose. "I guess a man wouldn't need to be overly smart to see what you're up to."

"I *am* your wife."

She was right. They'd said their vows before God. She was his—as surely as if they'd repeated the words in church. But still . . . consummating their marriage would only lead to trouble. He just knew it.

Cass thought if he ignored the invitation she might go away. He lay down and turned his back on her. He felt her settle beside him, smelled the lilac fragrance of her hair. He rolled over to face her, and that was a mistake. Now there was no turning back. Her lips, satin soft, met his as the moon slid behind a cloud, and as surely as Adam succumbed to Eve, he surrendered to the serpent.

The wagon train left the next morning amid fervent handshakes, hugs, and tears. People got real close traveling together. Most would never see each other again. Cass had unexpectedly walked up on a tender scene: Ernestine Parker weeping in Aaron's arms. He backed away, regretting his intrusion on the young folks' final moments together, but not before hearing Ernestine promise to write.

The sun was a red ball on the horizon, and lacy rose-colored clouds floated overhead. Late October had a bite to it. The children wore light jackets and shoes, which they would remove when the sun climbed higher. Susanne pulled her worn sweater tighter around her. She hated what she'd done last night. What she had perpetrated had been deceitful and inexcusable. Once again she had tricked the man she loved. She couldn't say her morning prayers for fear God would strike her dead. Now they were truly man and wife, but would it make any difference to Cass? She feared it wouldn't.

Jesse strode alongside. "I like it being us again; don't you?"

"It's nice," Susanne agreed. "But I'll miss some of the people in the wagon train."

He considered this. "Do you think Cass will stay in Kansas with us?"

"No," she bit out. He would not change his plans—especially now.

"He might if I ask him," Jesse said. "He likes me."

"He won't stay—and I forbid you to ask him, Jesse. I mean it. Don't ask him."

"Yes, ma'am." Jesse eyed her curiously. Bryon wandered off the trail, and he pointed at him. "Guess I'd better help Doog. He can't keep an eye on Byron and Joseph too."

Susanne watched the ensuing tug-of-war between Bryon and Jesse. The younger boy determined to go his own way and the older just as determined to keep him with the wagon. They were good boys. She didn't see how Cass could ride away from them and never look back.

Corliss raised the back flap of the wagon and looked out. "Bryon! You quit giving Jesse trouble. You hear me?"

Phebia ran up to Susanne. "Me so tired."

"All right, I'll give you a lift." She squatted so Phebia could climb onto her back, clasping the child's legs in front of her. Thin arms circled her neck, and she felt a curly head resting against her shoulders. "Would you rather ride in the wagon?"

"No. Want to be with you."

Susanne's heart swelled with love. If God never gave her anything more, He had given her these children, and she was grateful. The travelers forded a small creek bordered by wild plum, which in early summer would have been loaded with fruit. Now the branches only bore leaves, which were drying and falling to litter the ground. They would reach Kansas too late to lay up food for winter. She remembered only too well the blizzards that could sweep across the plains. They would need so many things, and her supply of cash was pitifully low.

The prairie was flatter than Susanne remembered and covered with tall grass, taller than the younger children. Phebia, Bryon, Joseph, and the twins needed to stay with the wagon. If they wandered out in that waving sea of grain they could be lost, unable to find their way back.

She sighed. Seemed like she just traded one set of worries for another.

Late morning, Cass rode up beside Susanne and Phebia. "Do you like Kansas any better this time around?"

"I'll make do," Susanne answered, unable to look at him. She felt so ashamed of her trickery. "I'm not the same person who left here."

"Really?"

She sensed that he had started to make a cutting remark about the way she'd changed, but didn't. Somehow the contrived wedding ceremony didn't matter that much anymore. It seemed so long ago and involved two different people.

"Is your father expecting you?"

Susanne hitched Phebia up higher on her back. "I wired him we were on our way, but he has no way to send a reply. He's willing to take us in, though."

He pointed to a strange little animal sitting up on its high legs staring at them. The twins made a dash in that direction, and immediately there was a shrill whistle, which seemed to come from a dozen different places. The little animal disappeared.

"Prairie dog," Cass said. "A colony of them."

"Dogs cute," Phebia said. "Get me one, Mr. Cass."

"I'm not fast enough to catch a prairie dog," Cass said. "Besides, you don't want one. They're wild animals."

"I do so want one." Phebia stuck out her lower lip in a familiar pout.

"When we get to Cherry Grove I'll find you a puppy. That will be better, won't it?"

Phebia cocked her head to one side, considering. "That will be better. Let me down, Miss McCord." Once on the ground she ran toward the wagon, good spirits restored.

Cass grinned at Susanne. "She's a charmer."

Susanne didn't smile. "What are you going to tell her when you leave?"

Color rose to his cheeks. "I'll stay if you want me to, Susanne."

She remembered their agreement. Pretty words, softly murmured words, but no misconceptions. "What do you want, Cass?"

He shook his head. "I'm not ready for marriage and responsibilities—I know I'm a little late, but you want the truth."

Yes, she wanted the truth. "I'll keep my part of the bargain," she promised. "However, it's possible you're making a mistake."

He fixed his gaze straight ahead. "I'll stay. You say the word."

She finally lifted her eyes. "We need to be going. We're holding up the group."

His eyes sought hers. "Do you want me to stay?"

"Not until and unless you choose to make a life with me."

"Susanne—"

She turned and walked off before she could change her mind.

They had been on the trail to Cherry Grove for a week. One of the oxen had pulled up lame and delayed them. The day started out warm for October. The air was heavy, muggy. A dark line of clouds outlined the western horizon, and a scorching wind whipped the grass in undulating waves. Cass felt the hair rise on his arms, a sure sign of electricity in the air. From all indications this was going to be a raging Kansas thunderstorm.

He rode up beside the wagon, calling to Harlon, "Think it's going to rain?"

"Like pouring water on a rock. Better find a place to weather the storm."

"Storm?" Susanne looked up, shading her eyes with her right hand. "The sky is clear—not a cloud to be seen."

"Look over there." Cass pointed west, and she looked where he indicated. Clouds foamed toward them. A sullen rumble of thunder reached her ears. A forked tongue of lightning licked the sky.

"Put Phebia and the twins in the wagon. The rest of you keep up. I don't want to lose you."

Susanne didn't argue; she followed his instructions. After putting the younger ones in the wagon, she scooped up Lucy and carried her. "Margaret Ann, you and Doog and Jesse get behind the wagon and keep up, you hear?"

"Yes, Miss McCord." Margaret Ann's voice was as serene as if she'd just been offered a cup of tea.

Jesse and Doog looked apprehensive, but they fell in step.

Cass heard Corliss soothing the younger children. Clouds roiled like a boiling pot.

Aaron, following Cass's directions, drove the wagon into the shelter of a low limestone bluff, barely higher than the top of the wagon. They quickly unhitched the team and hobbled them under the lip of the bluff. Livestock taken care of, Cass ordered Susanne and the children to get inside the wagon.

"What about you?" she shouted above the rising wind.

"I'll stay with the animals!"

Aaron and Payne stubbornly refused to seek shelter. "We'll help."

Cass frowned. "It's going to rain like dumping water out of a boot." Huge drops splattered the ground, emphasizing the warning. "It's going to be a bad one."

"If you can take it, we can," Aaron replied.

A solemn-faced Payne grabbed the lead rope and pulled the oxen closer to the cliff. The storm struck with a blast of thunder that set the animals fighting the restraining ropes. A blaze of lightning blinded Cass. He pulled his hat lower and hunched his shoulders against the driving rain.

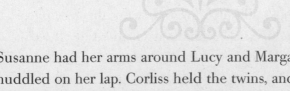

Susanne had her arms around Lucy and Margaret Ann. Phebia huddled on her lap. Corliss held the twins, and Doog and Jesse crouched close to Harlon. Each thrust of wind rocked the wagon until it seemed it would surely tip over. The canvas covering cracked and popped, and Susanne wouldn't have been surprised to see it tear apart, leaving them exposed to the storm's fury.

Thunder boomed like an explosion. Susanne's ears rang from the force.

Margaret Ann raised a tearstained face. "I really do not like Kansas, Miss McCord."

"Me want to go home," Phebia wailed.

Lucy shivered against Susanne. "Are we going to die?"

"Oh, no, darling. God will take care of us. Don't worry; the storm will pass."

"I do think God could do something about the noise." Margaret Ann jumped when another roar split the sky. "I believe I'll mention it to Him as soon as it's quieter."

Susanne stifled a hysterical laugh, imagining Margaret Ann facing God and saying, "I see." Having experienced her own interrogation, she knew exactly how He might feel.

The storm eventually blew past. Susanne climbed out of the wagon to face Cass and the boys. Payne looked shaken, a little pale, but he wore an air of quiet pride. They hadn't lost an animal, although Cass's horse had broken the rope. Aaron had caught it before it could bolt.

"Are you all right?"

"We're fine," Cass said. "I couldn't have held them by myself. The boys saved the day."

They made camp, building a fire to dry out their supplies. Corliss and Susanne fixed an evening meal, and they all retired early. Afterward she lay in her bedroll, staring up at a sky full of stars. The storm had passed; the night calmed.

But a storm still raged in her heart.

CHAPTER 11

A small party of buffalo hunters—one hunter, two skinners, and a cook—rode in late one afternoon. Their red wool shirts were dirty, their corduroy breeches stained, and the high Western boots they wore hadn't seen a coat of polish in years.

Corliss and Susanne, happy to welcome company, cordially invited the men to stay for supper. The hunters accepted their gracious offer and went about settling their stock for the night.

When Cass, Aaron, and Payne rode in from hunting, Susanne took one look at Cass and knew he was in a howling temper. He glared in her direction, looking like a Kansas thundercloud.

"Susanne, I want a word with you!" he ordered. He swung off his horse and handed the reins to Aaron, barely acknowledging the visitors' presence as he strode through camp.

Susanne rolled her eyes. Wiping her hands on her apron, she whispered to Corliss, "The king has bellowed."

Cass had been friendlier lately—not what you might call pleasant, but not inclined to snap like a chained dog every time she got close. There had been no chance for intimate talks or romantic moments, and she was relieved. Guilt hung heavy in her mind.

Evidently something had riled him now, though she had no idea what. She'd been careful not to cross him, but if Cass Claxton thought he could bully her he had another think coming. He might be her husband . . . yet he wasn't. So God's command about obedience to the husband didn't apply.

Cass's rules.

Corliss chuckled, and Susanne knew she was concerned and yet amused by Susanne's and Cass's open hostility to each other. Susanne had passed the wagon and heard Corliss and Harlon discussing the strange alliance one night when they thought everyone was asleep. Although they had no idea what was caus-ing the couple to behave with such animosity toward each other, they both seemed to feel that Susanne was attracted to Cass Claxton and that Cass was attracted to Susanne. However, they had agreed they were both so mulish that they'd go to their graves before either of them would admit it.

Susanne had burned at the thought. Well, she guessed it was true eavesdroppers never heard anything good about themselves.

Now Corliss placed her hands on her hips and frowned, a sure indication that she was getting ready to impart wisdom whether Susanne wanted to hear it or not. "You know, girl, Harlon's beginning to fret about the growing standoff between the two of you. He took an instant liking to that young man. Cass is doing a fine job. You might think about that."

"I do think about it, and I'm more than willing to be friends. I'm not the one causing trouble." Susanne knew Harlon hoped she might make a match with Cass. If the older man only knew the true situation he would be even more befuddled. *She* was confused, and she'd been the bride at that so-called wedding.

"Harlon thinks he's taking a shine to you. Why else is he busting himself to help us?"

"Harlon couldn't be more mistaken. Mr. Claxton wouldn't be helping us it weren't for the children. He's a softy where they're concerned."

Corliss lifted both brows. "Maybe so, but I've seen that look in a man's eyes before. He's got something on his mind, and it ain't driving us to Cherry Grove, Kansas. I know a man with a hankering for a woman when I see one."

"If he's 'hankering' for anyone, it's for the woman he left behind." Laure's lovely smiling face rose up to haunt Susanne. The young Frenchwoman had a captivating beauty she couldn't hope to compete against. Satin and lace did something for a woman that homespun never could.

She could see why Laure was interested in Cass, but there was a problem. Cass, even though he wasn't happy with the situation, was married, and he would be until he delivered his charges safely to Cherry Grove. If Susanne couldn't talk him into staying—convince him that she was the love of his life—then she would release him from what he considered a hateful alliance.

Cass bawled again, and Susanne took a deep breath, wishing she had the freedom to tell him what she really thought of his bossiness.

"Better go see what he wants," Corliss encouraged. "Margaret Ann and I will take care of the biscuits."

"It better be important," Susanne muttered under her breath. She handed the spoon to Margaret. She was at no man's beck and call, particularly Cass Claxton's.

Ignoring the watchful eyes of their visitors, she strode through the camp in the direction of his voice.

She found Cass preparing to wash for supper. He'd stripped his shirt off, causing her a stab of momentary distress. Why a bare chest should fascinate her so she wasn't sure. She just knew that it did.

"Don't you ever keep your clothes on?" she snapped.

He glanced up. "Who yanked your chain?"

"No one yanked my chain. . . . I'm worried that the girls will see you this way."

He lifted an inquisitive brow. "Is that the reason for your concern, or does it fluster *you* to see me without a shirt, Miss McCord?"

"The name is *Mrs. Claxton*," she reminded in a carefully controlled tone, "and no, it doesn't 'fluster' me to see you without your shirt. I'm from Missouri. I've seen mules without saddles before."

For a moment she thought she saw a hint of a smile twist the corners of his mouth, but then he turned away and started pouring water into the enamel washbasin. "I see you're in another one of your aggravating moods."

"Did you want me?" she said curtly. He had no right to ride into camp and bellow out for her as though she were his handmaiden and then act like he thought she was "flustered" by seeing him without a shirt. Granted, she had trouble looking away . . . and he knew full well they were more than friends.

"Afraid not, but it looks like I have you anyway." He reached for the bar of soap.

Susanne watched the tight play of muscles in his forearms

when he worked up a thick lather. "I don't have time for games. What do you want?"

"I see we have company."

"There's nothing wrong with your eyesight."

He leaned over and scrubbed his face and neck. "Do you know who those men are and what they do?"

Susanne wasn't sure if it was disapproval or mere curiosity she heard. Was this why he had called her away from her chores? Her eyes traveled the width of his broad shoulders and paused. "No . . . I mean, I assume they're probably family men who'll appreciate a hot meal and a bit of pleasant conversation."

Cass rinsed off his face and neck and reached for the towel. He rubbed the cloth over his face, eyeing her dispassionately. "Well, you assume wrong."

Tiny water droplets interspersed throughout the cloud of hair splayed across his chest. His dark curls clustered in damp ringlets, and her fingers itched to brush them back off his forehead. Exposure to the wind and sun had bronzed his complexion, making him—if possible—even more appealing.

Susanne caught her shameless reflections and averted her gaze. "Then who are they?"

Without taking his eyes off her, Cass reached for a clean shirt and slipped it on. "Buffalo hunters."

Her eyes lifted to meet his. The explanation was meaningless. "So?"

He finished buttoning the shirt and, with his eyes still firmly fixed to hers, casually tucked in the loose ends. She glanced away, uncomfortable in the face of his casual indifference. He treated her with the same offhanded manner he exhibited toward the children or Corliss. Not disrespectful, but as if he didn't think of her as a woman, or as if the other night had never happened. She felt a sudden urge to make him look at her the way she was sure he looked at Laure Revuneau.

"So," he mimicked, "by inviting those particular men to supper, we're now likely to attract the attention of every Indian within a fifty-mile radius."

She wasn't sure if it was the word *Indian* or her own wayward thoughts that caused her heart to suddenly hammer in her throat. Susanne knew only too well what a thoroughly aggravating creature Cass could be, but he was smart and experienced, and she knew she had better take him at his word.

She felt color flooding her cheeks. "I'm . . . sorry. . . . I didn't know."

It occurred to her that he might be deliberately amusing himself. He knew what she was thinking, and he loved to aggravate her, yet nothing in his manner indicated deliberate agitation. On the contrary, if Susanne hadn't known better, she would have sworn that he was looking at her with the same undeniable interest that she felt toward him.

For an electrifying moment, blue eyes seared deeply into violet ones, and Susanne was aware of nothing more than his overpowering presence and the uneven cadence of her breathing.

Then, as if they simultaneously realized what was happening, their gazes split. Cass reached for his hat, and Susanne eased to a safer distance on the far side of the makeshift washstand.

The incident left her puzzled and shaken. She found it hard to concentrate. Cass picked up the conversation in a tone that made her wonder if the events of the past few minutes or the time they had spent together had touched him. How could something so life-altering to her have meant so little to him?

"We'll have to hope there isn't a scouting party on the hunters' tails."

Susanne was confused. "Why would Indians follow them?"

"Because they hate them. Unlike the Indian, who kills the buffalo for his own survival, the white man kills for business and pleasure." He picked up his gun belt and buckled it around his waist. "The Indians depend on the buffalo to supply medicine, cooking utensils, blankets, garments, boats, ropes, and even their tents. They use the sinews to make bowstrings and thread for sewing. After the tribe has enjoyed the fresh meat of the kill, the women cut the rest of the meat into strips and hang it on racks to dry in the hot sun."

"To make jerky?" She knew that but had forgotten.

"Later they pound it into powder and make pemmican, which will keep for years. There's still plenty of buffalo roaming the plains, but every buffalo killed is a threat to the Indians' existence. The white man's irresponsible slaughter continues to drive the herds farther afield, and I've heard some predict that the time isn't far off when the vast herds roaming the land will be only a memory."

"That seems impossible," Susanne mused. "I've heard my father tell stories of seeing thousands of buffalo moving across the plains."

"That's true, but it will change if the white man continues to kill buffalo for personal gain. How many will be left in ten, twenty years? Trust me; the Indian will do everything in his power to kill the men who threaten his survival."

"So if the Indians discover that we befriended the hunters, then our lives may be in danger?"

He absently dusted his hat against the side of his legs. "No 'may be' about it. Our lives *are* in danger."

"Oh, Cass . . . I'm sorry. Corliss and I were just trying to be neighborly when we invited the hunters to stay for supper."

"Susanne, I want you to listen to me." His tone was firmer than she'd ever heard it. "There's something else you need to know. By their appearance, I figure these men have been on the trail for a while. My guess is they've been on a hunt somewhere in Kansas, Colorado, or Oklahoma, and they're on their way home. Now, I want you to heed what I'm about to say: a beautiful woman will be hard for them to ignore." His eyes locked with hers. "I want you to go out of your way to avoid any personal contact with these men. Serve supper, then disappear and let Corliss and the girls clean up. These men have no morals; you've never been around this sort."

"All right." Her pulse fluttered. Did he really think she was beautiful? She'd been around men all her life and was used to being admired and appreciated. But if Cass Claxton ever had a good thought regarding her, she had yet to notice it.

"With a little luck, the hunters will move on in the morning, and nothing will come of your misplaced hospitality."

"What about the Indians?"

"You let me worry about the Indians. You do what I say and leave immediately after the meal. I don't want to have to save you if one of those men gets out of line."

"You think they'd be disrespectful?"

"I think that would be the least of your worries. I hope you're smart enough to see the wisdom of my advice."

She knew he was waiting for her chin to lift with her usual rebellious pride. Just for that, she'd show him. "You sound as if you honestly care what happens to me."

"*Me* care about *you?*" He threw his head back and laughed.

Susanne gritted her teeth in an attempt to control her temper.

"Honey, if I were looking for female company, I'd find me a sweet-talking woman."

"Like Laure Revuneau?"

His sly grin spoke louder than words. "Now, there's a fine woman. Soft-spoken. Godly. Slow to anger, holds her tongue—a real lady."

"Are you going to marry the 'lady'?" She was glad to see the question momentarily stilled him. "You didn't answer my question."

He tipped his head subserviently. "How could I marry anyone, my lovely, when it seems I am already encumbered by a previous commitment?"

"My dear Mr. Claxton. You don't have to worry about me," she snapped. "I do not plan to 'encumber' you, so rest easy."

"I'm not worried. Even if a man took a wild fancy to you and dragged you away, you wouldn't be gone long. Once he'd spent a few hours with your spunk he'd be bringing you back so fast it'd make your head swim."

"Is that so?" She could feel herself slipping, but he was downright exasperating. Squaring her shoulders, she took a deep breath and volleyed back. "You don't believe God has a say in who you'll marry?"

"Well, sure . . . when I ask Him."

"You polecat. I've never had a problem attracting suitors."

He grinned, but he didn't rise to the bait. "Tell me—" his gaze moved over her dispassionately—"is there anything in particular that I'm supposed to find impressive?"

Her eyes narrowed with warning.

"Oh . . . I'm supposed to notice how pretty you are . . . or no, wait. It's your hair, isn't it? Lovely. Never a hair out of place."

Her hand shot up to smooth the messy locks.

"I suppose you *could* catch a man without resorting to a shotgun," he allowed.

She squelched a rising rush of anger. "I don't reckon I'd need a shotgun," she said. "The man I'd marry would be smarter than that."

"Touché."

Susanne knew that Aunt Estelle was rolling over in her grave right now, but she was determined to get his goat. He was the only man who had persistently ignored her. Men had been known to fawn over her, shower her with extravagant compliments to snare her attention. They had begged for her hand in marriage, but she had blithely broken their hearts. She had never met a man who matched her in spirit, with maybe the exception of this lout, and he wouldn't even concede that she was a woman!

"I've never been interested in you, and I don't see why you would expect me to be interested now, so what are we arguing about?" he asked, his voice only mildly polite.

Their gazes met in a defiant deadlock. "Can't you at least admit that I *frustrate* you?" Surely she had *some* effect on him! He couldn't be that apathetic.

"Nope. Unless you count right now. You're in my way and delaying my supper."

Determined to beat him at his game, she edged closer. "Most men would be interested in their *wives*. But, then, maybe you're not like most men."

He picked up the wash pan and slung the water against a handy tree trunk.

"I am not married," he calmly stated.

"Hogwash."

"And I'm not like most men. The men I know would have wrung your pretty little neck long ago. Considering the circumstances, I've shown remarkable restraint."

"Restraint!" she choked out. "Why . . . *you* . . ."

"Precisely." He grinned. "I feel the same way about you, dear 'wife.'"

"I've apologized for my behavior and you haven't. Don't you know what the Bible says about forgiveness?"

"I certainly do, but no sooner do I forgive you for one thing than you do something else downright unfriendly. Forgiving you is a full-time job. I do not have the patience of Job."

Susanne pulled the tattered remains of her dignity around her like a cloak. The man was marking time until he could safely dump her and the children in Cherry Grove.

She must quell her hope. *Dear God, I'm through. Through trying to make him care.* Hope *is only a word now; a meaningless word. You are not going to honor my hope.* Cass was lost to her. She had to accept that.

But defeat hurt so much.

Cass wondered why he liked to antagonize her so much. With her cheeks flushed and those violet eyes snapping sparks, she was about the cutest thing he'd seen in a long time. Pity she was such a spitfire—and even more regretful they'd started out on the wrong footing. Susanne McCord was a force to be reckoned with, and he reckoned he didn't know what to do about her.

Susanne Claxton, he corrected. She had tricked him into giving her the name, and he admitted it had a certain ring to it. He brought his thoughts sharply into line. What was he thinking? This woman had deceived and manipulated him every time he got near her, and now he was in deeper than ever. It was too late for an annulment; now a divorce would have to take place. Not exactly something the Lord would approve of. What would Ma say? And Beau and Cole?

His life would decidedly be less of a challenge without Susanne around. Still—he liked to aggravate her.

"A buffalo hunter might want you," he said.

Her hand came up to strike him, and he caught it, holding fast. She tried to pull away, and he blocked the effort. Caught off balance, she fell against him, and his arms caught her.

He looked down, meeting her startled expression. Violet eyes gazed up at him; her parted lips were soft, sweet, and he felt a surprised flicker of—what? Interest? Attraction?

Love.

God, please, no. Not that.

He felt her go limp against him, and the sudden realization

that she was not immune to him pleased—and worried—him. He shifted her closer, surprised to discover that she was tiny. She felt exquisite and delicate in his arms. Things he had barely noticed before.

He lowered his head until his lips brushed hers, light as the silken seeds of the milkweed plant growing alongside the trail. The touch of her mouth against his sent a longing racing through his veins. He kissed her again, slow, sweet. So this was the feeling. The one he'd heard described so often. The one he'd never believed possible.

Susanne stiffened, pulling away. "What do you think you're doing?"

He drew a deep breath. He tried to brazen it out by guilelessly staring back at her. "Why . . . isn't this what you want? I'm only trying to keep my wife happy."

"You're disgusting." She spat out the words. "You act as if you despise me one minute then the next you try to take advantage of me."

Cass's mouth dropped. "Take *advantage* of you? You've been chasing me for weeks."

"I never."

"You *know* you did. I can't turn around without stumbling over you."

Her face turned so red he thought she would explode. "You brute! *You* called me over to warn me about the hunters."

His gaze lightly caressed her mouth. "Now who's being cranky?" He tweaked her cheek.

She jerked free. "Miserable skunk!"

He flashed an exasperating grin. "I thought I was a weasel."

"Skunk is only one name for your miserable species!"

She whirled and stumbled over Margaret Ann, who had silently approached the warring couple.

"What is it, Margaret Ann?" she demanded, her voice shaky.

"Corliss said to tell you supper's ready."

Shooting Cass a dismissing glance, Susanne picked up her skirt and marched off, leaving Cass not as unscathed by the encounter as he would have hoped. His eyes followed her as she walked back to camp. He could still taste her kiss, and he had a feeling that sleep wasn't going to come easily tonight.

"You comin', Mr. Cass?"

"I'll be along in a minute, Margaret Ann," he said absently. Shaken, he reminded himself that Susanne McCord was not a woman for him to get involved with. She had bested him in every confrontation they'd ever had. A Claxton was supposed to have enough sense to know when to cut his losses. With Susanne, he'd never been ahead. She'd outthought him, out-maneuvered him, and just plain outfought him every time.

He tried to sort out his confused feelings and turned up empty-handed.

Actually most men would find his wife desirable. Too desirable.

After supper the children gathered around the hunters' wagon. They looked over the .45 Sharps rifles, along with Winchesters, Remingtons, and Springfield Trapdoor models. The boys were full of questions.

Payne picked up one of the more than fifty Green River and Wilson skinning knives lying in the bed of the skinners' wagon and reverently turned it over in his hands. The wagon had too many bull, calf, and cow hides to count.

"You say you've been in Colorado?" Harlon hobbled over to sit next to the fire. Cass figured the old cook would soon have their visitors reciting the tall, adventurous buffalo tales that were designed to make the children's eyes round with wonder.

"Yep, up near the border." Hoyt Willis stretched his long legs out before him and propped his head back on the seat of his saddle.

Cass thought the buffalo hunter had his stomach full of home-cooked grub, and judging from the foul odor it was the first time he'd taken off his boots all week. Cass assumed the hunters had observed the Indians' custom of hunting buffalo in September when the cows were fat.

"We'll go back once we've had time to visit our families and collect our money for the hides."

"You independent, or working for someone?" Not that Cass really cared. He was making conversation, keeping an eye on the man.

"Independent."

"Got a wife?" Harlon asked.

"A wife and ten young'uns just waitin' for their pa to come home."

Cass judged the hunter to be close to forty. The man stank like a polecat. His shirt was saturated with animal blood and dried pieces of flesh where he'd wiped the skinning knife, his beard matted to his face. Cass hoped Hoyt would be considerate enough to take a bath and change his clothes before he saw his family again. Although judging from the man's rough exterior, he didn't hold out much hope.

Cass got up from his seat at the fireside and moved back into the shadows, far enough away not to be noticed, but close enough to observe. Hoyt Willis, like Joe Killen, was the one to keep an eye on. Killen, by all signs, had moved on and was no longer a threat. But Willis was a new one. Cass had seen the disappointment on the buffalo hunter's face when Susanne had obediently disappeared after supper.

The night sounds closed around the camp and the men relaxed. Wood popped, sending showers of sparks flying.

"Where did the woman go?" Hoyt casually asked Harlon.

"Corliss? Why, I imagine she's getting ready for bed."

"Not your wife. The other one."

"Susanne?"

"Yeah, Susanne."

Harlon filled his pipe, lighting it with a coal from the fire. "I'm not rightly sure. . . . Why?"

"No reason." Hoyt tipped his hat over his eyes. "She and the Claxton man hitched?"

Harlon chuckled. "Nope."

"He seems right protective of her."

"Yes, that's his job."

A slow smile curved the corners of Hoyt's mouth. "She's not married, huh?" The hat brim hid his eyes.

"Nope, she's not married."

Hoyt rolled to his side and settled his head more comfortably against the rolled blanket. "Right nice-looking woman," he commented.

"That she is. Imagine Cass thinks so too."

"Yessir." Hoyt's mouth curved into a satisfied smile. He settled deeper under the blanket. "Right nice—you say Claxton has no claim on her?"

"No claim, but he wouldn't take nicely to a man showing any disrespect."

Cass stood in the shadows, fighting the urge to call the man out and teach him some manners. Problem was Hoyt had friends, and all Cass had was Harlon. Not real good odds. Just the same, if this unwashed, coarse-smelling specimen of humanity laid a hand on Susanne he would personally break his arm. She was a Claxton—even if no one knew it and she had come by the name dishonestly.

Claxtons took care of Claxtons.

CHAPTER 12

The Maison Des Petites Fleurs Orphanage arrived in Cherry Grove a little before noon on Wednesday. Skies were overcast, and a bone-chilling wind blew from the north. October had finally gotten down to business.

The wagon rolled down Main Street, and Susanne took in the familiar sight of Miller's Mercantile. She breathed her first sigh of relief since she'd left Saint Louis. The journey was finally over. The Lord—and Cass Claxton—had seen them safely through.

She pulled the team to a halt.

Corliss lifted the flap, a big grin dominating her rawboned features when her eyes took in the row of storefronts. "Well, bless my soul, am I ever glad to see this!"

Susanne sighed, her own smile rather happy. "We've made it, Corliss. We've finally made it."

"Amen and praise the Lord!"

Edgar Miller was sweeping off his porch. He squinted, apparently trying to make out the new arrivals. Susanne saw his balding head bobbing up and down with curiosity. She lifted her hand to give him a friendly wave. "Hello, Mr. Miller!"

Eyes widening, Edgar nearly dropped his broom when he recognized her. He suddenly turned tail and shot back inside the mercantile, slamming the door firmly behind him.

Cass rode up beside the wagon and stopped. Resting his hand on the saddle horn, he grinned at Susanne.

"Better raise a white flag, Miss McCord. I believe the troops are getting nervous."

Meeting his laughing eyes with an impervious look of her own, Susanne firmly gathered the reins in her hands. "Very funny, Mr. Claxton."

Cass was still chuckling when she clucked her tongue and set the wagon into motion.

Nothing had changed in Cherry Grove. The sleepy little town wasn't much, but she knew there were a lot of good, God-fearing people living here, people who would see to the children's physical and spiritual welfare. She saw that the Havershams still had their restaurant, and it looked like Doug Kelly still ran his saloon and gambling house. She wondered if the saloon still served as a church on Sunday mornings. The town wasn't nearly as bad as she'd thought it was six years ago. It was a nice place, actually, one she was sure that she and the children would grow to love.

Once they were settled, the children would come to know and respect Leviticus, and she and Cass could—

An unsettling realization overshadowed her resurrected hope. In days now Cass would ride out. He had become so much a part of all their lives that it was hard to imagine how she and the children were going to manage without him. Susanne didn't want to imagine a day without him, let alone the rest of her life, but she admitted that she had no power to prevent him from leaving. She'd used every trick—God forgive her—in her arsenal, and she had lost the war.

The wagon turned the corner, and Reverend Olson's house came into view. Susanne could see Rebecca standing on a chair, cleaning windows. The parson's wife glanced up, seemingly startled when she recognized Susanne driving the wagon. She quickly recovered and began tapping on the panes of shiny glass, making staccato sounds. Smiling, Susanne waved at her.

The door to the parsonage flew open, and Reverend Olson hurried out, struggling into his jacket.

Susanne was anxious to see her father. Though they'd corresponded regularly, she hadn't seen him in six long years. She wondered how much he'd changed. He'd always had a penchant for gooseberry pie and lemon cake, and she giggled when she pictured her wiry little father having developed a round belly and rosy cheeks. She couldn't wait until the children met him. Susanne knew they would adore him, and Harlon and Corliss would welcome the hours of companionship Leviticus would provide.

Although he didn't always know how to relate to children, he was generous to a fault. At Christmastime, he would see to it that the orphanage had the biggest, brightest, most beautiful tree in town. There would be apples, nuts, and oranges to fill each stocking, and the house would be bursting with the mouthwatering smells of succulent roast duckling, tasty mince pies, delectable spice cakes and—

Her thoughts wavered when Leviticus' house suddenly

came into view. She sawed back on the reins, halting the team. For a moment she sat, dumbfounded, staring at the scene before her.

Susanne heard Corliss's sharp intake of breath, then her awestruck prayer: "Dear God in heaven. Have mercy on us all."

The chimney, silhouetted against the gray sky, was the only thing left of Leviticus McCord's house. The rest had burned to the ground.

Cass rode up beside the wagon, grave faced.

Susanne stared up at him, too shocked to speak.

He climbed off the horse and onto the wagon seat, drawing her into his arms.

"Cass . . ."

"Shhhh. It will be all right, Susanne."

Reverend Olson briskly approached the wagon.

The reverend appeared momentarily taken aback when he saw Cass Claxton holding Susanne McCord in his arms. "Oh, Miss McCord . . . I'm so sorry I wasn't able to warn you."

Lifting her face from the haven of Cass's chest, Susanne stared back at the reverend, still unable to comprehend what was happening. "Warn me?"

"Yes . . . your father . . . he's . . ."

His words slowly began to penetrate her numbed senses, and her face suddenly crumpled. "Papa?"

Reverend Olson glanced at Cass. "You'd better bring her to the house. We can talk there."

"Come on, sweetheart." Cass lifted her gently off the wagon seat and drew her protectively against his side. "Corliss, you'll see to the children?"

"Of course."

"Aaron, drive the team and follow us back to the reverend's house."

"Yessir."

Cass remounted his horse, then reached down and pulled Susanne up behind him.

She wrapped her arms around his waist and held on tightly, terrified to let him go. Papa was gone. She had no one now. "Cass . . . Papa . . . ?"

Nodding solemnly at the children who stood staring up at him with open curiosity, Cass reined the horse around and walked the animal back to the parsonage.

Rebecca was waiting with a pot of hot tea and a heart filled with compassion. The reverend suggested that he and Susanne step into his study.

Alarmed, she glanced to Cass for assurance.

He nodded. "You want me to come with you?" he asked.

She shook her head dazedly. "No . . . I'll be all right." She followed Reverend Olson into his study, and the click of the door closing was like a blow to her heart.

Rebecca reached out and pressed a reassuring hand on Cass's shoulder. "Come sit beside the fire. You must be weary."

Cass belatedly removed his hat. "Thank you, ma'am."

When they were seated, Rebecca reached to pour the tea, but Cass suddenly jumped to his feet, his tormented eyes focused on the study door. The sound of Susanne's anguished cries broke his heart.

"Please, Mr. Claxton," Rebecca urged softly. "This is very difficult. . . . Later she will need you more."

Cass slowly sank down, stunned by the unexpected event. His blue eyes pleaded with Rebecca, trying to make sense of it all. "How . . . when . . . ?"

"Two weeks ago, in the middle of the night. No one is sure how the fire started. By the time it was discovered, it was well out of hand."

"And Susanne's father? He wasn't able to escape?"

Rebecca shook her head. "They found Leviticus still in his bed."

Cass woodenly accepted the cup of tea she offered.

"We knew that Susanne and the children were on their way here. That's all Leviticus talked about once he'd gotten the news she was coming. We've felt so helpless knowing we could do nothing to prepare her for the tragedy that awaited her."

Rebecca blotted her eyes. "My, how Leviticus looked forward to seeing his only child again, and the children she was bringing to fill the emptiness in his life." Overcome by emotion, Rebecca tried to stem the flow of tears rolling from her eyes. "He had such fine plans, such high hopes. He would sit for hours and tell anyone who would listen how they were all going to be so happy . . . and now . . . now what will happen to them? Leviticus and the home they were coming to are gone. Everything is gone."

Cass's gaze went back to the study door. Rebecca's words drove deeply into his heart.

The children were homeless. Again.

Later that afternoon Susanne asked Cass if he would take her to visit her father's grave. He said he would, and they left right after supper. Rebecca had insisted that they stay the night at the parsonage, saying that they'd all put their heads together in the morning and come up with a solution.

At the sight of the fresh mound of dirt, Susanne caught her breath and turned away, realizing that she'd been praying all afternoon that it wasn't true. But it was. Her father was dead without ever knowing the transformation that had taken place in his daughter. She had wanted to surprise him, to let him actually see how she had changed.

Cass silently drew her back into his embrace and held her tightly. Her anguish overflowed, and her tears came again.

"He never really knew me," she whispered brokenly. "And I never really knew him."

She was forlorn that Leviticus would never know how much she'd loved him, how much she'd appreciated the love and devoted care he'd given to her. And she had never once thought to say thank you.

Was it possible for a child to fully realize how deeply and unselfishly a mother and father gave their love, never asking, but freely sacrificing whatever was required to see their child happily and safely to adulthood? What other relationship on this earth could boast of such love, such unending commitment that asked nothing in return? How strange, she thought, that children failed to understand such love until they had young ones of their own.

She recalled how one day she had selfishly demanded that her papa walk through snow up to his hips to buy a silly little bauble she'd decided she had to have. He'd worked all day hauling water to the cattle and walked home, but at her insistence he'd trudged to the mercantile in a blizzard to do her bidding.

Hours later he'd returned, cold and exhausted, bearing a red peppermint stick and the shiny spinning top she'd wanted. She'd jumped up and down with joy in their warm, cozy parlor while Leviticus had shed his sodden clothing and Mama had wrapped a warm blanket around his shoulders. Susanne could still hear the way Leviticus's teeth had chattered. He'd stuck his feet into a basin of hot water to thaw out.

Mama had raced around the kitchen, fixing tea and liberally lacing it with brandy to keep him from catching his death, while Susanne had watched the colorful top twirl round and round in the middle of the floor, unconcerned about her father's near-frozen state.

She recalled thinking she was the luckiest girl in the world to have such a fine papa who would buy her such extravagant things. Now she knew how fine Leviticus had really been, not because he could afford to buy his daughter a spinning top but because he'd loved her enough to walk three miles in the snow to purchase a silly toy that meant nothing to him but everything to a five-year-old child.

"Leviticus McCord," Susanne could still hear her mother scolding, *"you're spoilin' that child somethin' terrible!"* But Leviticus had only laughed and candidly admitted that it was true, but he didn't care. Then he had taken Susanne onto his lap, opened the family Bible, and as her chubby fingers had worried the top

round and round in her hands, he'd begun to read her favorite story to her, the one about Mary and Joseph and the little babe born in a manger.

The tears came faster now, and Susanne desperately wished she were that child again. After her mother's death the relationship between father and daughter had changed. Each had been wrapped in their own individual grief, and they had grown apart rather than closer. She was aware that a good part of the blame lay with her. She had hoped they would have a chance to get to know each other as adults, but that dream had now been denied her.

Drawing her gently away from the graveside, Cass supported her slight weight back to the reverend's buggy. He lifted her up onto the seat, and their eyes met and held.

"Tell your papa good-bye, Susanne."

Drawing her shoulders up determinedly, Susanne turned, and with tears streaming down her cheeks, she said loud and clear, "Good-bye . . . and thank you, Papa!"

She glanced back to Cass, and a radiant smile suddenly broke through her tears. "Do you think he heard me?"

Cass smiled. "I think he heard you."

Darkness closed around them. Cass picked up the reins, and the horse began moving away, leaving only Leviticus—and the good Lord—to know for certain.

"My stars! Look what the dogs have dragged up!" Beau Claxton stood gazing at his brother, shocked to find him standing in the doorway of his cabin.

The two brothers slapped each other on the back, laughing and whooping like two young boys. Charity, Beau's wife, moved away from the stove, smiling. Cass swept her up and swung her into the air.

"Cass Claxton, put me down!"

"Great day, girl, you're fat as one of Ma's old sows!"

"Beau!" Charity wailed. "Tell your *brother* that I'm not fat; I happen to be carryin' your babies!"

Retrieving his wife's squirming body in midair, Beau lowered Charity to her feet, kissing her soundly on the way down.

"Another set of twins?" Cass teased, his eyes pivoting to the three children looking up at him with wide-eyed innocence. "Great day in the morning!"

Beau looked at Charity and winked. "Just obeying the commandment to go forth and replenish the earth."

"He didn't mean all by yourself, Brother," Cass admonished with a grin. "What's for supper? I can only stay for a short while."

"You'll stay the night!" Charity protested. "We haven't seen you in years!"

"Sure." He reached out and ruffled the oldest child's head of red hair. "I have to get acquainted with my nieces and nephew, don't I?"

"You'd sure better!" Wrapping his arm around Cass's shoulder, Beau walked him over to the fire. "What are you doing here? Children! Come over here and meet Uncle Cass." Beau motioned for the children to come to him. "You remember Mary Kathleen? She was just a baby last time you saw her, and these are the twins, Jason and Jenny."

Cass grinned and shook each child's hand solemnly. "Nice-looking family, Beau."

"Thank you." Beau beamed with fatherly pride. "It is, isn't it?"

While the men caught up on the news, Charity fixed supper. After they'd eaten the thick slices of cured ham, hot corn bread, and steaming bowls of brown beans, Charity hugged each man and then discreetly excused herself, saying she wanted to put the children to bed early.

When she'd disappeared to the loft, Cass sat staring pensively into the fire. Beau got up to wind the clock.

"I see you've built on to the cabin."

Beau grinned. "Had to—the young'uns started coming and we ran out of room. Put the loft on last year. So, what brings you back in our direction?" Beau asked as he finished with the clock and added a few more chips to the stove.

"It's a long story, but at the moment I'm trying to find a home for nine children."

Beau's hand paused in midair, and he grinned. "Nine, huh? Your women all catch up with you at one time?"

"No, my women didn't all catch up with me at one time," Cass mimicked.

"Whoa!" Beau's brow lifted curiously. "We're a little touchy, aren't we?"

Cass supposed that he was, but he was tired and he had to get the children settled somewhere. Phebia had cried for two days, wanting the home she'd been promised. "I'm in one big mess, Beau."

"You're serious, aren't you?"

"Dead serious."

Beau sat down to give his full attention. "All right, I'm listening."

Cass took a deep breath and then began to tell of his recent journey from Saint Louis—of the orphanage, the children, and the fire. He was candid about everything except Susanne McCord and her forcing him to marry her six years ago. That was too humiliating to admit, even to Beau.

"Why would *you* agree to escort a pack of orphans to Cherry Grove?" Beau wondered aloud.

"I did it as a favor."

"For the older couple you mentioned—Harlon and Corliss?"

"No, it wasn't for them. I agreed because the woman who runs the orphanage was in a bind."

"Really." Beau stared into the fire thoughtfully. "What's her name, and how good-looking is she?"

"That didn't have anything to do with it."

"I'll bet!"

"Seriously, Beau, it didn't. I ran into their wagon outside of town on my way to—on a trip I was taking." He wasn't going to mention Susanne or the problem yet. "They hadn't gotten two miles out of town, and already they were stuck in a mud hole. When I stopped to help, the woman made me see how desperate they were for a man to help them make the trip to Cherry Grove. I couldn't just ride off and leave them stranded, now could I?"

"Since when?"

"Come on, Beau, you know me better than that."

Beau chuckled. "A year ago it wouldn't have surprised me one bit to hear you'd left twelve people stranded along the road. Maybe there's hope for you yet. So you agreed to bring nine children, two seventy-year-olds, and the woman back to Cherry Grove. You know, I really have to wonder about that."

Cass sat up straighter, his face animated. "You wait until you meet these kids—you're going to love them! There's Aaron—he's sixteen—and Payne—he's fourteen. I've been teaching them all about hunting! Then there's Jesse, Doog, Bryon, Margaret Ann. . . . Wait until you meet Margaret Ann—you won't believe this child. She thinks she's thirty years old—and you will too once you talk to her—but she's only six. Then there's Lucy and Phebia. Phebia is three and still sucks her thumb, although we've all been trying hard to break her of it. And then there's Joseph, who's as cute—"

"Whoa! Wait a minute! Are you *sure* these aren't your kids?"

"Of course they're not my kids, but lately I've been thinking it wouldn't be so bad having a couple of my own," Cass admitted.

Beau grinned. "Ma would insist you marry first."

Cass sighed. "I'm aware of that."

"So, you were bringing the kids and the old people and the woman from Saint Louis, and when you got here, you found that the house that was meant to be the new orphanage had burned down?"

"That's right. And I've looked everywhere for the past two days to find a house large enough to serve as an orphanage, but there isn't anything." He had debated about taking them all back to Saint Louis and giving them Josiah's house, but with the first snows approaching, he realized that Harlon and Corliss would be in no shape to make the return trip.

Beau seemed pensive as he thought about the problem. "I can think of only one fire that's happened around here lately, and that was Judge McCord's house over in Cherry Grove—you remember him? He had a daughter named . . . what was it? . . . Susanne? You had that run-in with her at Miller's Mercantile."

Cass looked away. "Seems like I do recall something like that."

"You *recall* meeting her?" Beau hooted. "Why, she knocked you upside the head with her purse. Left a knot the size of a goose egg, didn't she?"

"I *said* I remember Susanne McCord," Cass interrupted tersely. How could he forget her? She was on his mind day and night; now she and her nine kids were in his heart.

"I just asked. You all right? I don't believe I've ever seen you so edgy."

"Look, I might as well tell you because there's no way I'm going to be able to keep it from you. Susanne McCord runs the orphanage. I said I would help her get the children to Cherry Grove safely."

Beau cocked his head, eyebrows raised.

"It's the truth."

"How many guns did she have pointed at you?"

"None!" Actually one, but not that day.

"All right, all right, you don't have to take my head off!"

"I need your help, Beau. Stop messing around and get down to business. I'm running out of time."

"How can I help? I don't have a house big enough for three kids—soon to be five—let alone nine!"

"Then you're going to help me build one."

"You and me? Build a house that big?"

Cass nodded. "And however many men I can hire to help us. Susanne needs a home for those kids, Beau, and I'm not going back to Saint Louis until I know they have one."

"Well, well, how about that?" Beau said softly. "What's your main concern here—the kids or Susanne?"

Cass refused to look up. "Just be in Cherry Grove first light tomorrow morning."

Susanne walked down the street from the parsonage to the ruins of her father's house. Evidently the fire had roared through the old frame structure, giving Leviticus very little chance of escaping. She wondered how it had started, then realized it didn't matter. Papa was gone.

Aunt Estelle's words came back to her. *"You have to keep moving and hope in the Lord."*

Hope. Susanne realized she had no hope left. She was bone-dry. Nothing had gone the way she planned.

My plans.

The words echoed in her mind. Perhaps that had been the trouble. She had made the plans and then expected God to bless them, running ahead of what God had in store for her. Her mind traveled back over a long list of transgressions. When had she ever truly hoped in the Lord? Sitting in church, it was easy to hope. Going about her life, faith came easy. Her hope had been centered firmly in her belief in Susanne McCord's ability to have her own way.

She regretted misleading her father about Cass. He had gone to his grave believing the lie she had told. Not only had she hurt Cass, she had deceived the one person who had trusted her.

That wasn't all she had done either. She'd manipulated Cass into bringing them to Cherry Grove, and she had taunted and teased him and manipulated him into consummating their marriage vows. Well, her chickens had surely come home to roost. What was she going to do now?

She thought of the Bible study Reverend Olson had conducted in his home last night. They had gathered around the big kitchen table, eager to learn. The text was on Abraham and how he'd run ahead of the Lord. Growing tired of waiting for God to provide the promised heir, he had taken matters into his own hands, creating a problem for everyone concerned.

She thought back to all the times she had promised to place her hope in the Lord. She'd even asked God to grant her the courage to hope in Him, but every time she had turned away to follow her own plans. Running ahead of God, so sure she knew what was best, had handed her a problem for which she had no solution. Tears ran down her cheeks as she realized she had never really trusted Him. A part of her had always held back, wanting to be in control.

She, Susanne Claxton—she would use the name privately— had taken matters into her own hands and made a royal mess. She stared at the blackened chimney pointing an accusing finger at the sky, knowing she had reached the end of her rope.

"I'm sorry, so sorry," she whispered. "Forgive me." The words caught in her throat.

"Lord, maybe I had to arrive at the place where You are all I have to realize You are all I need. But I'm ready now to submit to Your will. Show me what You want me to do, and, Lord, I promise, no matter how much it hurts, I'll give Cass his freedom. I never should have deprived him of it to start with."

She took a deep breath. "Take charge of my life. Show me what You want me to do. I promise from now on I'll wait for Your leading."

She thought of what she had admitted and realized something else needed to be said. "I was wrong to put my wishes ahead of Your plans for me and for the children. I was so sure I had to have a certain house, so sure I had to come to Cherry Grove, so sure Cass had to bring us. I've done a lot of damage to a lot of people. It's too late to ask forgiveness from some of them. But I beg You to forgive me. And . . ."

She sighed. There was one more thing. And it would hurt more than anything she'd ever done before.

"And, Lord, I will never again do or say anything to bind Cass to me against his will."

CHAPTER 13

With Beau, Aaron, Payne and the twenty additional men that Cass was able to hire, the house was under roof in three and a half weeks. It took a crew of five men to build the fireplaces alone. The orphanage could move in, though the house wouldn't be completed for months.

And what a glorious house it was. Fifteen rooms, seven fire-places, five spacious bathrooms complete with claw-footed tubs, and the most modern, up-to-date kitchen conveniences Edgar Miller could have shipped from Hays, depending on weather. The house had running water piped straight to the bathrooms and kitchen, sparking the envy of every housewife in Cherry Grove.

Cass wouldn't let Susanne see the house until it was almost completed. But her excitement and anticipation surpassed even the children's, so late one Saturday afternoon Cass borrowed the reverend's buggy and drove her out to the building site.

Situated on thirty-five acres of prime land, the house was built in a grove of towering oak trees that would encourage cool breezes in the summer and provide a sturdy shelter against winter winds.

The horse's hooves clopped up the winding drive as Susanne's hands came up to cover her mouth, on the verge of squealing when she saw the magnificent sight spread before her.

Cass grinned, watching her turn speechless in wide-eyed wonder. "I wanted it to be larger—and it will be eventually. The carpenters require several months to complete the interior. When we need additions, they'll build on for us, but since you're so crowded at the reverend's I told them to just get you into the house. I figured Rebecca and the reverend need a little peace and quiet."

Having thirteen unexpected guests for nearly a month couldn't be pleasant, Cass had reasoned, especially since four of the children were either ill with chicken pox or coming down with it.

"Oh, Cass, I've never seen anything like it!" Susanne's eyes lit with joy. "It must have cost a fortune!"

He reined the horse to a stop in front of the house, and they sat for a few moments, admiring the carpenters' craftsmanship. The dwelling was superb, both in quality and construction. Two stories of wood and stone supported tall columns and sweeping verandas.

"The men will finish up the stonework by late tomorrow. The remainder of the furniture will be here Monday, and we should be able to get you moved in on Tuesday morning," Cass said as he set the brake and stepped out of the buggy. "You won't have all conveniences for a while, but you'll be comfortable."

"Oh, it's lovely . . . simply lovely. . . ."

He turned to lift her down but instead held her suspended in the air for a moment, his dancing eyes teasingly meeting hers. "Is that all you can say—that it's lovely?"

She smiled down at him. "How about, thank you, Sir Galahad, because you surely must be the noblest knight in all the land."

Cass shook his head, indicating that she needed to do better. She shook her head inquiringly. "No?"

"No."

"Then perhaps a kiss from the fair maiden?"

"Perhaps you know one?"

"Sir—" she dropped her gaze demurely—"I was one, until Sir Galahad rode into my life." Her mouth dipped to brush his lightly. Cass could feel the thunder of his heartbeat.

"I should apologize, fair maiden. I don't know what came over me," Cass said. "Can you forgive me?"

"The fair maiden not only forgives you, sir, but pledges her undying love," Susanne whispered.

He drew back, the teasing light in his eyes gone. Once he had her and the children comfortably settled, he would be gone, taking with him only a memory of days that meant more to him than he liked to admit. "I believe you were interested in seeing the house?"

"Oh yes . . . I can hardly wait."

Tucking her against his side, he led her up the steps leading to the circular veranda.

"Cass, has Reverend Olson said anything to you about why we're together?"

"I've noticed that he and Rebecca have exchanged a few inquisitive looks." Cass chuckled at the kindly minister's confusion. Though the reverend had presided over their hasty vows six years ago, neither Cass nor Susanne had given him reason to think their marriage would last.

"I should sit him down and explain what's happened," he conceded.

"I think you should." Susanne looked up at him and grinned. "Then come and tell *me*, because I still can't understand it."

"Someone will have to explain it to me first." Cass had lain awake nights, wondering how he'd suddenly found his life so entwined with Susanne's. They shared an easy camaraderie now, one that he knew he was going to miss.

They opened one of the two large doors and stepped into the front parlor. Long, elegant windows lined the room, bringing light in from the east. A stone fireplace to lend warmth in the winter centered on the west wall.

Susanne's hands flew up to cover her mouth again when she saw the mammoth room. "Oh, my . . ."

"Come Christmas Eve, I want Aaron and Payne to cut the biggest, nicest tree they can find," Cass told her. "When they bring it home, I want you to make it a night the children will never forget. They can string popcorn and berries and make chains from colored paper. I'll send some of those tiny candles they can put on the branches, but you'll have to watch and be sure that they don't burn themselves. And be sure to make Phebia take a nap that day, so she won't be so cranky that she can't enjoy it. And have Jesse and Doog hold Joseph up to the tree, so he can get his share of the fun and—"

Susanne laughed. "Cass Claxton, I never dreamed you were so sentimental!"

He grinned sheepishly. "Christmas is a special time for family. I want this year to be the best the children have ever had."

They strolled to the kitchen, holding hands. Susanne was taken aback when she saw the long work counters, two cookstoves, three sinks, and a colossal icebox to cool milk, butter, meat, and vegetables.

"I've never seen such luxury," she murmured, her eyes taking in the rows and rows of copper-plated pots and pans hanging over the cookstoves.

Cass took her arm and led her to the window, pointing to a large structure still under construction behind the house. "That's going to be the washhouse. I wanted it to be away from the main quarters so that you and Corliss won't be bothered."

"Bothered?"

"I've arranged for three women to come in four times a week to do the wash."

Susanne turned, flabbergasted. "For how long?"

"From now on."

"But Cass, I can't afford to pay three women to do our wash!"

"I know you can't, but *I* can. There'll also be a couple of men who'll do the yard work, two who'll keep you in wood, a tutor for the children, a man who'll supply fresh meat year-round. Three local farmers will keep you in fresh vegetables, milk, eggs, and the fruit in season. Sadie Withers and Wanda Mitchell will be coming in daily to do the cooking so that you and Corliss won't have any thing to do but look after the children. I've arranged for you to have unlimited credit at Miller's Mercantile, so you can buy staples and the children's clothing and shoes. Use it. I've spoken with the doctor in town, and he's been instructed to forward any bills pertaining to the orphanage to my offices in Saint Louis, including those incurred by Harlon and Corliss and yourself. Every month, you'll get a sizable check for incidentals you might need."

He paused and lifted an inquiring brow. "What have I overlooked?"

She looked at him in awe. "Your sanity! I can't accept such generosity."

He drew back, affecting a mock bow. "It isn't for you; it's for the kids." And for her, but she wouldn't take it unless he stretched the truth.

"Cass . . . I don't know what to say. Your kindness is overwhelming, but—"

He took her arm again and guided her to the next room. Their footsteps echoed across the gleaming pine floor. "No *buts*. You should know by now you're not going to win an argument with me."

Like he had ever had an argument with her *he* hadn't lost.

The dining room was large and airy with space enough to seat fifty guests. "The children will need the extra room for the friends they'll be bringing home over the years," Cass explained.

An adjoining room with back-to-back fireplaces looked out over a meadow, providing the children with restful surroundings to do their schoolwork. Next to it was a medium-sized study where Susanne would transact business pertaining to the orphanage. The room had a smaller, more intimate feel, with a cozy fireplace tucked into one corner and four large windows across the south wall.

To the left, a separate wing housed Susanne's and Corliss and Harlon's bedrooms.

Cass suggested that they view Susanne's quarters after they'd taken a tour of the upstairs. Leading her up the long, winding staircase, Cass then led her down the hallway, where they peeked into each of the children's bedrooms. Every room was large, bright, and cheerful. Susanne could visualize the astonished looks on the children's faces when they saw their new home.

Susanne thought her heart would burst from happiness. There was only one thing to mar her joy: the knowledge that Cass would not be there to share it with them.

"Now. The best part," he said.

"There couldn't be more."

"Ah, but there is."

They went back down the stairway, arm in arm. At the bottom Cass turned her in the direction of the wing he had left for last. "I thought you might enjoy having the bedroom on the left, though you're free to choose any one you want."

He paused before a closed door and gave her a wink that threatened to stop her heart. "This is the only fully completed room, and for some reason, I am partial to this one." He reached out, turned the handle, and the door swung open.

Susanne was unprepared for the sight she found. The four-poster bed, the armoire, the chiffonier, and the dressing table were made of the finest, richest walnut. The draperies, the bedspread, the pillows, the fabric on the settee in the adjoining sitting room, the chaise lounges, and the numerous chairs scattered about were sewn in delicate shades of lavender and blue. Lush baskets of ferns hung in the corner windows where fading rays of sunlight shone through the windowpanes. Outside the window was a large pond where a couple of waterfowl paddled through the peaceful water. Susanne's eyes took in the small dressing room, a closet the size of a room, and the private bath with gold-plated handles and faucets.

The room was so beautiful that tears welled in her eyes. "Oh, Cass, it's wonderful. I don't believe it."

Cass leaned against the doorway, watching her. "The lavender reminds me of your eyes; the blue warns me how much I'm going to miss you and the children," he said softly.

Not daring to look at him, she kept her eyes fixed on the waterbirds and said in a broken voice, "You're leaving, aren't you?"

"First light, Wednesday morning," he verified softly.

She wouldn't hold him; he'd stay because he loved her or not at all. She was through manipulating.

"Susanne . . . if you want—"

"I won't stop you. . . . I only wish you wouldn't go."

"There are times I wish I didn't have to go. But I do."

Swallowing the lump crowding the back of her throat, Susanne turned, smiling. She had made God a promise; she would honor it. "We'll miss you."

Placing her hands on either side of his face, she closed her eyes.

He pulled her to him, his lips skimming hers. Suddenly he drew back when salty wetness slid down her cheeks. "Don't cry," he probed gently.

"I'm sorry. I'm doing exactly what I promised I wouldn't do."

"Getting weepy on me?"

"Yes."

Stemming the flow of tears with his thumbs, he reminded softly, "I haven't gone yet."

Her heart was in her eyes. "You've brought me here to say good-bye, haven't you?"

He sighed, tenderly drawing her head back down to his chest. "It's not easy for me, Susanne."

She understood; it wasn't easy for him to walk away. He had deep feelings for the children—she knew that, but the knowledge didn't make it any easier for her.

For a long moment they said nothing; then he gently tipped her face up to his and kissed her. Her breath fluttered unevenly through her lips to his, "I never knew it could hurt so badly."

"What?"

"Loving you."

"Please, don't make this any harder," he whispered raggedly.

Tears ran unabashedly down her cheeks. "I'm afraid I'll never see you again."

His breath was warm and sweet against her mouth. "I'll never be very far away if you or one of the children needs me."

"Oh, Cass, how will I ever let you go?"

"You have to, Susanne. Don't try to force me to stay."

No, she wouldn't do that. She'd learned the hard way you couldn't hold anyone if they didn't want to stay. She wouldn't stand in the way of his leaving, but it would break her heart to let him go. Particularly now when she held the one weapon that would bring Cass Claxton to his knees. And she'd promised God she wouldn't use it.

Cass had hoped the house would ease Susanne's pain over their parting. He realized now that while it might help, nothing would make it easier for her. Or for him. How had they come to this point? Sometimes he wanted to stay, but he wasn't sure if he *could* love only one woman after so many years of running from them. He knew what he felt for her must come powerfully close to lasting.

They wandered out on the veranda, sitting down in the cane-bottomed rockers provided there. Cass watched her out of the corner of his eye, half expecting her to beg him to stay. He hoped she wouldn't; it was hard to deny her anything. He'd enjoyed building the house, taking pleasure in imagining her and the children enjoying the luxury and comfort they'd never known. He'd pictured Phebia running through the house, Jesse and Doog sliding down the banisters, Margaret Ann's common-sensical remarks.

Most of all he'd pictured Susanne moving through the rooms, going about her work, resting on the spacious veranda. Now he realized he'd pictured himself there too.

She rested her hand on his arm. "I do appreciate all you've done for us. Life will be so much easier now."

"It's not enough, is it?" He hadn't meant to ask the question. The words had popped out.

"It has to be."

"It will be all right; you'll see."

"No, it won't. Being back here where it all started makes me realize how badly I behaved. God must be punishing me for what I did to you."

He was silent for a moment, searching for words. "In that case, He must be punishing me too. My part in this hasn't been all that admirable either."

She smiled. "I wonder what it would have been like if we'd started differently. Would you have found me desirable?"

He chuckled. "Well, I sure do at this moment." The smile faded. "You are lovely, dedicated, and wise—far wiser than I."

Unshed tears sparkled in her eyes.

For the hundredth time Cass wondered if he was doing the right thing. Could he leave her—ride away and not think of her and the children day and night?

She reached out, touching his face. "I'm afraid you'll forget me."

"Forget you?" He clasped her hands and held on tightly. "I make you this promise, Susanne. Until I draw my last breath, I will never forget you."

He couldn't forget. It would be better for them both if he could.

CHAPTER 14

Winter's first snow sifted down in fine, powdery flakes when Bryon, Joseph, Lucy, and Phebia huddled around Susanne's skirt, their eyes openly indicting Cass for desertion. He stoically saddled his horse, dismissing the silent pleas. Even Margaret Ann had shed some of her sophistication when the cold fact that he was leaving became evident.

A cold wind whipped the tails of the heavy sheepskin jackets that Cass had recently purchased for the boys. Jesse, Doog, Payne, and Aaron stood by, watching his departure in stony silence.

Delaying as long as prudent, Cass summoned enough nerve to turn and face his accusers. The forlorn faces he found waiting weren't encouraging.

He cleared the goose-egg lump in his throat and adjusted his hat, settling it lower on his forehead, carefully avoiding any particular gaze. "Well, guess that about does it."

Corliss offered him the sack of food she and Susanne had prepared earlier. "Just some chicken and biscuits—won't last long, but it'll be more appetizing than jerky."

"Much obliged, Corliss. I appreciate it." Cass tucked the food away in one of the saddlebags. "I talked to Harlon earlier, but tell him I said good-bye again."

"Shore will . . . you take care now, you hear?"

His eyes softened. "I will, Corliss."

"How long will it take you to ride to Saint Louis?" Susanne asked, finally stepping forward.

Cass was forced to meet her gaze, though he didn't want to. They had said their good-byes last night, and it hadn't been easy. "Ten, twelve days . . . depends on the weather."

"You could sell your horse in Westport and take a boat the rest of the way," she said. "It'd be faster."

"I don't mind. I need the time."

A faint smile touched her lips, and he knew she was trying to make it easier for him. "You take care of yourself. Snow's going to be deep."

He gazed down at her. Was he doing the right thing? He came up with the same unyielding answer: he didn't know.

"You'll write?" she whispered.

"Yes . . . you do the same."

"Of course."

Turning to face the children, he looked at the faces he had grown to love, fighting the building emotion that was pressing heavily against his chest. "You kids mind your elders."

There was a combined mumbling of "yes, sirs" before Phebia buried her face in Susanne's skirt and began to sob.

Reaching out, Cass lifted her into his arms and forced her to look at him. "You're a big girl now, Phebia. Big girls don't cry."

Tears of misery rolled silently out of the child's eyes. There were many things the three-year-old couldn't comprehend, but he knew Phebia sensed that he would no longer be there to patch her hurts and make them better. "They do when their daddy leaves," the little girl whispered.

"You want to pinch my nose?" Emotion clouded his speech. Phebia shook her head no.

"Will you give me a kiss before I go?"

She nodded. Cass removed the thumb from her mouth, and she leaned over and pecked him on the mouth.

He winked at her. "Not bad. With a little practice, you'll be breaking some man's heart before we know it."

Margaret stepped forward shyly to offer him a kiss. She was joined a few moments later by Lucy. How he loved these kids, he thought. He held tightly to the three small bodies.

Phebia suddenly backed away and extended Marybelle to him. Cass grinned and obediently gave the chosen one a kiss. But Phebia emphatically shook her head. "Marmarbelle go with Papa," she said firmly, extending the doll to him again.

Cass lifted his brows. "You want me to take Marybelle?"

Her face broke into a radiant smile. "You Marmarbelle's papa!"

He nearly broke down. "You sure you don't want Marybelle to stay here and live with you?"

She shook her head again.

"All right. I'll be a good papa to Marybelle." He carefully tied the doll onto his saddle horn.

Openly shaken now, he turned and knelt down to hug Joseph, then Bryon. Rising to his feet again, he shook hands with Doog and Jesse. "You boys behave yourselves."

"Yessir."

"Yessir."

Cass could feel his eyes mist. He reached out and clasped Payne's hand—a man's hand now. "I'm counting on you to keep the smaller ones under control."

"I will, sir."

"You see that you do."

And then it was time for Aaron.

Aaron's eyes remained stoically fixed straight ahead as Cass, too overcome by his deep feelings for this young man, simply reached out to squeeze his thin shoulder. Then he turned and walked blindly to his horse.

"Cass."

His foot paused in the stirrup at the sound of Susanne's voice.

"Yes?" he answered without turning around.

She was suddenly by his side, her hand gently on his arm, silently willing him to turn and look at her.

But he refused. Keeping his head down, he said in a voice gruff with emotion, "Susanne . . . let's get this over with."

Wordlessly she pressed an envelope into his hand.

Recognizing the significance of the long, legal envelope, a blanket of pain suddenly settled over him. The divorce papers.

"These are the papers I promised you. All they need is your signature," she said softly. "I signed them last night."

He swung up onto the saddle, tucking the envelope inside his jacket. "See that you write."

Her eyes confirmed her love, told him that she would always love him. "You do the same."

He kicked the horse. The children stood huddled against the driving wind, watching him ride out of their lives as simply and as suddenly as he had ridden in.

"*Mon cheri*, I do not know what has gotten into you!" Laure Revuneau paced the floor of Cass's study, wringing her hands with frustration. "I did not hear from you the entire time you were gone. And now that you're back, you've been ignoring me for weeks."

Cass sat at his desk, staring out the window. Heavy snow was falling in sheets. But it was no heavier than the sense of depression that had plagued him since he'd left Cherry Grove ten weeks earlier.

Laure crossed the room to stand before him. "You have not been to see me since you returned. Have I done something to offend you, *mon cheri?*"

He pushed back from his desk, hoping to avoid the question in her eyes. He didn't know why, but Laure wasn't the woman for him. He had started to compare each one he encountered with Susanne, and it annoyed him. "You haven't done anything wrong, Laure. I've been distracted lately." He walked to the fire and picked up the poker.

She followed him. "You are not so terribly busy now, *n'est-ce pas?*"

He studied the fire, realizing that the time had long passed to be honest with her. He had told her nothing of Cherry Grove or Susanne McCord, and he didn't plan to. But he also realized that he had no plans to continue their relationship. "I'm sorry, Laure." He knelt to stir the fire. "I'm leaving for Atlanta within the hour."

He knew she was stung by his rejection; her expression showed her displeasure. "You're leaving again?"

"My business has suffered in my absence. I will be traveling often in the next few months."

"But . . . what about us?"

Cass straightened, turned to face her. "I think you would be happier if you sought more reliable companionship."

She lifted her head proudly. Laure Revuneau had more dignity than he thought. She inclined her head. "If that's what you want."

"Laure . . ." He heard the familiar note of despondency creeping back into his voice. "I don't know what I want."

A tap sounded at the door as Laure gathered her ermine cloak and prepared to leave. "Perhaps you will reconsider when you return from Atlanta."

"I won't reconsider."

Laure opened the door to find Sar waiting. She turned back to Cass and smiled, her eyes issuing a challenge. "I do not give up easily."

Cass smiled wanly. "Take care, Laure."

Her eyes softened with perception. "Whoever she is, I hope she deserves you."

Sar stepped back to allow Laure room to exit. When she was gone, he walked into the room and Cass turned back to the fire.

"Another letter has been delivered, sir."

Cass glanced up expectantly.

"Again it's postmarked Cherry Gro—" Sar didn't get to finish before the letter was snatched from his hand.

Cass tore into envelope eagerly.

"Will there be anything else, sir?"

Cass wasn't listening. He strode to his desk, his eyes hungrily roving over the piece of paper.

"Very good, sir." Sar closed the door behind him.

Seating himself at the desk, Cass's eyes focused on Susanne's neat penmanship:

Dearest Cass,

I hope this letter finds you happy and well. The Christmas tree fit in the window as beautifully as you predicted it would. Aaron and Payne took the smaller boys, and they scouted the woods on Christmas Eve, looking for the perfect cedar.

That evening we placed the lovely candles on the tree, and the children strung popcorn and made chains from the colored paper you sent them. When they were finished, the tree was truly a magnificent sight.

Aaron and I took turns holding Phebia and Joseph so he could place the star of Bethlehem on top. Joseph was so proud. Later we gathered around the tree and I read the story about the angel appearing to the Virgin Mary, telling her she had been chosen to be the mother of the Christ child, and how Joseph and Mary had made the long trip to Bethlehem only to find no room at the inn.

For days afterward, our Joseph was quite adamant that he had a wife named Mary and that they had journeyed to Bethlehem on a donkey, where they'd developed a case of bad sniffles because they'd had to sleep in a stable.

Corliss and I finally got the children to bed and asleep by midnight, only to be up again before five. The older boys were ecstatic over their new rifles, and the girls simply adore their dollhouses. Of course, Bryon and Joseph thought their bicycles topped everything. Where in the world did you find such silly contraptions?

Well, I must close and get to bed. Tomorrow Doog and Jesse are in a spelling bee at school. Can you imagine that?

We think of you every day, and your name is mentioned quite frequently in Margaret Ann's prayers.

Respectfully yours,
Susanne McCord

The first buds of spring were bursting open on the oaks when Doog came running up the drive, waving a letter in his hand.

"It's here!"

Susanne dropped her sewing, and children flew out every door. Making her way carefully down the steps, she prayed that it was news from Cass. "Is it from him?"

"Yes!" Doog answered.

When the letter was in her hand, Susanne closed her eyes and held it close to her heart for a moment, imagining that she could smell his familiar scent. Of course she couldn't, and at the children's indignant insistence, she ripped into the letter and began to read aloud:

Dearest Susanne, Harlon, Corliss, Aaron, Payne, Doog, Jesse, Bryon, Joseph, Margaret Ann, Lucy, and Phebia,

Please do not take in any more children until I can acquire a longer pencil.

Susanne paused to glance up sheepishly. "He's silly, isn't he?"

"Read us more," Joseph demanded.

"All right." She went on:

I have been traveling for many weeks now, and I am very weary. At times I think I will sell everything I have and retire, but after a good night's rest, I change my mind again. Hope you children are minding well and keeping up with your homework.

Take care of yourselves.

Love,
Cass

Margaret Ann frowned. "Is that all?"

Susanne sighed. Cass couldn't be accused of being long-winded. "That's all."

Dearest Cass,

Is it ever hot! If we owed someone a hot day, we could have paid him back a hundred times lately. The temperature has soared dreadfully for days, and the children are getting cranky. Aaron and Payne have taken the smaller ones to the pond to swim every afternoon, though I had to scold Joseph again today. He chases my pretty swans until they are exhausted.

Harlon is up and about. Feeling right perky, he says to tell you. Corliss says she's feeling tuckered out because of all the heat. Phebia has just about stopped sucking her thumb, though she does have an occasional relapse.

I received the signed divorce papers. Thank you.

I trust you are well. I had a spell last week of not feeling so well, but I'm much better now.

We thought of you the other night at supper; we were enjoying that stew you like so much.

Take care.

Respectfully,
Susanne McCord

P.S. I almost forgot! Bryon and Lucy wanted me to tell you that they've each lost another front tooth. You should see them when they grin! They insisted that I enclose their teeth—hope you don't mind.

The oaks were bursting with color as Doog came running breathlessly up the drive again.

Susanne ran out of the washhouse. "Is it here?"

"It's here!"

She flew across the yard, her heart thumping erratically. "Give it to me."

Not waiting for the other children this time, she tore into the letter, her eyes eagerly devouring his words:

Dear Ones,

Since I'm in California, I decided to visit the ocean today. I sat for a long time looking out across the water, thinking of you. I was reminded of what a great distance separates us. Sometimes I worry that you don't have every-thing you need, and that makes me worry even more. If you should ever want for anything, you have only to ask. Don't worry about money. I have all we could ever need and more. I used to think money could make a man happy, but I'm beginning to realize that there are more important things in life.

Take good care of yourselves—I miss all of you in a way I find hard to put on paper.

Love,

Cass

P.S. Susanne, be sure that the kids have big pumpkins for Halloween. I mean it. I'm getting tired of you being so frugal.

Dear Cass,

The children had the biggest pumpkins in town; I hope you're happy. Do you realize you are spoiling these children shamelessly?

Take care.

Respectfully,

Susanne McCord

Dear Susanne,

   I'll spoil the children if I want to. I miss you all.

Cass

"The old-timers are predicting at least nine inches by morning," Sar remarked. He set a tray filled with sandwiches and a pot of tea on the study table.

Cass answered absently. He sat staring into the fire, his fingers folded above the bridge of his nose, staring unseeingly at the glowing embers. Susanne was on his mind constantly lately. Her memory tortured him at night, and today he'd passed a woman on the street who'd reminded him of her. The response had been painful.

What was he going to do about Susanne McCord? about the children?

He got up and walked to the window to pace restlessly. It had been close to a year since he'd seen them. Eleven months. How much the children must have grown! Why didn't he go to them? How much longer was he going to feed his senseless pride that no longer required feeding? he wondered.

Regardless of what Susanne had done to him in the past, he

could no longer deny that he was in love with her. She had changed. He had seen her change from a spoiled brat to a compassionate, loving woman. So what was he waiting for? Why did he keep torturing himself like this? The reasons he'd given for leaving her didn't seem to make sense anymore. He didn't want to be a footloose bachelor, and he'd trade all the money in the world to feel Phebia tugging on his nose again.

Suddenly he stopped pacing. He wasn't going to wait any longer. He was going to go after her.

His eyes caught sight of a buggy pulling up in front of the house, and he groaned.

Company—the last thing he needed or wanted. He was about to tell Sar that he wouldn't see anyone when he noticed a boy stepping down from the carriage.

Cass leaned closer to the window, his face wreathing with happiness when he recognized the visitor.

"Aaron!" He bolted from the sill.

Sar glanced up from pouring the tea. "I beg your pardon, sir?"

"Sar, it's Aaron!" he exclaimed. He briskly walked across the room and out the door.

"Aaron?" Sar lifted his brow curiously.

Aaron was coming up the walk when Cass flung the door open. The boy broke into a grin as Cass rushed out to engulf him in a warm embrace.

Clapping him heartily on the back, Cass exclaimed, "Aaron, what are you doing here, son?"

"Come to pay you a visit."

Cass held the boy away from him to get a good look. He'd grown at least two inches! "It's good to see you—"

His smile suddenly froze. "Is everything all right at the

orphanage? Has anything happened to Susanne or one of the children?"

"No, sir, they're all doin' fine," Aaron insisted with a good-natured grin.

"Are you sure?"

"I'm positive."

Cass began moving the boy toward the house, keeping his arm firmly around him as if he might somehow slip away. "How did you get here?"

"By boat."

"Boat? From Westport?"

"Yessir. I have a part-time job working at Miller's Mercantile, and I used some of the money I've earned to buy a ticket."

"You didn't need to do that. I would have sent you the money to come for a visit."

"I couldn't do that, sir. Miss McCord says I need to be man enough to stand on my own two feet."

"Well, she's right, of course—are you hungry?"

"Yessir."

They walked inside the house, and Cass shouted for Sar to bring more food.

"It's cold out there—and snowing." Cass drew Aaron closer to the warmth of the fire.

"Yeah, but Missouri's not as cold as Kansas."

"Take off your coat and warm yourself. How did you find me?"

"I asked around. You weren't hard to find."

Sar returned with a large tray laden with food. Cass began to fire a million questions at Aaron about the other children.

When he'd answered all of them to Cass's satisfaction, Aaron tore into the slice of steaming apple pie that Sar had set before him.

Cass lit a cheroot and settled behind the desk. "Well, how have you been?"

"Real good. You remember Ernestine Parker?"

"Sure. I remember Ernestine Parker."

Aaron grinned. "Well, me and her might be marrying up next spring."

"Is that so?"

"We've been writing back and forth, and I'm thinking real strong about asking for her hand."

Cass shook his head. It was hard to realize that the boy was old enough to think about such things.

"How old are you now?"

"Seventeen. Ernestine is younger, but I plan on taking real good care of her."

Cass smiled. "Ernestine's a fine choice, Aaron. I'm sure she'll make you an excellent wife."

"Thank you, sir. I hope she feels the same."

"Where do you plan to live?"

"In Cherry Grove. I think Miss McCord can use my help raising those kids. Corliss and Harlon are getting older, and the kids are a handful at times."

Cass nodded, glancing out the window, fondly recalling how there was rarely a moment's peace when the children were around. "How are Corliss and Harlon?"

"Holding up."

"And Susanne?" Cass's turned and leaned forward in his chair. "How is she?"

"She's fine, sir. Had you a fine son a few months back."

LORI COPELAND

"Oh yeah? Well, that's good—" Cass started to lean back when he suddenly froze, his face draining of color. He sat up straighter. "Had me a *what*?"

Aaron's tone changed from friendly to critical in the blink of an eye. "I said, she had you a fine son, sir."

Cass couldn't find his voice.

Moving the slice of half-eaten pie aside, Aaron stood up and drew a deep breath. "Sir, I want you to know I've thought a lot about what I'm about to say—and I know you might not be real happy to hear it, but I've come a long way to say it, so don't try to stop me."

Cass glanced up, in shock at the news that he had fathered a son.

"I don't mean any disrespect, sir, but you've got this coming."

"All right." Cass stood up to meet Aaron's stringent gaze. "Say what you've come to say."

"You're a no-good, sorry piece of trash . . . sir." Aaron doubled his fist and struck out.

Cass lifted a hand to his smarting cheek, astounded by the boy's actions. His eyes narrowed. "I've whipped men for less than this."

Aaron braced himself, looking fully prepared to fight. "Then you'd better get to whipping, sir, because it's the truth." The boy's face reddened with anger.

"The truth!"

"Yessir, the truth."

"You want to tell me why you think it's the truth?"

"Because of what you did to Miss McCord."

"What do you think I've done to her?"

"Sir, I may not know a whole lot, but I think it's plain to everyone what you did to her."

Cass had the grace to blush. "What's all this nonsense about me being a worthless piece of trash?"

"You are one, sir, sure as I live and breathe." Aaron kept his eyes solidly fixed to the snow falling outside the window. "You told me you'd been taught that if a man trifles with a woman and then walks away, he's nothing but a piece of trash."

"And you think that's what I've done?"

Aaron's gaze focused on Cass accusingly. "I *know* it is."

Cass leaned back in his chair, trying to grasp what had happened. He was quiet for a long moment, trying to muddle through the boy's accusations. "Does Susanne know you're here?"

"No, sir! And she'd skin me alive if she knew. She thinks I've gone to visit Ernestine, but I had to do this for Sammy."

Cass looked up. "Sammy?"

"Samuel Cass Claxton. I believe Miss McCord figured you might want your son named after you and your pa, seeing as how he's dead and all."

Samuel Cass Claxton, Cass thought. *I have a son.* Susanne had had the perfect way to trap him again, and she hadn't. She *must* have known or at least suspected that she was carrying his child when he'd left her. She'd let him ride away that day, divorce papers in hand, and never said a word.

"Aaron—" Cass's voice broke with emotion—"believe me, I didn't know. . . . She never told me. . . . I never dreamed . . ."

"You mean, she really didn't tell you?" Aaron asked.

"No . . . she never said a word. I wouldn't have left if I had known. . . ." Cass's eyes turned pleading. "You have to believe me, Aaron. I didn't know."

Aaron laid his hand on Cass's shoulder. "Well, then, I think it's time you met your son." He smiled, and Cass saw that the smile was no longer that of a child but of a man.

"I think so too. You think Susanne will forgive me?"

"Shoot, yes. She's always been downright silly about you."

A proud grin spread across the new papa's face. "When's the next boat leave?"

Reaching into his back pocket, Aaron drew out two tickets. "Tomorrow morning—and I'd be much obliged if you would pay me back for your fare, because I'll need the money for my wedding—" Aaron flashed him an embarrassed grin—"sir."

CHAPTER 15

Fire popped in the grate; the orphanage had settled down for
the night. Susanne cuddled her son in her arms, one hand
supporting the head of dark, curly hair. She gazed into an
achingly familiar pair of blue eyes and sang softly: "Hush, little
baby, don't you cry; I'm gonna sing you a lullabye. . . ."

It had been a long, hot summer and fall. She recalled the
day she'd finally drawn Corliss, Harlon, and the children aside
to explain her expanding waistline. The older boys had taken
the news grim faced.

"I'm carrying Cass's child." She had stilled the horrified
looks with a hasty "We're married—been married for over six
years." Then she'd gone on to explain the hopelessly entangled
mess she'd made of her life—and Cass's. "I'm so ashamed. I have
led that poor man a merry chase."

Harlon cleared his throat and then spoke up. "Does Cass
know about the child?"

"Certainly not—and he isn't to know. Ever."

"But, Susanne—you can't deny a man his son or daughter. It
isn't right."

She'd thought about that, but the child wasn't his child. It was her child. Cass wanted nothing to do with marriage or responsibility. He'd said so time and again.

"If I were to tell him, Harlon, he would be back in an instant. But it wouldn't be because he loved me or the baby. It would be because he felt an obligation to us." She had looked up, her eyes brimming with tears. "I want him back on his own accord. I want him to love me, Harlon. Truly love me when—if— he ever returns."

Corliss had shaken her head, deep lines etching her forehead. "Don't seem right, child."

It wasn't right, but it was the only solution to the problem. She had been selfish and out of the will of God. Disobedience sometimes demanded a high price.

Susanne glanced up when she heard the sound of the door opening behind her, and her heart leaped to her throat when she saw who was standing in the doorway.

Cass leaned against the frame, his gaze fixed on her. "Forgot to mention something, didn't you, Miss McCord?"

She managed to still her pulse long enough to return his gaze. "No, Mr. Claxton, not that I can think of."

His eyes motioned to the child. "No?"

"No."

"Where did you get the baby?"

Susanne smiled. "Oh . . . he just sort of came . . . late one rainy afternoon."

"Really."

Susanne realized that, somehow, Sammy's father had found out about him. "Who told you?" she asked softly.

"Does it matter?" Cass crossed the room and came to kneel

beside her chair. His presence suddenly filled the awful emptiness in her heart, and she murmured a silent prayer, thanking God for sending him back, if only for a visit.

He gazed down on his son, his eyes wet with emotion. "He's a handsome boy."

She drew the blankets aside to allow him a closer look. "We do good work, don't we, Mr. Claxton?"

"We sure do." Cass reached out and lightly touched a finger to his son's chin. "Hi, Sam."

The child puckered up, threatening to break into tears.

Mother and father laughed, momentarily easing the tension.

"How old is he?"

"Four months."

"No kidding! He's big for his age, isn't he?"

"Of course." She avoided meeting his eyes, struggling to keep her emotions in check. The past year had been an emotional seesaw. "Samuel Cass Claxton is going to be exactly like his father. A fine, strong man."

Cass leaned closer, and she felt faint when she detected his familiar smell. She longed to throw herself into his arms and let him kiss away the loneliness of the past year, but she knew she wouldn't. Not this time.

His gaze returned to the infant. The shock of dark hair and arresting blue eyes. "He favors me. Ma will be pleased."

Susanne sighed. He didn't have to remind her of how much the baby looked like him. Sammy was a daily reminder of the man she loved. "Yes, he does, and he has your streak of orneriness too."

"Mine?" Cass grinned, that affable crooked grin that tore at her heartstrings. "I'd say he gets that from his ma."

"Oh, now, now," she cooed when the child began to sob harder. "Is this any way to act in front of your papa?"

Cass suddenly caught her hand, turning her to face him. "Why, Susanne? Why didn't you tell me about our son? How long did you plan to keep this from me?"

Susanne swallowed the constricting knot in her throat. "I don't know—I wasn't sure how you would feel about him, Cass. I know you aren't ready to settle down, and a baby calls for permanence in one's life."

"Feel about him? He's my *son*."

Susanne drew a long breath. "Yes, but he's my son too, Cass. How does *that* make you feel?"

"Maybe that makes him even more special," he admitted in a shaky voice.

"Maybe?" She wasn't sure what he was trying to say. Was he here to claim his son? If he was, he'd have to claim her too. She wanted Cass Claxton, and this time she was willing to fight for him. "I didn't tell you about our child because I didn't want you to think I was trying to trick you again."

"I wouldn't have thought that—"

"Yes, you would have. You know you would have."

"Well, I don't think that now," he said gently.

"Cass, I love you so deeply it's a physical ache at times," she confessed. "I pray every night that someday you'll return my love, but I'm tired of using tricks and deceit to hold you. I'm afraid if you want your son, you have to take me too."

"I'd be grateful to have the both of you."

His ready acceptance failed to register. "And you'll have to want *me* and agree that our lives will be empty and meaningless without each other," she warned. "I'll settle for nothing less."

His gaze traveled adoringly over her, then on to his son. "You'll have nothing less. I'm sorry it's taken me so long to realize how I feel, but I had to be sure—for both our sakes. I love you, Susanne Claxton—love you so much—and I'm miserable without you."

"Well, as I say, if you ever want—" She paused, his words finally sinking in. Her eyes widened. "You love me?"

He nodded, slowly drawing her mouth up to meet his. The kiss was long and filled with urgency and longing.

"Oh, Cass, why did you leave?" she whispered against the sweetness of his mouth.

"I had to. It's taken me almost a year to realize what's important in my life, but not a day has gone by that I didn't know that I loved you. I said many things to you, Susanne—spiteful things, words spoken in bitterness and anger. I ask you to forgive me— allow me to make amends for my bad behavior."

"But you signed the divorce papers."

"Because I wanted the *old* marriage over and done with. I want us to start again. I want God and our love to be the ruling forces this time, not manipulation. I'm deeply in love with you, Susanne." His hand reached out to touch her face and her eyes reverently. "Can you forgive me?"

"Oh, Cass, if you only knew how long I have waited to hear you say those words."

His smile was as intimate as a kiss. "Get used to it—you're going to be hearing it a lot for the next fifty years."

When their lips parted many long minutes later, she prompted softly, "Does this mean you're home to stay?"

"It does."

"What about your business—?"

He laid a silencing finger across her lips. "I've consolidated most of my holdings, and the remainder of my business can be handled from here in Cherry Grove. I'm closing the house in Saint Louis, and I've arranged to have Sar brought here to help with the children—if you have no objections."

She gazed back at him, her heart overflowing with joy. "Of course I have no objections, but . . . are you sure it's me you want, or is it because of your son—and the children—that you've changed your mind?" She had to know for sure.

"I want you, my love, and my son . . . and my nine other children."

"Oh, Cass . . . are you sure? The children will be overjoyed. They love you as much as I do. . . ." She paused and smiled, drowning in the familiar blue of his eyes. "Well, nearly as much."

"Woman, I've never been surer of anything in my whole life—and don't start arguing with me." His lips pressed and then gently covered her mouth.

"Then each and every one of us is yours," she said a moment later. "You don't mind being hog-tied and branded?"

"Not by you."

He reached out to pull her and the baby onto his lap.

"Hey, Sam, me and your ma are getting married—not in the middle of a road at the point of a shotgun, but she and I and our ten children are going to plan the biggest, rowdiest wedding this town has ever seen!" Cass told his son. "I want the whole world to know she's mine, and she's going to stay mine for the rest of her life!" He paused and grinned engagingly at his son. "What do you think about *that*, Samuel Claxton?"

Sammy Claxton burped.

Cass and Susanne laughed and indulged in another long kiss. Afterward, Susanne whispered. "That means your son thinks your idea sounds simply grand."

He frowned. "No . . . Susanne, a man doesn't use words like *simply grand.*"

She nodded and revised. "Well, partner, your son thinks that sounds mighty fittin'."

He kissed her. "Better, but we'll work on it."

Three weeks later, Cass stood at the upstairs window, looking down on the activity, shaking his head with amazement. The orphanage was decked out in its very finest. Greenery and colored ribbons adorned each room, while the smell of cedar filled every nook and cranny. The weather had held; the day was crisp and cold. The men he'd fought with—become good friends with over the years—had come. Trey McAllister and others too numerous to name.

The parlor was filled with tables stacked high with gaily wrapped presents awaiting the bride and groom's attention.

A magnificent eight-tiered wedding cake kept Corliss busy trying to keep the children's fingers out of the icing.

There had been a solid stream of buggies arriving for the past hour, with people alighting from the carriages in their Sunday best to witness the exchange of vows between Miss Susanne McCord and Mr. Cass Claxton.

A knock sounded and the door opened.

"Hello."

Cass turned, a smile surfacing on his face as Susanne swept into the room as bright as a ray of summer sunshine on this snow-covered winter afternoon. "It's about time you got here. Come here, woman."

She went willingly to him, and his arms encircled her, one hand at the small of her back. His kissed her. "Ready to marry me?"

"More than ready, darling."

"Then let's do it—the right way this time. With God's blessing."

There was a lot of backslapping and hugging when the Claxton family reunited.

Cass drew his mother, Lilly, into his arms and held her tightly. He hadn't seen her for more than five years.

"Now, where are all my grandbabies?" Lilly turned to Cole's children, engulfing them in big grandmotherly hugs.

"Ma, you better ease up," Cass warned. "You still have my ten to go."

Lilly threw her hands up in despair. "I always said you'd be the one to turn my hair gray!"

Willa, the family housekeeper who'd been like a mother to the Claxton boys, was here, beaming with pride. She swept Cass into her arms and gave him a big kiss.

Wynne was standing by and, by the look in her eyes, eager

to talk to the lothario who had jilted her at the altar many years ago. "I can't wait to meet the woman who's finally snagged you," she teased, going into Cass's open arms.

With a good-natured grin, Cass drew his sister-in-law into a tight embrace. "Wynne, sweetheart, look at it this way: if I hadn't left you standing at that altar, and you hadn't traipsed all over the country looking for me, why, where would my brother be today? In the arms of another woman—"

Wynne Claxton poked him soundly in the ribs. "All right, all right. How many times do I need to say thank you?"

Cass laughed and knelt down to greet his nieces and nephews. "Jeremy, look how you've grown—and your sisters, Tessie and Sarah!" He stood up again, shaking his head with disbelief. "They make you realize you're getting old, don't they?"

Cole was suddenly forced to sidestep when Doog, Jesse, Bryon, Joseph, and Lucy hurtled down the staircase. "Did school just let out?"

Cass threw his head back and hooted. "No, those are just more of mine!"

Beau and Charity arrived with their five children, and the hugs and kisses started all over.

"You're expecting again!" Wynne exclaimed.

Charity nodded, her eyes sparkling with happiness. "Beau says it's boys again."

"It better be; I need more help with the work," Beau teased, giving his wife an adoring squeeze.

Events blurred. Handshakes and greetings were exchanged. Cass grew more nervous. He anxiously checked the time, dragging his timepiece in and out of his pocket.

When he was sure he couldn't wait another moment, the

music suddenly sounded the wedding march. He straightened his tie, took a deep breath, and stepped into place next to Aaron and Payne beneath the wide arch of greenery in the parlor.

Phebia, dressed in a miniature replica of the bride's gown, had confiscated Marybelle, and she now carried the doll down the stairway. She entered the parlor scattering dried petals along the pathway, sneaking an occasional suck on her thumb.

Margaret Ann and Lucy followed, dressed in long lavender-blue gowns and wearing circlets of dried flowers around their hair.

Jesse, Doog, Bryon, and Joseph were next, looking spit-shined and polished in their Sunday best. Corliss followed, carrying Sam, who didn't appear to care much for all the commotion. The latter didn't have an official role in the wedding, but it had been agreed by all that the ceremony should be a family affair.

And then the moment Cass had been waiting for arrived.

Susanne descended the stairway, a vision of loveliness in an ivory bridal gown.

Cass's eyes locked with hers as she walked slowly toward him, supported by Harlon's steady arm. They smiled at each other, and Cass savored the heady moment.

Reverend Olson officiated over the nuptial ceremony, and this time he didn't have to prompt the groom to accept his vows or kiss his bride. In fact, the assembled guests had reason to wonder if the groom was ever going to stop kissing her.

Susanne finally broke the embrace and covered her face with embarrassment amid the sound of hoots and applause.

Corliss cut the wedding cake. Guests crowded around when the groom lifted his glass, his eyes overflowing with love, and made the first toast to his bride. "Darling Susanne—love of my life. Here's to our first happy year of marriage." He winked, then leaned closer and whispered in his bride's ear. "One out of seven's not bad, huh?"

She laughed and kissed him soundly.

"Well, little brother." Cole cornered Cass when they caught a rare moment alone. "Looks like all these years I've worried about you have been for nothing."

Cass's eyes fixed on his new bride, who was busy trying to excuse herself in order to slip away. "She's something, isn't she?"

Cass had finally told his family about his earlier marriage to Susanne and how he'd grown to love the orphans as much as he loved his own son. He'd had to. Lilly had swooned when he told her he had ten children.

Beau drifted over to join his brothers. "I guess Susanne will do in a pinch, but have you two really looked at Charity? Now, gentlemen, there's a woman!"

Cole hooted. "Brothers, no disrespect intended, but Wynne's got your women beat, hands down."

Beau and Cass both turned to give him a dour look.

The three brothers suddenly exchanged identical devilish winks.

"Yeah," Cole said softly, "it looks like the Claxton boys have done just fine."

Samuel Claxton Senior would have been right proud of his sons.

Dear Reader,

Well, we've come to the end of the third story in the Men of the Saddle series, and I hope when you close this book, you'll feel your hope has been renewed. Just as Susanne struggled with her old nature, we struggle with ours. Day by day we must renew our hope in the Lord Jesus Christ and wait for His perfect plan for our lives. His time is not our time, but in due time, joy will come in the morning!

In your daily devotions, take time to read the following Scripture passages on hope: Psalm 9:18; Psalm 119:114; Psalm 103:5; Jeremiah 17:7; Proverbs 13:12; and Lamentations 3:24. Then stand back and watch God work in your life.

Lori Copeland

ABOUT THE AUTHOR

Lori Copeland, Christian novelist, lives in the beautiful Ozarks with her husband and family. After writing in the secular romance market for fifteen years, Lori now spends her time penning books that edify readers and glorify God. She publishes titles with Tyndale House, WestBow, and Steeple Hill. In 2000, Lori was inducted into the Springfield, Missouri, Writers Hall of Fame.

Lori's readers know her for Lifting Spirits with Laughter! She is the author of the popular, best-selling Brides of the West series, and she coauthors the Heavenly Daze series with Christy award–winning author Angela Elwell Hunt. *Stranded in Paradise* marked her debut as a Women of Faith author.

Lori welcomes letters written to her in care of Tyndale House Author Relations, P.O. Box 80, Wheaton, IL 60189-0080.

the Plainsman

"Mr. McAllister, please. If you'll sit still this will get over with a lot sooner."

Trey twisted in the hard seat; the cape around his neck felt like a noose. He'd enjoyed the bath. The women had filled a tub with hot water and left him with a man-size bar of lye soap, clean towels, and—thank goodness—his privacy.

Now the haircut—and who should be wielding the scissors but none other than the young Cajun girl with the crazy father.

"I should be halfway to Kansas by now," he groused.

"Kansas? I thought you told Dee you hailed from New Orleans. How much do you want taken off the top?"

He didn't correct her. "Not much." This was the second haircut in a month. He'd be bald if he wasn't careful.

She laughed—a clear, pleasant sound. In spite of her heavy French accent, she had a good command of English. Trey suspected she'd been schooled more than most young women.

She wagged her finger at him. "I see you are a tease." With that she drew a good three inches through the comb and snipped. He winced. "Such beautiful red hair," she murmured.

Trey hated it when people talked about his hair. Silence hung between them as Mire went about her work. He'd learned that she had a natural gift. She cut hair for everyone who came through the small town—anyone who wasn't scared to stay that long. He was afraid to glance at the mirror lying on the kitchen table. He liked his hair collar length, brushed over at the forehead, and he had a hunch it would be a while before he saw that image again.

"What will Trey McAllister do when he reaches home?" she asked softly.

"Go back to living."

No more sleeping on the hard ground. No more eating dried meat and moldy bread. No more drinking bitter chicory coffee and listening to the sounds of friends dying at his side.

"Yes. I would imagine the last few years have been terrible."

Trey had thought about the future a lot lately. What did he plan to do? First he had to ensure his sisters would have a home. Now that the war was over and men were drifting back it probably wouldn't be long until some or maybe all of them got married. He could say one thing for his sisters: they were good-looking women. Great cooks, too. A man could consider himself lucky to win any one of the bunch.

As for him, likely he would settle in and start working the land. Maybe even give some serious thought to starting a family. Maybe.

Most men his age had made the decision early, but Trey had missed his opportunity six years ago. He concentrated on the quiet *snip-snip* and suddenly found himself wondering what Mire planned to do. Would she fight her father until her dying breath? Didn't seem like much of a future for a pretty young thing. "What about you?"

The scissors paused. *"Mon cheri?"*

"What about you? Are you going to fight your father until you win?"

"I will never win," she admitted. She sat down, staring at the scissors. "But I will keep on fighting until either Jean-Marc or I can fight no longer."

"That doesn't sound sensible."

"No, *mon cheri*, it is not." She stood up and the blades on the scissors flew again. "But what is life without freedom? Have you not just spent part of your life fighting, in part, for other people's freedom?"

"Slavery's different. And the war was about more than slavery. It was about differences of opinions between the government and state."

"Oh?" She paused again, lifting her dark brows.

Trey had never seen more beautiful eyes on any woman. Coal black, sparkling with life and headstrong determination. He'd wager that Portier had the same stubborn look.

Like father, like daughter.

"Why do you say this? When a person's freedom is taken away what else can it be called other than slavery?"

Trey shifted, uncomfortable with her fierce defense. Actually, she was right. He had spent three years of his life fighting for exactly what she was fighting for, but somehow her spat with her father seemed insignificant when contrasted to the War Between the States.

"Can't you find a way to make peace with your father without all this fuss? It seems to me that the other women are paying for your family dispute."

According to Grandma Speck, Sassy Gap lived in a continual stage of siege, and the siege would not let up until Mire surrendered. Trey didn't know why that should bother him, but it did. Much more than he wanted it to.

"I do worry about that." The scissors paused. "But I cannot give in to Jean-Marc. If I do, my life will be over."

"You call him Jean-Marc. Why not Father? Or Papa?"

"Never! I will never acknowledge him as Papa." Her eyes burned brightly. "Never!"

Trey eyed the flying scissors nervously. He'd lived around women long enough to recognize theatrics; he had serious doubts that her life would "be over," yet the woman was a stranger to him and he had no evidence of the true nature of the dispute. From what he knew it sounded like a family row, one best solved by the folks involved.

"You do not know Jean-Marc," she accused as though she had read his thoughts. "He is not a good man. People admire him because of his money and big house and plantation. Some even admire his ruthlessness and the power he has amassed. But they do not know him. I—" she stabbed a finger dramatically toward her chest—"only I know him, and that is why he is determined to force me back under his control. It is also why I must fight him. He leaves me no choice."

Trey found himself starting to be drawn into the dispute regardless of his indifference. "Then why not leave? Move so far away that your father can never find you unless you want him to."

"I would not want him to, but Jean-Marc would find me no matter how far I ran." She shook her head. "So, I cannot run. I must stand and fight, although it would be easier to run and sometimes I long to do so. But it is impossible. You surely see this. He must be made to understand that I am no longer a child to be ordered around, but a woman who will not be silenced."

"Seems to me he'll be more likely to make trouble for you if you stay here."

She visibly stiffened. "I will stand and *fight*. Only cowards run."

Jean-Marc's words, no doubt. Still, Trey teetered on the edge of sympathy. Maybe the girl was right; maybe she had to fight for her independence. He'd known daughters whose lives were rules by their fathers.

Even been engaged to one once.

If it hadn't been for Abel Wilson's iron hand Trey would be a married man now with a child or two.

Bitterness burned the back of his throat.

The scissors paused a third time and Mire's eyes grew distant with thought. "But if I were willing to leave—perhaps you would take me with you?"

Trey choked and then cleared his throat to cover it. Take her with him? She couldn't be serious. A single woman and a single man traveling together? Grandma Speck had said Mire had been married briefly, but no matter. He couldn't take her anywhere. It just wasn't done.

"I couldn't do that."

She knelt to face him, eyes wide with expectation. "You said that I should put more distance between me and Jean-Marc."

"Your father. Call him your father!" Trey could see why the man would be annoyed.

"Never!"

Trey backed off. "Okay. I didn't mean that *I* wanted to get involved. This argument is between you and your father."

"But he has made it an argument between him and the women of the town."

Trey stood, ripping the cape off his neck. This conversation was going nowhere.

"I wish I could help, but I can't. My advice to you is to meet with your father and settle this matter once and for all."

"Never," she stated.

He walked out of the kitchen, feeling heat from more than the cookstove. He could feel her gaze following him through the doorway. He'd tried to talk sense into a bullheaded father once and met with no luck. There were some men who couldn't be reasoned with, and he suspected he knew of two: Abel Wilson and now Jean-Marc Portier. Yet he admired Mire for fighting. Sharon had surrendered after the first shot.

Remorse filled the back of his throat when he remembered how little his love had meant to Sharon Wilson.

But that water had gone over the dam a long time ago, and he had learned a valuable lesson—you couldn't count on a female. God had been good enough to let him learn that lesson and learn it well. *But, Lord, You are my shield and wonderful God who gives me courage.* That should have meant that he'd stay and help fight. But strangers? And females? He'd best ride on.

"Mr. McAllister!" Mire called. "I have not finished cutting your hair!"

"Looks good enough," Trey called over his shoulder. He was out of this town.

BOOKS BY BEST-SELLING AUTHOR
LORI COPELAND

TYNDALE
FICTION